HALICHOS
BAS YISRAEL
A Woman's Guide to
Jewish Observance

Rav Yitzchak Yaacov Fuchs

HALICHOS BAS YISRAEL

*A Woman's Guide to
Jewish Observance*

the English edition of
הליכות בת ישראל

prepared by
RAV MOSHE DOMBEY
in collaboration with the author

I

*From the Hebrew edition,
Chapters 1-14*

TARGUM PRESS
Oak Park, Michigan

FELDHEIM
Jerusalem/New York

First Published 1985
ISBN 0-87306-397-X

Phototypeset at Nachal Ltd. and Gefen Ltd.

Published by:
Targum Press, Inc.
14500 Park
Oak Park, Mich. 48237

Distributed by:
Philipp Feldheim Inc.
200 Airport Executive Park
Spring Valley, NY 10977

96 East Broadway
New York, NY 10002

Feldheim Publishers Ltd.
POB 6525 / Jerusalem, Israel

Printed in Israel

הסכמות רבותינו הגאונים שליט"א

יצחק יעקב וייס
רב ואב"ד
לכל מקהלות האשכנזים פעיה"ק ירושלם תובב"א
מח"ס שו"ת מנחת יצחק
ירושלים, רחוב ישעיהו 20

בס"ד, ירושלים פעיהקת"ו

הן כבר איתמחי גברא רבא ויקירא מוכתר בנימוסין הרה"ג ירא ושלם
חו"ב מורה"ר יצחק יעקב פוקס מפעיהקת"ו בספרו החשוב והנכבד
התפלה בצבור שנתקבל באהבה אצל לומדי התורה, וכבר יצא טיבו
ותהילתו בספר הנ"ל.

ועתה עלה במחשבתו והעלה על הכתב ספר חשוב ומאד יקר אשר
בשם "הליכות בת ישראל" יכונה, והוא ע"ד המעשה אשר יעשון בנות
ישראל חיוביהן ופטוריהן, ושאר דינים ומנהגים המיועדים להן, ואסף
כעמיר גורנה מדברי רבותינו הפוסקים וסידרן בסידור יפה דבר דיבור על
אופניו בטוב טעם ודעת, וגם הוסיף הערות והארות בהשכל ובדעת
והעלה תמצית הדינים שבירר בידיעתו וביגיעתו בתוה"ק, וכאשר מבואר
בדברי ידי"נ הגאון המפורסם שלשלת היוחסין כש"ת רבי משה
הלברשטאם שליט"א מגדולי וחשובי מורי ההוראה בפעיה"ק, אשר האריך
הרחיב בשבח הספר והתועלת המרובה אשר יפיקו רצון ויאותו לאורו הני
רבנן ותלמידיהון וידעו את המעשה אשר יעשון והדרך אשר ילכו בה.

לכן ראוי המחבר הה"ג שליט"א להחזיק לו טובה שזיכה את בנות
ישראל בספרו יקר ונעלה זה, ואמינא לפעלא טבא אייש, וידי תיכון עמו
להוציאו לאור לזכות את הרבים, וכל המזכה את הרבים זכותו גדולה
מאד שיזכה לברך על המוגמר בס"ד ויבואו רבים ויביאו ברכה בביתם.

וכבימים ההם יראנו הקב"ה ניסים ונפלאות בבנין בית מקדשנו
ותפארתנו בב"א.

הכו"ח לכבוד התורה ומצוותי' זאת חנוכה תדש"ם.

יצחק יעקב וייס רב ואב"ד פעה"ק ת"ו.

שמואל הלוי ואזנר
רב אב"ד ור"מ
זכרון מאיר, בני ברק

ב"ה יום א וישלח תשד"מ לפ"ק

הנה כבוד ההה"ג המושלם הרבה זוכה ומזכה הרבים הרב יצחק יעקב
פוקס שליט"א, יושב באהלה של תורה בירושלים תוב"ב — כבר זכה
משולחן גבוה בספרו היקר התפילה בצבור שנתקבל באהבת תורה היות
כי המחבר שואף אל מטרת האמת, ועתה הוסיף לחבר ספר יקר "הליכות
בת ישראל" והמה הלכות כמסמרות נטועות הנוגעים להנהגת בת ישראל
נשואה ופנויה — יום יום שבת ויו"ט — הלכות צניעות הנחוצות, וגם
הרבה דברים חדשים אשר לקט המחבר החשוב מבין גן שושנים של
גדולים אחרונים — והיות כי ספרים כאלה המה קרובים מאד לזכות
הרבים וגם נתחבר לשם שמים וביגיעות הרבה, הרני מסכים להעלותו על
מכבש הדפוס ויפוצו מעיינותיו חוצה.

ע"ז בעה"ח מצפה לרחמי ה'
שמואל הלוי ואזנר
ראב"ד ור"ק"מ זכרון מאיר בני ברק

הרב משה הלברשטאם

מו"ץ בהעדה החרדית

ראש ישיבת "דברי חיים" טשאקוע

פעיה"ק ירושלים תובב"א

רחוב יואל 8

בס"ד

הן הובא לפני עלים לתרופה מספר נעלה יקר וחשוב עד מאד —
"הליכות בת ישראל", שיסדו וטיפחו משך שנים מרובות ביגיעה עצומה
הי ניהו הרה"ג ירא ושלם מחבר חיבורים יקרים מורה"ר יצחק יעקב פוקס
שליט"א מגדולי הלומדים באהלה של תורה פעיקת"ו, ומטרת הספר
לדעת הני נשי במאי קא זכיין במצות ד' ברה, ובמאי פטרוה חז"ל
והמסתעף, והרב המופלג הנ"ל נחית לעומקא דדינא הדין בבירור אחר
בירור בעיון מרובה ובכובד המשקל הראוי לצורבא מרבנן.

עברתי על רובו ככולו של הספר, ונהניתי לראות ולהוווכח שדבר טוב
ומועיל פעל ועושה עמנו להוציא דבר זה לאור עולם ולזכות בזה את
הרבים. ומעלה יתירה בספר זה ששם דגש מיוחד על חילוקי הדינים
והמנהגים בין העדות השונות שלדידן הוה מומא ולדידהו לא הוה מומא,
וכן להיפר, כמו"כ דן בהרחבה בשאלות מעשיות לבעלי תשובה אשר ב"ה
לשמחתנו רבו מאד באחרונה, כן ירבו. גם מצאתי שאלות רבות
שנתחדשו בימינו, ובעיקר בנושא הצניעות של בנות ישראל הכשרות אשר
רבות וכן טובות נכשלות שלא בכונה וגבהו בנות ציון ותלכנה הלוך
וטפוף וכדרשתם ז"ל, ובטוחני כי רבים יברכוהו על המעשה הטוב אשר
זכה להציל בנות ישראל הצנועות מכל סיג ופגם בהליכתן ובתלבושתן
ואשר כל רואיהן יעידון ויגידון כי הם זרע ברך ד', ובזכות נשים צדקניות
נגאלו אבותינו ממצרים, ובזכותן נגאל במהרה בימינו בביאת גואלנו צדק,
אמן כי"ר.

וח"ש בפרוס יומא דחנוכה, שנת גדולה האורה של ימי חנוכה לפ"ק
פעיה"ק והמקדש שיבב"א

משה הלברשטאם

בע"ה

אודה ה' בכל לבב על כי ספרי "הליכות בת ישראל" במהדורתו בלשון הקודש, נתקבל בברכה, ונדפס מאז הופעתו בס"ד פעמים רבות.

לבקשת רבים וטובים, אשר השפה האנגלית שגורה יותר בפיהם, נתתי ליבי לתור ולמצוא שלוחים נאמנים אשר יטו שכם לעסוק במלאכת התרגום והעריכה — משימה לא קלה כשהמדובר בספר הלכה הכולל אלפי פרטים בעניינים שונים ומגוונים.

והנה הקרה ה' לפני, אנשים חכמים וידועים, העוסקים בעבודת הקודש — חינוך בנות ישראל לתורה וליראה, ידידי היקרים, הרבנים החשובים: ר' יעקב מרדכי רפפורט, ר' משה דמבי ור' טוביה קרביט שליט"א, אשר קיבלו על עצמם עבודת התרגום וחברי הוצאת "תרגום" בארה"ב שנטלו על עצמם כל הקשור בהוצאת הספר ובהפצתו בשפה האנגלית, ולא חסכו עמל וטורח להוציא מתחת ידם דבר נאה ומתקבל.

תודה מיוחדת לכב' ידידי הרב ישראל בערל שליט"א, אשר היה לנו לעיניים והואיל לעבור על הספר ולהעיר הערותיו המועילות. וכן לכב' הרב משה דמבי שליט"א על השעות והימים הארוכים בהם בררנו וליבננו גופי ההלכות לפרטי פרטיהן להתאימם לענות על מציאות הבעיות ההילכתיות השכיחות במדינות ארה"ב ואירופה.

בירכתי ותיקוותי, כי בס"ד נזכה לראות ברכה בעמלינו, וזכות זיכוי הרבים תעמוד להם ולכל בני ביתם ויזכו להגדיל תורה ולהאדירה.

יצחק יעקב פוקס

ערב ראש השנה ה'תשמ"ו
פעיה"ק ירושלים ת"ו

Rabbi CHAIM P. SCHEINBERG
KIRYAT MATTERSDORF
PANIM MEIROT 2
JERUSALEM, ISRAEL

הרב חיים פנחס שיינברג
ראש ישיבת "תורה אור"
ומורה הוראה דקרית מטרסדורף
ירושלים טל. 3151952

I have seen the valuable book *Halichos Bas Yisrael,* which was excellently compiled by the young Torah scholar, HaRav HaGaon Rabbi Yitzchak Yaacov Fuchs, whom I have known for many years in our neighborhood, Kiryat Mattersdorf, and who spent many hours discussing many of the topics therein with me.

The purpose of this work is to educate and inspire the public to perform all of the complex details of the commandments incumbent on the "House of Jacob — these are the women". It excels in its clear presentation, concise language, and efficient organization, especially in its description of the laws of modesty, a basic area in which it is very necessary for women to be knowledgeable, proficient and cautious, and whose importance requires daily re-emphasis. Praised is the share of the author whom Providence has merited with the rare opportunity to successfully disseminate this important information. He has been doubly blessed with the opportunity to have his work presented in English, thus allowing a much wider audience to benefit from it. The English edition in no way deviates from the standard of excellence found in the Hebrew edition.

Since this book is a compilation of delicate halakhic opinion and conclusions drawn from a wide variety of differing authorities, I must be hesitant about expressing my absolute agreement with all of its contents; this would require a scrupulous and meticulous analysis of every sensitive detail. In no way, however, does this detract from the compendium's value as a medium for the aforementioned goals.

Many Torah giants have already praised the author's previous work, *HaTefillah B'Tzibur,* and my hand joins his present endeavor as well. I praise his strength in spreading, strengthening, and glorifying Torah, and may the Almighty grant him the stamina for many other worthwhile projects.

I sign with respect for the Torah and Her students, here in the Holy City of Jerusalem, on the 20th day of Cheshvan, 5746.

Rabbi Chaim P. Scheinberg

Publishers' Preface to the English Edition

Before the publication of *Halichos Bas Yisrael* by the distinguished Jerusalem educator Rav Yitzchak Yaacov Fuchs, there was a dearth of accessible material on that most important subject, practical observance for the Jewish woman. The original Hebrew edition quickly became the most widely-read book of its kind. It manages to be popular and scholarly at the same time.

Halichos Bas Yisrael follows a format typical of the halakhic guides which proliferated in the Jewish world in recent years. The rules of practical halakhah are clearly set forth in the text — with comprehensive annotated sources, differing opinions and variant customs fully discussed in accompanying notes. This method of presentation, with its balance between theory and practice, has proved invaluable to both layman and scholar.

At the Targum Press, we have departed from the usual way of translating guides of this nature, which is to render the basic text in English while leaving the explanatory notes in Hebrew. In translating the notes as well as text, we are convinced of the importance to the English-speaking public of practical halakhah with clear exposition of the underlying principles and varying opinions. Many readers of English with neither the time nor the background to study the Hebrew notes have been, until now, deprived of valuable resources and have had to contend themselves with a needlessly superficial knowledge of the subject matter.

It is therefore with deep satisfaction that we present this complete translation of *Halichos Bas Yisrael*. We are confident that it will meet the needs of a wide range of readers: the high school student; the professional seminary teacher; the young woman seeking an authentic guide to practical observance; the housewife; the adult reader with limited Hebrew; and the *kollel* scholar, who may lack all the original sources or the time to investigate them thoroughly.

Because the book is addressed to women, the laws are often presented in the female gender. The reader should be aware, however, that many of these laws apply to men as well.

Since certain readers might be unfamiliar with some of the basic concepts referred to in the original work, the notes have often been supplemented with brief explanations. For the sake of clarity, this added material has been incorporated into the translation rather than presented separately. Nothing has been added, however, without the consent and encouragement of Rav Fuchs. We hope and pray that the material is presented so that more advanced readers will also benefit.

In both text and notes, wherever Ashkenazic and Sephardic practices differ significantly, it is duly noted. A number of contemporary authorities, Ashkenazic and Sephardic, were queried in the preparation of the original work, and the author has cited many of their verbal answers. All halakhic decisions cited in the names of HaGaon Rav Shlomo Zalman Auerbach, HaGaon Rav Yosef Sholom Eliashiv, HaGaon Rav Ben Zion Abba Shaul, and HaGaon Rav Chaim Pinchus Sheinberg were formulated in accordance with their directions and were checked by them personally.

We wish to emphasize that this translation was undertaken in close collaboration with Rav Fuchs. Any changes in the organization or order of the material were made with his consent, and their only purpose was to make the book as readable as possible in another language. All halakhic questions which arose in the course of the project were discussed with him, and his decisions guided us. We hope that we have in no way modified the author's meaning, and we apologize for any shortcomings in the translation.

With respect to particular applications of *halakhoth* outlined in this book, we can only reiterate the author's advice in the Preface to the Hebrew Edition: Since many halakhic matters inspire much discussion and disagreement among authorities, when in doubt, "Make for yourself a Rav", and consult him for direction in personal observance.

Halichos Bas Yisrael is the first of a number of translations of Hebrew works in Jewish law and thought currently being prepared for publication by the Targum Press. It is published with the hope that *HaShem Yisborakh* will guide our minds and hearts to produce works *L'hagdil Torah U'l'hadirah.*

Targum Press
Oak Park, Michigan
Kislev, 5746

Acknowledgments

The publishers wish to express their sincere appreciation to all who gave so much time and effort to prepare *Halichos Bas Yisrael*:

Rav Moshe Dombey, who translated the original Hebrew work and saw the manuscript through its many stages to completion.

Rav Yaakov Rapoport, who reviewed the entire translation and offered many suggestions which were incorporated in the final version.

Rav Yisrael Berl, who reviewed the translation and offered many suggestions concerning the presentation of many *halakhoth* in English.

Reb Tuvia Krevit, who was deeply involved in shaping and editing the manuscript at every stage of its preparation.

Chaim Phillips and Susan Efros for their valuable editorial help.

Debra Applebaum for preparing the index and glossary.

A special word of thanks is due to Rav Yitzchak Yaacov Fuchs. Without his warm encouragement, this translation could never have been completed.

Table of Contents

Contents

The Contents of Volume 2

Author's Preface to the Hebrew Edition

"Who can find a wife of excellence?" asks King Solomon, the wisest of all men. "A God-fearing woman," is his answer, "she is the one to be praised."

The *Chazon Ish* teaches, "The function of fear is scrupulous observance of the Law." Our holy Torah is not found in the heavens. It is a guide to life, instructing us in the actions we are to perform. Conscientious observance of practical *mitzvoth* and care in preserving the halakhah are true expressions of a complete fear of God residing in the heart.

"Anyone who studies Jewish Law each day is assured a place in the World to Come," our Sages tell us. The foundations of the Jewish home, the pillars on which it stands, are halakhah and minhag. They must be constantly studied and reviewed in order for us to train our children properly in the observance of Torah and *mitzvoth* — training so crucial for the establishment of a new generation of upright Jews. If these words pertain to the father of the family, how much more to the mother. Says the wisest of men, "Listen, my son, to the *mussar* of your father, and do not forsake the *Torah* of your mother." How puzzling is this advice. Do not words of *mussar* — guidance — issue from one's mother's mouth as well? Why does the verse single out the father as the one to be listened to?

The father traditionally shapes the household's framework by ensuring that the family does not overstep certain physical and spiritual boundaries. He gives form and direction by deciding what and how the children will study. This guidance is referred to as *mussar*; hence, listen to the *mussar* of your father.

The mother begins educating her children while they are still in the crib — when they still "do not know how to ask". She opens up the child's mind, planting in the child's soul the values of Torah and *mitzvoth* — more through example and other non-verbal influence than through words. With keen sensitivity, young children imbibe her patterns of behavior. They are nurtured on the holy atmosphere and spirit of modesty that prevails in the home. They watch her light the *Shabbath* candles and pray *Shemoneh Esrey*. They listen to her recite *Birkath HaMazon*. They imitate her actions when she separates *challah* from dough and cares for guests. This Torah, about which it is said, "Do not forsake the Torah of your mother", is the rich source on which a Jew draws throughout his life. The mother's Torah of actions in the informal classroom of the home is a "Torah of life" in its most literal sense.

The *Chazon Ish* often remarked that a mother has much greater power to implant full-hearted love of Torah in her children than a father, for love does not express itself in words alone. Indeed, love finally comes to dwell in a person's heart only through actions.

Without doubt, the ability to educate by action and example depends on diligent study of the laws — their general concepts and specific details. It is the sacred duty of every Jewish girl and mother to prepare herself for the lofty role of rearing children who will be dedicated to the study of Torah and fulfillment of *mitzvoth*.

With all my heart, I give thanks to God that I have merited to gather together the materials presented in *Halichos Bas Yisrael*. In it I have attempted to include a summary of the opinions of all the major *poskim* in those areas of halakhah relevant to the Jewish woman and girl.

Recent generations have merited an abundance of literature in all areas of Jewish Law pertaining to every segment of Jewry.

May it be God's will that this book draws all those who seek His word — the halakhah — to the sources for the laws and customs presented here.

It is hoped that the addition of comments of contemporary *poskim* will give the researcher the key to comprehending the writings of earlier authorities and enhance his ability to understand points which are not so explicit in those works. Where differing opinions are mentioned without a final decision, the reader should adopt the dictum of the Sages: Make for yourself a Rav. Discuss these questions with him and obtain his counsel.

As in my earlier work, *HaTefillah BeTzibbur,* the halakhic decisions of the *Mishnah Berurah* have been my guide. They serve as the basis for the text itself. Varying opinions are referred to or discussed in the footnotes.

With the kindness of God, our generation has begun to witness the fulfillment of the words of the Prophet: Behold, days are coming, says God, when I will send a hunger into the land. Not a hunger for bread and not a thirst for water, but to hear the word of God.

The benches in the houses of study are becoming daily more crowded as are seminaries and educational institutions for girls. Women and girls who are searching a life of Torah and *mitzvoth* often encounter new halakhic questions: What is the correct way to choose a *nussach* for prayer? May one serve food to a person who does not recite a blessing? What should be done with immodest clothing? Is it possible to fulfill the *mitzvah* of *Kiddush* by listening to someone who is unaware of the halakhic requirements surrounding it? Is it permissible to shake hands with family members of the opposite sex? In this book, I have placed particular emphasis on resolving these kinds of practical questions by citing relevant sources, with the advice and counsel of the foremost authorities of our day.

To women embracing a Torah life let it be said that full adherence to halakhah is often fraught with difficulties and challenges from the society around us. Our Sages have taught, "A person should not be ashamed in front of people who mock serving God." After some experience, a woman who faithfully follows the halakhah will merit great assistance from Heaven.

Not only she, but all around her, will be influenced to guard and uphold the mandates of the Torah. Finally, the Name of God will be sanctified through her.

Yitzchak Fuchs
Jerusalem
6 Kislev, 5740

Acknowledgments

First and most important, an obligation which I approach with a great deal of pleasure is to thank my master and teacher, HaGaon Rav Shlomo Zalman Auerbach, who encouraged and assisted me greatly by giving of his valuable time to answer, both verbally and in writing, the many questions I put to him concerning areas dealt with in this book. May God grant him health and strength to continue his great efforts in the proliferation of Torah.

Special blessing to HaGaon Rav Ben Zion Abba Shaul, who guided me and answered my many questions concerning Sephardic halakhic practice. God, in His boundless mercy, has restored him to good health. May He sustain a speedy recovery so that he can continue his holy work for many years to come.

Thanks and blessings are also due to others who assisted me — to HaGaon Rav Moshe Halbershtam of Jerusalem, who reviewed the entire work; to Rav Zvi Weber and Rav Pinchus Wiener; to all my colleagues at the Beith HaMidrash for Torah and Halakhah Kollel Beith HaTalmud, led by HaGaon Rav Shiloh Raphael; and particularly to my close friends and confidants, Rav Yaacov Pels and Rav Yisrael Zisman. May God grant them all their wishes and bless them with all good things.

My sincere gratitude and thanks to my mother Rivka, who has

guided me from early childhood, with devotion and faithfulness, to devote all my energies to the study of Torah. May God grant her length of days and a life full of pleasantness. May she merit to derive much *nachas* from all her children.

May God also bless my in-laws, Rav Yehudah Zvi Glick and his wife. May God grant them much *nachas* from all their children. May they be blessed with health and happiness for many years.

Finally, a special blessing for my wife, Esther, of whom it can be said, "She lights my eyes and stands me on my feet" (*Yevamoth* 63a). In the merit of her selfless devotion and boundless love for our holy Torah, this work has been published. May it be the Will of God, whose kindness has not left us to this day, that we might merit to raise our precious children to a life of Torah and fear of Heaven, with much *nachas*. May He grant us the strength to learn and to teach, to guard and perform and fulfill.

HALICHOS
BAS YISRAEL
*A Woman's Guide to
Jewish Observance*

INTRODUCTION

A Woman's Obligation in Mitzvoth

1. Many laws of the Torah are expressed in the masculine form — but men and women are equally obligated in all of them unless there is a specific source to suggest either a total or partial exemption. With certain exceptions, women are exempt from time-bound, positive *mitzvoth*. All prohibitions, however, apply to women.[1]

2. Women are exempt from any *mitzvah* which must be performed at a specific time.[2]

---

1. Tractate *Kiddushin* 35a: "It is written, 'A man or woman who commits any sin' (*BaMidbar* 5:6). The Torah here equates women with men with respect to all punishments... 'These are the laws that you shall place before them' (*Shemoth* 21:2). The Torah here equates women with men with respect to civil law...'And it [an ox] shall kill a man or woman' (*Shemoth* 21:29). The Torah here equates women with men with respect to the death sentence."
2. Tractate *Kiddushin* 29a. *Tosafoth*, in Tractate *Eruvin* 96b, adds that women do not even have a Rabbinic obligation to perform time-bound *mitzvoth*.

3. There are exceptions to the rule. Women must
a) eat *matzah* on the first night of *Pessach*,[3]
b) rejoice on *Yom Tov*,[4]
c) gather for *Hakhel*,[5]
d) observe all *mitzvoth* connected to *Shabbath*,[6] and
e) perform *mitzvoth* whose time for performance is seasonal and not tied to a specific date or hour.[7]

---

3. Tractate *Kiddushin* 34a and *Pesachim* 43b. A woman's obligation to eat *matzah* is deduced from the inclusion in the same verse (*Devarim* 16:3) of the prohibition against eating *chametz* on *Pessach* with the obligation to eat *matzah* on the first night of the holiday. This juxtaposition teaches that everyone included in the prohibition is also included in the obligation, even though it is a time-bound positive *mitzvah*. (Outside of *Eretz Yisrael*, this requirement is binding the first *two* nights of *Pessach*.)
4. Tractate *Kiddushin, Ibid.*, based on the verse, "And you shall rejoice on your Festivals, you and your sons and your daughters" (*Devarim* 16:14).
5. This is the commandment that all Jews gather in the *Beith HaMikdash* once every seven years to hear the king read the Book of *Devarim*. The Torah explicitly obligates women to participate in this *mitzvah* with the verse, "Gather the people, the men, the women..." (*Devarim* 31:12).
6. Tractate *Berakhoth* 20b. This exception is based on the tradition that the words *zakhor* (remember [the *Shabbath*]) (*Shemoth* 20:8) and *shamor* (guard [the *Shabbath*]) (*Devarim* 5:12), both found in the Ten Commandments, were uttered simultaneously by God. The tradition teaches that everyone included in *shamor* — the negative commandments of *Shabbath* — is also included in *zakhor* — the positive commandments of *Shabbath* — although it is a time-bound, positive *mitzvah*.
7. For example, the *Mishnah, Bikurim* 1:5, states that women are obligated to bring their first fruits to the *Beith HaMikdash*. Elsewhere in the *Mishnah*, we learn that this *mitzvah* may only be fulfilled between *Shavuoth* and *Channukah*, which would make it appear to be a time-bound *mitzvah*. The *Turey Evven*, in his commentary on Tractate *Megillah* 20b, explains that the time factor is a function of the growing season and not intrinsic to the

Time-Bound Rabbinic Mitzvoth

4. The rule exempting women from time-bound positive commandments applies to *mitzvoth* instituted by the Rabbis as well.[8]

5. Certain time-bound Rabbinic commandments, which were enacted to commemorate miraculous events, are incumbent on women because, "They, too, were included in the miracle."[9] This group of Rabbinic commandments includes drinking four cups of wine at the *Pessach Seder*,[10] lighting *Chanukah* candles,[11] and all the *mitzvoth* of *Purim*.[12]

Reasons for the Exemption

6. Many commentators offer reasons why the Torah exempts women from time-bound *mitzvoth*. The

---

mitzvah. Therefore, in spite of its time limits, it is not considered a time-bound *mitzvah*, and women are obligated to perform it.

8. *Tosafoth*, Tractate *Berakhoth* 20b and *Pesachim* 108b. Also see *Birkey Yosef, Orach Chayim* 291:8; *Teshuvoth Rabbi Akiva Eiger*, No. 16; *Sdeh Chemed, Kelalim* 40:135. Some authorities disagree with this view, maintaining that women are indeed obligated in time-bound · Rabbinic *mitzvoth. Tosafoth, Berakhoth, Ibid.*, understands the latter opinion to be *Rashi*'s. Also see *Sefer HaManhig, Hilkhoth Shabbath*, No. 44.

9. Tractate *Pesachim* 108b. *Tosafoth*, citing the Talmud *Yerushalmi*, explains that women were also saved from the dangers that threatened the Jewish people in Egypt and in the days of Persian and Greek oppression. *Rashi* and the *Rashbam* attribute their obligation in these *mitzvoth* to the fact that women were instrumental in bringing about these miracles.

10. Tractate *Pesachim, Ibid.*; *Shulchan Arukh, Orach Chayim* 472:14.

11. Tractate *Shabbath* 23a; *Shulchan Arukh, Orach Chayim* 675:3.

12. Tractate *Megillah* 4a; *Shulchan Arukh, Orach Chayim* 689:1.

Avudraham[13] notes that it is the woman who assumes responsibility for managing the household, attending to the physical needs of the Jewish family, and playing a major role in rearing and educating young children at home. Because many of these responsibilities must be attended to at unpredictable times, the Torah exempts women from obligations which must be performed at set times.

The *Maharal*[14] gives as an additional reason the basic psychological difference between men and women: Men, with their natural aggressive tendencies, cannot attain the peace and serenity of the World to Come unless they sublimate these tendencies through constant involvement in Torah study and the performance of *mitzvoth*. Women, however, are naturally more peaceful and serene and do not need this constant involvement in order to attain their reward.

Rabbi Samson Raphael Hirsch[15] explains that men's constant interaction with society at large and their pursuit of a livelihood may cause them to forget the true goal of life. Only with the help of regular reminders — time-bound *mitzvoth* — are they able to subordinate the attainment of physical comforts to the higher goal of divine service. Women, whose primary roles are domestic, are not as subject to the lure of physical pursuits and consequently do not need these regular reminders to develop sensitivity to spiritual values.

Voluntary Fulfillment of Mitzvoth

7. Women may fulfill any *mitzvah* from which they are

---

13. *Seder Tefilloth Shel Chol.* See also *Kol Bo*, No. 73, and *Sefer Chassidim*, No. 611.
14. *Drush Al HaTorah.*
15. Commentary on *VaYikra* 23:43.

halakhically exempt,[16] except those specifically restricted to men.[17]

8. Ashkenazic women follow the ruling of the *Remah,* who permits the recitation of blessings over the voluntary fulfillment of *mitzvoth.*[18]

9. The general Sephardic custom follows the opinion of the *Beith Yosef,* who forbids women to recite blessings over *mitzvoth* from which they are exempt.[19]

---

16. *Tosafoth,* Tractate *Rosh HaShanah* 33a; *Rambam, Hilkhoth Tzitzith* 3:9; *Shulchan Arukh, Orach Chayim* 589:6; *Remah, Orach Chayim* 17:2.

17. *Birkey Yosef, Orach Chayim* 38, based on the *Kol Bo,* No. 21; *Remah, Orach Chayim* 17:3. The only two *mitzvoth* women are not permitted to perform are *Tzitzith* and *Tefillin.*

18. *Remah, Orach Chayim* 589:6 and 17:2, based on the view of Rabbenu Tam, cited in *Tosafoth,* Tractate *Eruvin* 96b. Rabbenu Tam argues that these are not blessings recited in vain because a woman who fulfills a *mitzvah* receives reward whether she is obligated or not.

19. *Shulchan Arukh, Orach Chayim* 589:6, based on the *Rambam, Hilkhoth Tzitzith* 3:9 and *Hilkhoth Sukkah* 6:13. As explained by the *Smag, Asin* 42, this opinion is based on the fact that the blessings contain the word *v'tzivanu* (and He has commanded us); a person who is not commanded to perform the *mitzvah* cannot use this word truthfully.

The *Shibuley HaLeket,* No. 295, cites an alternative explanation of the *Beith Yosef*'s view in the name of Rabbenu Yeshayah. He explains that a woman who recites such blessings gives the impression that she is obligated to fulfill the *mitzvah,* and this may be a violation of the prohibition against adding to the Torah (*Bal Tosif*).

A number of Sephardic authorities rule that women may recite blessings over time-bound *mitzvoth.* See the *Chiddah* in *Devash LePhi, Ma'arekheth Nun* 14; *Zekher LeAvraham* (Alkalay), *Orach Chayim,* Vol. 1, *Hilkhoth Berakhoth,* No. 50; *Kaf HaChayim, Orach Chayim* 17:40 and 589:23.

10. The distinction between Ashkenazic and Sephardic practices is not so clear cut; certain halakhic authorities point to various blessings which the *Remah* would forbid women to recite,[20] and others find examples of blessings which the *Beith Yosef* would permit women to recite.[21] Each case will be dealt with separately in the text.

Positive Mitzvoth Which are Not Time-Bound

11. All positive *mitzvoth* that need not be fulfilled at a particular time, such as sending away the mother bird from her nest (*Shiluach HaKen*), building a partition on a roof (*Ma'akeh*), or returning a lost object (*HaShavath Aveidah*), are incumbent on women.[22]

12. Exceptions to the preceding rule include
a) *Talmud Torah* (Torah study),[23]
b) *Pidyon HaBen* (redemption of the first born son),[24]
c) *P'ru U'R'vu* (procreation),[25]
d) all *mitzvoth* related to the judicial system, and
e) all *mitzvoth* related to the waging of war.

---

20. The *Magen Avraham* 296:11 maintains that whenever the recitation of the blessing is itself the performance of a time-bound *mitzvah*, i.e., *Havdalah* and *Kiddush Levanah* (blessing for the new moon), women do not recite it — even according to the *Remah*.
21. Many Sephardic authorities rule that women may recite blessings that do not contain the word *v'tzivanu*.
22. Tractate *Kiddushin* 34a.
23. The exemption of women from the *mitzvah* to study Torah is discussed at length in Chapter 9.
24. "All your first born *sons* you shall redeem" (*Shemoth* 34:20). *Chazal* deduce that just as a daughter does not have to be redeemed, so a woman is not obligated to redeem her children.
25. *Shulchan Arukh, Evven HaEzer* 1:13, based on Tractate *Yevamoth* 65b.

Negative Commandments

13. Women are obligated in all negative commandments of the Torah, including those which apply at specific times.[26]

14. Exceptions to the preceding rule include
a) the prohibition against "shaving hair off the corners of the head",
b) the prohibition against a *cohen* becoming defiled through contact with a dead person,
c) all negative commandments regulating the judicial system, and
d) all negative commandments regulating the waging of war.[27]

Special Responsibilities of Women

15. The *mitzvoth* of *Niddah, Challah* and Candle-lighting were designated particularly for the woman.[28] She alone is trusted to count the seven clean days following her menstrual period.[29] Although men and women are equally capable of separating *Challah* and lighting candles before *Shabbath* and *Yom Tov*, women, by virtue of their special role in the home, are entrusted with these important tasks.[30]

The Sages, in the Talmud *Yerushalmi, Shabbath* 2:6,

26. See paragraph 1, note 1, where the source for this rule is cited.
27. See *Sefer HaChinukh* 3, 7, 74, 117 and 411.
28. *Mishnah, Shabbath* 2:6; Talmud *Yerushalmi, Shabbath* 2:6.
29. Tractate *Kethuboth* 72a.
30. *Shulchan Arukh, Orach Chayim* 263:3, and *Mishnah Berurah; Kaf HaChayim, Orach Chayim* 242:24.

have commented on the deep connection between women and these commandments: "Why were women commanded in these three *mitzvoth*? God said, 'Adam was the first of my creations. He was commanded not to partake of the tree of knowledge. But of Eve it is written, 'And the woman saw...and she also gave to her husband...and he ate' (*Bereshith* 3:6). She caused him to be subject to death, which is as if she spilled his blood. In the Torah it is written. 'One who spills the blood of man, his blood shall be spilled' (*Bereshith* 9:6). Let her blood be spilled, and by guarding the laws of *niddah*, she will atone for the blood she has spilled.'

"From where do we know [that women are especially commanded in the *mitzvah* of] *Challah*? She defiled the *challah* of the world [man, who was separated from the rest of creation for divine service]. R. Yose ben Katzarta said: 'Just as a woman mixes the dough with water and then lifts the *challah*, so did God do with Adam, as it is written, 'And a mist went up from the ground and watered the face of the earth' (*Bereshith* 2:6). It is then written, 'And the Lord God formed man dust from the earth' (*Bereshith* 2:7).'

"From where do we know [that women are especially commanded in the *mitzvah* of] candle-lighting? She extinguished the light of the world, as it is written, 'The candle of God is the soul of man' (*Mishley* 30:25). Therefore, she should fulfill the *mitzvah* of candle-lighting."

These *mitzvoth* do more than expiate the sin of Eve. They embody the essential role of the Jewish woman in the home. The *Midrash (Bereshith Rabbah* 60:15) relates that in the homes of Sarah and Rivkah, a candle burned from *Shabbath* eve to *Shabbath* eve, a constant blessing was found in the dough, and a cloud covered the entrance to to the tent.

The *Shabbath* candles spread light and joy, enabling us

to transcend the trials and tribulations of the week. By lighting these candles, women create the special *Shabbath* atmosphere, compared by *Chazal* to a taste of the World to Come. A God-fearing woman, who walks in the way of her righteous ancestors, builds this special atmosphere into the fabric of her home, to be felt by her family during the week. In establishing a home filled with joy in the performance of *mitzvoth* and Torah study, she spreads the light of the *Shabbath* candles to all who enter her home. As burdened as they may be with their daily worries, they find it a place of refuge. The true Jewish woman is thus endowed with the power to "burn her *Shabbath* candles" all week until the time comes to light them again.

Chazal teach that the charitable acts of a Jewish woman bring greater satisfaction to their recipients than those of men. A kind word and some freshly-cooked food bring greater comfort to the destitute than a few coins dropped in their palms by anonymous passers-by. *Chazal* express this idea in the saying, "One who gives a coin to a poor man is blessed with six blessings. But one who consoles him receives eleven blessings" (*Bava Bathra* 16b).

The blessings that come to a home depend on the extent to which that home is open to needy outsiders. A family which gives with a generous heart and a good spirit — ready to feed the hungry and speak to them pleasantly — true blessing "will be found in their dough". It is the Jewish woman who is primarily responsible for setting this tone for her household.

If a woman illuminates her house with the light of Torah and *mitzvoth,* bringing to it the blessings that come through charity — surely a "cloud will cover her tent". Just as the cloud protected Sarah and Rivkah, her home will be protected from the storms of this world, which can alienate and estrange a person from all that is holy. The spirit of modesty which a woman brings to her home turns it into a fortress. The light which emanates from it grows stronger and stronger until it can dispel the darkness that covers the world. Just as our forefathers were redeemed from Egypt by the merit of righteous women, so shall we be redeemed with the coming of *Mashiach*, speedily in our days.

CHAPTER 1
Washing the hands in the morning

Washing the Hands

1. *Chazal* teach us that an impure spirit (*ruach ra*) settles upon a person while she sleeps. When she awakens, this *ruach ra* departs from every part of the body except the hands. In order to remove the remaining impurity, one must pour water three times over each hand — one hand at a time — the first thing in the morning.[1] *Chazal* warn us to be careful not to touch any orifice of the body or handle food until this washing has been performed. Since women are often involved in the preparation of food, they should be particularly scrupulous in this regard.[2]

---

1. Tractate *Shabbath* 109a. The washing of the hands in the morning to remove *ruach ra (netilath yadayim* in Hebrew) is popularly known by its Yiddish term, *negelvasser* (literally, "water for the nails"). The proper sequence for washing is first the right hand, then left; right-left; right-left. The Vilna Gaon adds a fourth time for each hand to remove the impure water left over from the third. See the *Mishnah Berurah* 4:10.
2. *Chazal* warn that *ruach ra* can have a harmful effect if one touches the eyes, mouth or nose while it is still on the hands. The *Mishnah*

2. Food which has been touched by someone who has not washed away *ruach ra* should be rinsed three times.[3] If it is a type of food that cannot be rinsed, it may still be eaten.[4]

3. A woman who awakens in the middle of the night need not wash for *ruach ra* if she intends to go back to sleep immediately. She must still avoid touching any orifice of the body.[5]

4. A woman who gets up for a short time during the night to eat or drink is obligated to wash her hands before reciting the appropriate blessing over her food. The purpose of this washing is to clean the hands, which have become unclean during sleep.[6] All blessings must be said in a state of cleanliness.

Berurah 4:12 and 4:13 cautions against touching the eyelids or the rectum before *negelvasser*. The *Zohar* also warns against allowing *ruach ra* to remain on the hands for any period of time, requiring that a person wash before walking four cubits. (See Chapter 2, note 21.) Because of the urgency of removing this impure spirit, many people keep a basin and cup beside their beds so that they can wash immediately on awakening.

3. *Mishnah Berurah* 4:14.

4. *Mishnah Berurah, Ibid.*

5. *Eshel Avraham (Butchach)* rules that someone awakening briefly in the middle of the night is even permitted to touch the eyes, ears and other orifices of the body without washing. Most authorities, however, seem to disagree with this view, maintaining that touching of the orifices is forbidden. HaGaon Rav Chaim Pinchus Sheinberg has ruled that the view of the majority should be followed in this matter.

Sephardic women should take note of the view of the *Ben Ish Chai* that one who awakens during the night, even for a short time, should wash to remove *ruach ra*, even if no orifices are touched.

6. The hands have become unclean since one invariably touches normally-covered parts of the body during sleep. Since the purpose

5. It is preferable for a woman to remove any rings from her hands before washing,[7] but this is not necessary if it involves a hardship.[8]

Washing the Hands When a Woman is a Niddah

6. When a woman is a *niddah*,[9] her husband is permitted to bring water to her for washing in the morning. He may also bring her water to wash before eating bread.[10] Some authorities forbid her to bring water to her husband for these purposes,[11] while others permit it.[12] But all

---

of this washing is to remove dirt, and not *ruach ra*, it is not necessary to pour water three times over each hand.

7. The *Shulchan Arukh, Orach Chayim* 4:7, explains that it is proper to fulfill the *mitzvah* of washing the hands in the morning in accordance with all the requirements for washing the hands before eating bread. One of these requirements is that no object should come between the water and the hand.

8. An example of a hardship would be if one's fingers are swollen, and the rings are difficult to remove. The *Remah*, in his glosses to the *Shulchan Arukh*, comments that although it is proper to act in accordance with the above-mentioned view of the *Shulchan Arukh*, it is not absolutely essential. The *Mishnah Berurah* 4:16 interprets the *Remah* to mean that where there is an extenuating circumstance, one need not be particular to conform to all the requirements of washing before eating bread.

9. *Niddah* refers to the halakhic status of a woman from the onset of her menstrual period until she purifies herself through immersion in a *mikvah*. Jewish Law severely limits the types of activities a husband may perform for his wife when she is a *niddah*.

10. *Minchath Yitzchak*, Vol. 7, No. 72. The *Kaf HaChayim, Orach Chayim* 159:74, adds that a man whose wife is ill and has no one else to assist her may even pour the water over her hands. He is permitted to do so only for the *mitzvah* of *Netilath Yadayim* and only if she is unable to wash by herself.

11. *Shakh, Yoreh De'ah* 195:16. Many authorities interpret the *Shakh* only to forbid her to bring water to her husband where no *mitzvah*

authorities agree that she is forbidden to pour the water over his hands.[13]

Washing the Hands and Child Care

7. A woman should be careful not to attend to children before cleansing herself of *ruach ra* in the morning, for we are cautioned that it can be harmful to the mouth, nose, ears and eyes.[14]

8. One should refrain from touching a child's food, even if it is inside a bottle,[15] until the hands have been washed.

9. A woman who awakens in the middle of the night to cover a child or place a pacifier in his mouth is not required to wash her hands, as long as she is careful not to touch the above-mentioned parts of the child's body.[16]

10. One should be careful to wash the hands of even small children in the morning before they are allowed to touch food.[17] Some people have a custom to wash the hands of infants every morning, even when they are too

---

is involved. If the water is brought for him to wash for the *mitzvah* of *Netilath Yadayim*, the *Shakh* would permit it. But under no circumstances may she pour the water over his hands. See *Pardes Simchah* 195:12 and *Be'er Moshe*, Vol. 3, No. 141.

12. *Taz, Yoreh De'ah* 195:8; *Orukh HaShulchan, Yoreh De'ah* 195:14; *Darkey Teshuvah* 195:12. These authorities permit her to bring water to her husband even where no *mitzvah* is involved.

13. *Shulchan Arukh, Yoreh De'ah* 195:12.

14. See note 2.

15. *Rivevoth Ephrayim*, Vol. 2, No. 6.

16. See paragraph 3.

17. *Mishnah Berurah* 4:10.

young to handle food — and this custom is praiseworthy.[18]

11. Someone who has touched any part of a child's body that is normally covered should wash her hands before praying, reciting blessings, studying Torah or eating.[19] One need not wash the hands after touching normally-exposed parts of a child's body, even if those parts would normally be covered in the case of an adult.[20]

12. After putting on or removing a child's shoes, the hands must be washed. Since this and the washing described in the above paragraph are for reasons of

---

18. The *Pri Megadim, Orach Chayim, Mishbetzoth Zahav* 4:7, strongly advises that *ruach ra* be removed from children who are too young to be trained in the performance of *mitzvoth*. The *Kaf HaChayim, Orach Chayim* 4:22, comments that washing children's hands instills in them a spirit of sanctity and holiness.

The *Shulchan Arukh HaRav, Mahadurah Basra* 4, calls it praiseworthy for a mother to prevent her son from touching food with unwashed hands, beginning on the day of his *brith milah*. But he adds that, according to the letter of the law, the actual obligation to wash a child's hands does not begin until he is old enough to be trained in the performance of *mitzvoth* — the age of *chinukh* (education). *Tzitz Eliezer*, Vol. 7, No. 2, also rules that before the age of *chinukh* there is no obligation to wash a child's hands, but agrees that this practice is a good way to instill a spirit of sanctity in young children.

I have heard that HaGaon Rav Moshe Feinstein instructs women to wash the hands of infant children when they awaken in the morning, even though it is not obligatory. I am also informed that in the home of HaGaon Rav Yaakov Kamenetzky they are particular to wash the hands even of newborn infants.

19. *Shulchan Arukh, Orach Chayim* 4:21; *Mishnah Berurah* 4:38 and 4:57. Covered parts of the body tend to perspire. After touching them, the hands must be washed for cleanliness. Since this washing is not for *ruach ra*, it is not necessary to pour three times over each hand. The water should still cover the entire hand, up to the wrist.

20. This is based on a ruling of HaGaon Rav Yosef Sholom Eliashiv.

hygiene only, they may be delayed for a short time,[21] but blessings and prayers should not be said until after the hands are cleaned.[22]

13. After helping a child relieve himself in the bathroom, one should immediately wash the hands.[23]

The Blessings and Their Order

14. The blessing over washing the hands in the morning is *Al netilath yadoyim*.[24]

15. The blessing *Asher yatzar* is recited each time a person relieves herself.[25]

---

21. *Mishnah Berurah* 4:41. See note 3.
22. *Shulchan Arukh, Orach Chayim* 4:18; *Mishnah Berurah* 4:41 and 4:57. As above, one should wash the entire hand, up to the wrist.
23. *Shulchan Arukh, Orach Chayim* 4:18 and 4:21; *Mishnah Berurah* 4:39. A form of *ruach ra* rests upon a person when leaving a bathroom. The *Mishnah Berurah* cites a difference of opinion as to whether it is necessary to wash each hand three times to remove this impurity. Contemporary authorities also differ as to whether or not the standard bathrooms of today even require this washing since the excrement is quickly flushed away.

   It should be noted that a person who touches excrement (for instance, while changing a baby's diaper) during the course of a meal at which bread is eaten is obligated to wash again and repeat the blessing *Al netilath yadoyim*. This is only necessary if she still intends to eat the minimum amount of bread which requires washing with a blessing (a *k'betzah*, which is equivalent to about two ounces or 50 grams). See *Shulchan Arukh, Orach Chayim* 164:2, and *Mishnah Berurah* 164:13.

   I have been informed by HaGaon Rav Ben Zion Abba Shaul that the custom among Sephardic Jews is to omit the blessing *Al netilath yadoyim* upon washing a second time during a meal.
24. "[Who commanded us] concerning the washing of hands." We are required to recite this blessing once each day, apart from when we eat bread.
25. "Who created [man in wisdom]." This blessing is classified as a

16. If the intention is to pray first thing in the morning, the order of washings and blessings is as follows:

a) Immediately upon awakening, wash each hand three times in alternating fashion, without a blessing.[26]

b) Relieve oneself and wash each hand again as normally done when leaving the bathroom.

c) Recite the blessings *Al netilath yadoyim, Asher yatzar* and *Elokai n'shamah.*[27]

17. If a woman intends to wait until later to say morning prayers, she should wash her hands upon awakening (without a blessing), relieve herself and then wash again, *omitting* the blessing *Al netilath yadoyim.* Only *Asher yatzar* and *Elokai n'shamah* are to be recited, after the second washing. The blessing *Al netilath yadoyim* should be postponed until just prior to the recitation of morning prayers, at which time she should relieve herself again,[28] wash, and recite *Al netilath yadoyim* and *Asher*

---

birkath hoda'ah (blessing of thanksgiving), in which men and women are equally obligated. The *Ben Ish Chai, Shanah Rishonah, Parshath VaYetze* 15 states: "Women...should commit this blessing to memory, for it is extremely important to recite it. They should also learn the simple meaning of the blessing in order to understand what they are saying."

26. This first washing is for the purpose of removing *ruach ra.* The *Mishnah Berurah* 4:4 points out that it is improper to recite the blessing *Al netilath yadoyim* at this time because it is forbidden to recite a blessing while feeling the urge to relieve oneself.

27. "My God! The soul [You have bestowed in me]." The *Mishnah Berurah* 6:12 explains that it is preferable to say the blessing *Elokai n'shamah* immediately after *Asher yatzar*, and not after *Birkath HaTorah*, as printed in many prayer books. Because *Asher yatzar* thanks God for the body and *Elokai n'shamah* praises God for the soul, some authorities rule that the two blessings are connected and should be recited together.

28. If she does not feel the urge to relieve herself, she should still create the need to wash her hands, for example, by scratching the head or

yatzar together with the rest of the morning blessings (*birkhoth ha'shachar*).[29]

---

touching parts of the body which are normally covered.

29. *Mishnah Berurah* 6:9. To understand the reason for postponing *Al netilath yadoyim*, we must look at the halakhic rationale for the blessing itself. The *Rishonim* (early commentators) explain that from the perspective of *ruach ra* alone, washing the hands in the morning does not require a blessing. *Ruach ra* is considered a danger — and a blessing is not said over actions performed for the purpose of preventing harm, but only for those carried out in fulfillment of a *mitzvah*. Since *Chazal* do require a blessing when washing the hands in the morning, we can assume that it also involves a *mitzvah*. There are two opinions on exactly which *mitzvah* is involved. The *Rosh* explains that when a person sleeps, the hands become unclean from touching normally-covered parts of the body and cites the *mitzvah* of cleaning the hands before prayer as the reason why *Chazal* enacted the blessing *Al netilath yadoyim*. The *Rashba,* however maintains that the *mitzvah* of *Netilath Yadayim* in the morning is based on the obligation to begin each day on a note of sanctity. "Because in the morning a person is created anew," he writes, "we are commanded to give thanks to God Who created us in order to serve Him... *Chazal*, therefore, decreed that a person should sanctify himself at the start of each day by purifying his hands... just as a *cohen* would do at the beginning of each day's service in the *Beith HaMikdash*" (cited in the *Beith Yosef, Orach Chayim* 4). Clearly, then, while the *Rosh* views the *mitzvah* of *Netilath Yadayim* as a preliminary to prayer, the *Rashba* places it in the overall preparations for the day's activities. The *Mishnah Berurah* rules that in our practice we adopt both views, by postponing *Al netilath yadoyim* until morning prayer, when washing fulfills a dual function.

The controversy between the *Rosh* and the *Rashba* raises an interesting question discussed by *Machazeh Eliyahu*, No. 11: Should a woman who does not recite *Shema* or *Shemoneh Esrey* recite *Al netilath yadoyim* at all? The author concludes that she should not, following the *Rosh*'s view that the *mitzvah* of washing the hands only exists as a preparation for prayer. The *Rosh*'s view should be followed in this instance, because the blessing should only be said when both the *Rosh*'s and *Rashba*'s opinions are satisfied.

Although it is not discussed by *Machazeh Eliyahu*, it would appear that if the woman recites even a short prayer, such as the *birkhoth*

Some authorities[30] take issue with this sequence, maintaining that *Al netilath yadoyim* should always be recited early — after relieving herself upon awakening — regardless of whether morning prayers follow immediately.[31]

18. A woman who wakes up before dawn[32] and washes her hands should wash them again after dawn, without a blessing, even if she has stayed awake in the intervening time.[33]

If she returned to sleep or relieved herself, she may recite *Al netilath yadoyim* over the second washing provided that she did not already recite it over the first one.[34]

If she did not recite the blessing over the first washing,

---

ha'shachar, she may wash and say *Al netilath yadoyim* beforehand, provided she intends to fulfill her obligation of prayer through these blessings and does not plan to say *Shemoneh Esrey* later. (See Chapter 2, paragraph 2, for a discussion of a woman fulfilling her obligation of *Tefillah* by reciting a short prayer in place of *Shemoneh Esrey.*)

30. *Sha'arey Teshuvah,* cited in the *Mishnah Berurah* 6:9; *Shulchan Arukh HaRav* 4.
31. These authorities agree that the blessing should only be said after relieving oneself. See note 26.
32. Dawn begins approximately seventy-two minutes before sunrise.
33. *Shulchan Arukh, Orach Chayim* 4:14. The *Mishnah Berurah* 4:31 cites authorities who rule that *ruach ra* settles on a person at dawn, whether or not she is sleeping.
34. *Mishnah Berurah* 4:33. The ruling that if a blessing was recited over the first washing it should not be repeated over the second washing, even if the hands have become unclean, is based on the *Rashba*'s view, which connects the *mitzvah* of washing the hands to the obligation to purify oneself at the start of the day's activities. According to this view, a woman satisfies her obligation for the whole day when she recites the blessing upon awakening the first time, and it may not be repeated.

and she has not returned to sleep, she should relieve herself before reciting *Al netilath yadoyim* over the second washing.[35]

19. A person who remains awake the entire night should still wash her hands in the morning to remove *ruach ra*.[36] The blessing, however, should be recited only when washing after she has relieved herself or has made her hands unclean in some other way.[37]

---

35. *Mishnah Berurah, Ibid.* Since the *Rosh* links the blessing to the obligation to clean the hands for prayer, it can only be said when the hands are actually unclean. Otherwise, according to the *Rosh*, it is called a "blessing in vain".
36. Some authorities rule that *ruach ra* settles on a person at dawn, whether or not she has slept. Others link it to sleep, and therefore a person should wash for *ruach ra* without reciting the blessing, even after a daytime nap.
37. *Shulchan Arukh, Orach Chayim* 4:13; *Mishnah Berurah* 4:30.

CHAPTER 2
Prayer

A Woman's Obligation to Pray

1. Most halakhic authorities maintain that women are obligated to recite the *Shacharith* and the *Minchah Shemoneh Esrey* on weekdays, *Shabbathoth* and *Yamim Tovim*. In addition, they have an obligation to recite other sections of the Morning Service enumerated below.[1]

---

1. *Shulchan Arukh, Orach Chayim* 106:1; *Mishnah Berurah* 106:4. A woman's obligation to pray is first mentioned in the *Mishnah, Berakhoth* 3:2: "Women...are obligated in the *mitzvoth* of *Tefillah, Mezuzah* and *Birkath HaMazon*." The nature of this obligation is the subject of a dispute between the *Rambam* and the *Ramban*.

The *Rambam* maintains that although Torah Law requires a person to pray daily, "Torah Law does not indicate the number of times one must pray in a day, neither does it prescribe a formal wording for prayer or set a fixed time for this *mitzvah*. Therefore, women are required to fulfill this obligation since it constitutes a positive commandment that need not be performed at a specific time" (*Hilkhoth Tefillah* 1:1).

According to the *Rambam*, there is a Torah obligation of *Tefillah* which can be fulfilled by saying almost any kind of short prayer any

2. A woman who is so involved in caring for children that she cannot spare the short time necessary to recite *Shemoneh Esrey* is nevertheless obligated to recite a short prayer.[2] This prayer must begin with an expression of

---

time during the day. The time-bound aspects of this *mitzvah* derive from Rabbinic decrees, which set forth specific hours and wordings. In his view, the *mitzvah* requiring women to pray refers only to the commandment as required by Torah Law. The *Magen Avraham* 106:2 reports that, following the *Rambam*'s ruling, it was customary for women to say some short prayer each day but not the *Shemoneh Esrey*. (The necessary elements of these short prayers are discussed in paragraph 2.)

The *Ramban*, on the other hand, maintains that Torah Law only requires prayer when one is in actual distress. In his view, the requirement of daily prayer is entirely Rabbinic and equally binding on both men and women. Women must recite the *Shacharith* and *Minchah Shemoneh Esrey* in spite of the fact that these prayers are to be recited within specific hours. The *Ramban* overrides the general exemption of women from time-bound *mitzvoth* by interpreting *Chazal* (in Tractate *Berakhoth* 20b) to be saying that prayer, an act of requesting mercy from God, is equally incumbent on men and women, since they both need Divine beneficence.

The *Mishnah Berurah* rules: "The *Ramban*'s opinion is accepted by the majority of halakhic authorities...Women should therefore be instructed to recite the entire *Shemoneh Esrey* twice each day, in the morning and afternoon."

A similar view is found in *Yalkut Shimoni (Shmuel, Remez* 80): " 'And Channa prayed' — This is a source for a woman's obligation to pray, for Channa recited the Eighteen Blessings." (See also *Kaf HaChayim* 70:1.)

Most women do not recite the *Ma'ariv Shemoneh Esrey*. Although the Talmudic ruling that *Ma'ariv* is voluntary applies to men as well, men have accepted evening prayer as an obligation from early times. Women have not done so, and therefore it remains truly voluntary for them. See paragraph 31.

2. In *Sichoth Chafetz Chayim*, Chapter 1, par. 27, Rav Aryeh Leib, the son of the *Chafetz Chayim*, writes, "My mother, of Sainted Memory, hardly ever recited *Shemoneh Esrey* as long as we were in

praise to God (*shevach*), followed by a personal request (*bakashah*) and words of thanksgiving *(hoda'ah).*[3]

---

her care. She told me that my father had exempted her from this obligation because she was constantly involved in raising her children."

R. Dov Eisenberg, writing in *A Guide for the Jewish Woman and Girl,* p. 30, reports, "I have heard from HaGaon Rav Yaacov Kanievsky that a woman who is involved in child care has the halakhic status of one who is attending a sick person and is exempt from the obligation to pray." (See also *Mo'adim Uz'manim,* Vol. 1, Chapter 9.) Still, a woman who can find a few moments to recite *Shacharith* and *Minchah* is required to do so. In addition to fulfilling her obligations, she will be enriching the spiritual atmosphere of her home. Seeing their mother take time for prayer will definitely make a strong impression on children. She should not be overly concerned if she cannot concentrate properly during the entire *Shemoneh Esrey.* In strained circumstances, she can fulfill the *mitzvah* of *Tefillah* even if she only concentrates during the first blessing. See *Shulchan Arukh, Orach Chayim* 101:1.

3. According to the *Rambam*'s view, cited in note 1, a woman's short prayer must include *shevach, bakashah* and *hoda'ah* to satisfy the minimum criteria of the *mitzvah* of *Tefillah.* Although he maintains that Torah Law does not require fixed or formal prayers, he does insist that they conform to a specific structure: "The obligation of this commandment is as follows: A person should supplicate and pray each day by relating words of praise to God (*shevach*) and afterwards asking [God to grant] his individual needs (*bakashah*)...Afterwards, he should express praise and thanksgiving to God for all the good that He has bestowed upon him (*hoda'ah*)" (*Hilkhoth Tefillah* 1:2). See also *Mo'adim Uz'manim,* Vol. 1, Chapter 9.

The *Pri Megadim,* in his introduction to the Laws of Prayer, states that a woman who has recited a specific prayer, even *Ma'ariv,* three times in a row, must continue the practice, as she is considered to have taken a vow. She may be released from it only by having the vow formally annulled. But *Rivevoth Ephrayim,* Vol. 1, No. 173, cites the decision of HaGaon Rav Eliezer Yehudah Valdenberg, who takes an opposing view, maintaining that it does not constitute a vow. See also *Noam,* Vol. 12, p. 140.

The *birkhoth ha'shachar* (morning blessings)[4] and *Birkath HaTorah* (blessing over Torah) contain these elements, and both fulfill the requirements of a "short prayer".[5]

3. If a woman has additional time, she should add the following prayers, listed in order of priority: (Note that they are always *said* in the order in which they are printed in the *siddur*.)

a) *Shemoneh Esrey*

b) The first verse of *Shema* — together with the line *Barukh shem k'vod malkhutho l'olam va'ed*

c) The blessing *Emeth v'yatziv*[6]

d) *Barukh she'amar, Ashrey* and *Yishtabach*[7]

---

4. These blessings begin with *asher nathan la'sekhvi vinah* (Who gave the rooster understanding) and conclude with *ha'gomel chasadim tovim le'amo Yisrael* (Who bestows kindness on His people Israel).

5. The three blessings which constitute *Birkath HaTorah* contain these three elements: *shevach* ("Who has sanctified us...to be involved in the study of Torah"), *bakashah* ("May the words of Your Torah be sweet in our mouths...") and *hoda'ah* ("Who has chosen us from all the nations...").

6. "True and firm." This blessing, which runs for seven paragraphs in most prayer books, joins the end of the full *Shema* to the beginning of *Shemoneh Esrey*. It is the "Blessing after *Shema*" mentioned in Tractate *Berakhoth* 11a. Care should be taken to lead directly from the concluding words of the blessing, *ga'al Yisrael*, (Who redeemed Israel), to the opening of *Shemoneh Esrey* without a break.

7. *Barukh she'amar* is the introduction to *P'sukey D'zimrah* — the collection of psalms, prayers and Torah passages said as a preparation for the morning service; the full *P'sukey D'zimrah* is last on the list of priorities.

Barukh she'amar should not be said without also reciting *Ashrey* (Psalm 145), considered the most important of the *p'sukey d'zimrah*, and it must be followed by *Yishtabach*, the concluding blessing.

e) *Birkhoth ha'shachar*

f) *Birkath HaTorah* and the two passages that follow. ("May the Lord bless you and keep you," and the Mishnaic excerpt which begins, "These are things which have no fixed measure...")[8]

g) The two blessings which precede *Shema*[9]

h) The entire *Shema*[10]

i) The entire *P'sukey D'zimrah* (Verses of Praise)[11]

Eating Before Prayer

4. Both men and women are forbidden to eat or drink before morning prayers.[12] This restriction does not include

---

8. These verses, containing sections from both the Written and Oral Law, have the effect of combining actual learning with the blessings over Torah study.

9. *Yotzer ohr* (Former of light) and *Ahavah rabbah* (With unbounded love).

10. This includes all three paragraphs which follow the verses, *Shema Yisrael* and *Barukh shem k'vod...*

11. The order of priority for the various passages of *P'sukey D'zimrah* is given in the *Shulchan Arukh, Orach Chayim* 52.

    R. Dov Eisenberg, in *A Guide for the Jewish Woman and Girl*, p. 34, raises two objections to this order of priority (which follows *Birur Halakhah* 70). First, since the *Beith Yosef, Magen Avraham* and *Pri Megadim* clearly maintain that women are obligated to recite *Birkath HaTorah*, these blessings should take precedence over the *birkhoth ha'shachar*, where the obligation is less clear. Further, *P'sukey D'zimrah* should take precedence over *Shema* and the two blessings which precede it. All authorities concur that women are exempt from the *mitzvah* of reciting *Shema* and the preceding blessings, but many authorities do require *P'sukey D'zimrah*.

12. *Shulchan Arukh, Orach Chayim* 89:3, based on Tractate *Berakhoth* 10b: "If one eats and drinks before his prayers, of him Scripture says, 'And you have cast Me behind your back' (*Melakhim I* 14:19). Read not *gavekha* (your back) but *gey'eka* (your pride). Says God, 'Only after this person has first exalted himself does he then

water, tea or coffee, even with sugar.[13]

5. A person who feels weak is permitted to eat and drink as necessary before prayer.[14]

6. A girl who wishes to eat at home before going to school should pray before eating. If this is not possible, she should at least recite the *birkhoth ha'shachar* or *Birkath HaTorah*. It is also recommended that she recite the first verse of *Shema*.[15]

7. Children below *bar mitzvah* and *bath mitzvah* age are permitted to eat before prayer.[16]

---

come and accept the Kingdom of Heaven.' "

13. The *Mishnah Berurah* 89:22 specifies that one may drink water, tea or coffee and that it is our custom to permit the addition of sugar. The *Mishnah Berurah* emphasizes that before prayer one should refrain from drinking tea with friends, for then it becomes a social gathering.

14. *Shulchan Arukh, Orach Chayim* 89:4. The *Mishnah Berurah* 89:24 explains in this case that it is not a sign of arrogance to take a small amount of food or drink to regain strength in order to devote oneself more fully to prayer.

15. *Minchath Yitzchak*, Vol. 4, No. 28:3.

Many high schools and seminaries instruct their students to pray in their classrooms. This practice has great educational value since students often pray with greater devotion there than at home. As a result, many girls need to eat breakfast before *Shacharith*. HaGaon Rav Shlomo Zalman Auerbach points out that in practice it is customary to permit high school and seminary girls to eat before reciting *Shemoneh Esrey*, provided they recite a short prayer before eating.

Although women are halakhically exempt from the *mitzvah* of saying *Shema*, they are advised to recite at least the first verse before eating. See the *Mishnah Berurah* 89:22 and the *Biur Halakhah* beginning *V'lo le'ekhol*.

16. *Mishnah Berurah* 106:5. This applies even if the child is old enough to pray every day.

General Instructions

8. It is proper to designate a fixed place in the home for prayer.[17]

9. A woman should not engage in housework such as laundering, ironing, cleaning or cooking before reciting morning prayers.[18]

10. A woman should be sure that her clothes are neat and clean for prayer. One should not recite *Shemoneh Esrey* in a bathrobe or apron.[19]

11. A woman should wash her hands before prayer. The blessing *Al netilath yadoyim*, however, is said only once each day, before her first prayer in the morning. (For details, see Chapter 1, paragraphs 16 and 17.)[20]

12. When there is an infant or toddler in the house, a woman should not recite *Shemoneh Esrey* before checking the child's diaper. If she fails to do so and then discovers that the child has soiled his diaper, she must repeat *Shemoneh Esrey* if the child was less than four cubits away from her.[21]

---

17. *Mishnah Berurah* 90:59.
18. *Shulchan Arukh, Orach Chayim* 89:3, and *Mishnah Berurah.*
19. *Shulchan Arukh, Orach Chayim* 91:5, and *Mishnah Berurah.*
20. *Shulchan Arukh* 92:4.
21. *Shulchan Arukh, Orach Chayim* 76:7-8, and *Mishnah Berurah.* According to the conversion calculations of the *Chazon Ish*, four cubits is 2.34 meters (92.8 inches). According to HaRav Chaim Naeh, it is 1.92 meters (76.8 inches).

    If the excrement was exposed, she must repeat *Shemoneh Esrey* even if she smelled no foul odor. If it was covered, *Shemoneh Esrey* is only repeated if there was a foul odor.

    The *Shulchan Arukh* 81:1 explains that these laws apply "from

13. A woman should not pray while facing a naked child.[22]

14. A woman in the middle of *Shemoneh Esrey* is allowed to signal a child who is crying or disturbing her. She should, however, not interrupt the *Shemoneh Esrey* by speaking.[23] If the child is causing a disturbance which makes it difficult to concentrate, she may walk over and quiet him down, but she must not speak.[24]

The Morning Blessings

15. Women are obligated to recite the fifteen morning blessings (*birkhoth ha'shachar*) which begin with *asher nathan la'sekhvi vinah*[25] and end with *ha'gomel chasadim tovim l'amo Yisrael.*[26]

---

the age at which a child can eat a *k'zayith* of grain in the time it takes an adult to eat an *akhilath pras.*" A *k'zayith* of grain is a dry volume measurement equivalent to the volume of an olive; and *akhilath pras* is, variously, three or four times the volume of an egg. *Yosef Ometz* (Norlingen), No. 9, states, "I saw my father, of Blessed Memory, rule that these laws apply from the age of one year." Some authorities set an earlier age. The *Misgereth HaShulchan*, commenting on the *Kitzur Shulchan Arukh* 5:3, stipulates three months, and *Beith Barukh*, Vol. 1, p. 67, decides on two to three months. According to the *Magen Avraham*, cited in the *Mishnah Berurah* 81:3, it is proper to be stringent even with the excrement of an eight-day-old child. The *Shulchan Arukh HaRav* 81:2 interprets "eight-day-old child" to mean a new-born infant. If a woman adds cereal to a new born's formula, even *Yosef Ometz* might agree with the ruling of the *Magen Avraham.*

22. See Chapter 7, paragraph 14.
23. *Sha'arey Teshuvah* 104:1.
24. This is based on a ruling of HaGaon Rav Shlomo Zalman Auerbach.
25. "Who gave the rooster understanding."
26. "Who bestows bountiful kindness upon His people Israel." This is

Instead of the blessing *She'lo asani ishah,*[27] women should recite the blessing *She'asani kirtzono.*[28] According

---

the final line of the longer, concluding prayer that begins with, "Blessed are You...Who removes sleep from my eyes..."

Some authorities exempt women from reciting the *birkhoth ha'shachar*, maintaining that their recitation is a time-bound *mitzvah*. The *Rashba*, in the Responsa cited in Chapter 1, note 30, rules that the *birkhoth ha'shachar* should only be said in the morning. The *Derekh HaChayim (Hilkhoth Onen*, par. 5) infers from the *Magen Avraham* 70:1 that all the morning blessings, except for *Birkath HaTorah, She'lo asani goy, eved, ishah* and *She'asani kirtzono*, must be recited before the end of the fourth hour of the day. According to their view, most of the *birkhoth ha'shachar* falls outside a woman's obligations.

In *Ma'asey Rav* 9, on the other hand, it is explicitly stated that according to the Vilna Gaon the *birkhoth ha'shachar* may even be recited after nightfall, if they were not said during the day. According to his view, then, these blessings are not time-bound, and women are obligated to recite them. The *Mishnah Berurah* 70:2 infers that this is also the view of the *Shulchan Arukh, Orach Chayim* 46:4. The *Mishnah Berurah* concludes that even the authorities who exempt women from reciting the *birkhoth ha'shachar* agree that they may assume the obligation if they wish.

The *Mishnah Berurah* 46:1 cites the *Tur*'s explanation of the purpose of these blessings, which may serve as an additional reason for obligating women to recite them: "Because it is forbidden for a person to derive benefit from the physical world without a blessing...our Sages designated a blessing for each of the routine activities which we enjoy." Clearly, this concept applies to women no less than to men.

27. "Who did not make me a woman." A man recites this blessing to thank God for the extra *mitzvoth* that he, as a man, is required to fulfill.

28. "Who made me according to His Will." The *Shulchan Arukh, Orach Chayim* 46:4, implies that this blessing should be recited with *shem* and *malkhuth*. The *Pri Chadash* rules that it should be recited without *shem* and *malkhuth*, because this blessing is not found in Talmudic sources. The general custom is to include *shem* and *malkhuth* in the blessing.

There are several interpretations of the blessing *She'asani*

to many Sephardic authorities, the blessing *She'asani kirtzono* should be recited without mentioning God's name or the declaration of His kingship (*shem* and *malkhuth*). Their text is *barukh atah she'asani kirtzono.*[29]

The general practice is for women to say *she'lo asani goy* and *she'lo asani eved* as men do,[30] although some authorities rule in favor of the feminine forms *she'lo asani*

---

kirtzono. The *Tur, Orach Chayim* 46, and the *Avudraham* explain that it signifies acceptance of God's decree that they should have fewer *mitzvoth* to perform than men. According to Rav Samson Raphael Hirsch, this blessing expresses thanks to God for creating women more naturally attuned to His Will than men: "God's Torah takes it for granted that our women have greater fervor... for their God-serving calling and that they are less threatened by temptations which occur in the course of business and professional life. Accordingly, the Torah does not find it necessary to give women these repeated...reminders [of additional *mitzvoth*] to remain true to their calling" (Commentary to the Torah, *VaYikra* 23:43).

A novel interpretation is offered in *Yeshuoth Yaacov, Orach Chayim* 46:5. The *Midrash Rabbah, Bereshith, Parsha* 8, relates how God consulted the angels before creating Man. The world was to be arranged so that the Heavenly Hosts would suffer if Man sinned. They had to accept this great risk and give their consent to the creation of Man. Since Woman is less prone than Man to sin, God created her without consulting the angels. So the intention of the blessing *She'asani kirtzono* is to thank God, "Who has created [Woman] in accordance with His Will [alone]."

29. *Kaf HaChayim, Orach Chayim* 46:41, citing the *Chiddah; Ben Ish Chai, Shanah Rishonah, Parshath VaYeshev* 10. *Y'chaveh Da'ath*, Vol. 4, No. 4, concludes that teachers of Sephardic girls should instruct their students to recite this blessing without *shem* and *malkhuth*. The general custom, however, even in Sephardic communities, is to include them. See note 38.

30. The *Eshel Avraham* (Butchach) defends the masculine form, explaining that the words *goy* and *eved* are general terms which include women. The *Shulchan Arukh* also implies that the wording of these blessings does not change when they are recited by women.

goyah and *she'lo asani shifchah.*[31]

16. Women are required to recite *Birkath HaTorah* every morning.[32] If a woman wishes to study Torah before saying morning prayers, she must recite *Birkath HaTorah* first.

---

31. *Siddur Nussach Livorno* cites the feminine form, as does the *Kaf HaChayim, Orach Chayim* 46:42. It is also found in *Siddur Ya'avetz* of Rav Yaacov Emden. Many respected schools in Jerusalem do say it, keeping *shem* and *malkhuth* in the blessing. *Siddur Ya'avetz*, however, advises against including *shem* and *malkhuth*, because the feminine form does not explicitly appear in the Talmud.

32. *Shulchan Arukh, Orach Chayim* 47:14. *Birkath HaTorah* consists of the three blessings: *La'asok b'divrey Torah* (Who has commanded us to occupy ourselves with words of Torah); *V'Ha'arev nah* (Please make pleasant); and *Asher bachar banu* (Who has chosen us).

The *Shulchan Arukh* states that women are required to recite *Birkath HaTorah*. He bases this ruling on the view of the *Agur*, who notes that women are obligated to learn those laws which relate to them, even though they are exempt from the general commandment of study for its own sake. The recitation of *Birkath HaTorah* is therefore required as a prerequisite to studying these laws.

The Vilna Gaon rejects the *Agur*'s reasoning, maintaining that since women are exempt from the *mitzvah* of Torah study for its own sake, they are not *obligated* to recite the blessing over this *mitzvah*. The Vilna Gaon does *permit* women to recite *Birkath HaTorah* just as women are permitted to recite blessings for any *mitzvah* from which they are exempt. The Vilna Gaon's ruling follows the decision of the *Remah, Orach Chayim* 17:2. According to the Vilna Gaon, Sephardic women, who follow the decisions of the *Beith Yosef* (who maintains that women should not recite a blessing when voluntarily performing *mitzvoth* from which they are exempt), would not be allowed to recite *Birkath HaTorah*.

An original approach to the question of a woman's obligation to recite *Birkath HaTorah* is found in the Novellae of HaGaon Rav Yitzchak Ze'ev Soloveitchik on the *Rambam, Hilkhoth Berakhoth* 11:16. Citing his father, HaGaon Rav Chaim of Brisk, he explains that the blessing which precedes Torah study is essentially different

17. A woman may not exempt a man by her recitation of *Birkath HaTorah.*[33]

18. A woman who has forgotten whether or not she has included *Birkath HaTorah* in her prayers should not recite it out of doubt.[34]

Korbanoth and P'sukey D'Zimrah

19. Some authorities require women to say the sections of the morning service that describe the daily sacrifices

---

from those blessings which precede the performance of other *mitzvoth. Birkath HaTorah* is not a blessing over the *mitzvah* of studying Torah. Rather, the act of Torah study itself calls forth an obligation of praise and gratitude, regardless of whether or not it constitutes an obligation. Women must also recite this blessing in order to express appreciation for the precious gift of Torah that God has bestowed upon the Jewish people.

See also *Minchath Chinukh* 430; *P'nei Yehoshua, Berakhoth* 11b; *Yeshuoth David*, No. 1; *Chathan Sofer*, No. 1; *Rivevoth Ephrayim*, Vol. 3, No. 42.

At least one authority rules that women are actually forbidden to recite *Birkath HaTorah* altogether: See *Chikrey Lev, Orach Chayim,* No. 10.

33. *Biur Halakhah* 47, beginning *Nashim.* A person may fulfill the obligation to recite a blessing by listening to another person recite the same blessing provided that this is the intention of both parties and that the speaker has an obligation in the blessing at least as great as the listener's. Since the Vilna Gaon maintains that *Birkath HaTorah* is voluntary for women, they may not exempt men with their recitation, since the blessing is mandatory for them.

34. *Birkey Yosef, Orach Chayim* 47:8, cited in *Sha'arey Teshuvah* 47:1. If *Birkath HaTorah* is a Torah obligation (as it is with men according to many authorities), one is stringent in cases of doubt and recites it. Since a woman's obligation in this blessing is open to question, she should not recite it in cases of doubt.

(*korbanoth*) in the *Beith HaMikdash*,[35] but it is accepted custom to rely on other authorities who exempt women from these readings.[36]

20. Women are obligated to recite *P'sukey D'zimrah* (Verses of Praise).[37] Some Sephardic authorities rule that

---

35. The *Beith Yosef, Orach Chayim* 47, cites *Mahari Moellin*, who argues that since prayer is a substitute for *korbanoth* and women are obligated to pray, they are accordingly required to recite the readings which describe the *korbanoth*. See also *Biur Halakhah* 47, beginning *Nashim*, and *Shulchan Arukh HaRav, Orach Chayim* 47:10. *Yosef Ometz* (Azulai), No. 67, however, interprets *Mahari Moellin* to mean that the recitation of *Korbanoth* by women is permitted but not obligatory.

36. The *Pri Megadim, Eshel Avraham* 47:14, opposes *Mahari Moellin*. He finds evidence that the Torah specifically excludes women from playing a role in the daily sacrifices in the *Beith HaMikdash*; *Tehillah LeDavid* contends that it is also apparent from the fact that women were exempted from donating the annual half-shekel, which was used to purchase animals for *korbanoth*. These and other objections to *Mahari Moellin* lead us to the accepted custom of exempting women from saying *Korbanoth*.

   The view of *Tehillah LeDavid* is cited by the Vilna Gaon as a reason to exempt women from reciting *Mussaf* as well. (See paragraph 36.) See also *Mor U'K'tzi'ah, Orach Chayim* 47.

37. The *Mishnah Berurah* 70:2, based on *Chiddushey Rabbi Akiva Eiger, Orach Chayim* 52, explains that *P'sukey D'zimrah* were formulated as a preparation for *Shemoneh Esrey*, and since women are required to recite *Shemoneh Esrey*, they are also required to recite *P'sukey D'zimrah*. The *Sha'ar HaTziyun* footnotes to the *Mishnah Berurah* 70:4 quotes the *Shulchan Arukh HaRav* 70:1, which exempts women from these prayers. Also see the *Orukh HaShulchan* 70:1.

   HaGaon Rav Chaim Pinchus Sheinberg rules that since only the opinion of Rabbi Akiva Eiger is cited in the text of the *Mishnah Berurah*, women should not be lenient in this matter when it does not infringe with child care. But he comments, "When necessary they may omit the bulk of *P'sukey D'zimrah* and say at least *Barukh she'amar, Ashrey* and *Yishtabach,* adding to that as time permits."

women should recite *Barukh she'amar* and *Yishtabach* without *shem* and *malkhuth*. Those who do include *shem* and *malkhuth* have sound opinions to rely on.[38]

---

38. HaGaon Rav Ovadiah Yosef, writing in *Yabiah Omer*, Vol. 2, *Orach Chayim*, No. 6, and *Y'chaveh Da'ath*, Vol. 3, No. 3, cites the decision of the *Beith Yosef, Orach Chayim* 17 and 589, that women may not recite blessings over *mitzvoth* from which they are exempt. He deduces that *Barukh she'amar* and *Yishtabach* should be said without *shem* and *malkhuth* because a woman's obligation to recite *P'sukey D'zimrah* is open to question.

The *Kaf HaChayim, Orach Chayim* 70:1, however, takes note of the view of the *Shulchan Arukh HaRav* cited above and concludes, "Knowledgeable women are accustomed to recite the entire morning service beginning with the *Akeidah* (the Torah reading dealing with the binding of Yitzchak) and ending with *Aleinu l'shabei'ach.*" Most Sephardic women rely on this view and recite the blessings with *shem* and *malkhuth.*

The *Tzlach*, in his commentary on Tractate *Berakhoth* 26b, argues that the *Beith Yosef*'s opinion forbidding women to recite blessings over *mitzvoth* from which they are exempt only applies to those blessings which contain the word *v'tzivanu* (and He has commanded us). When someone who is halakhically exempt says *v'tzivanu*, it could be considered a falsehood. Blessings which do not contain the word *v'tzivanu*, then, may be said by women, even though they are exempt from the obligation to recite them.

Tzitz Eliezer, Vol. 9, No. 2, uses the *Tzlach*'s argument to refute the view of *Yabiah Omer* cited above. *Tzitz Eliezer* concludes that both Ashkenazic and Sephardic women may recite these blessings with *shem* and *malkhuth*. See also *Machazeh Eliyahu*, No. 16:2.

HaGaon Rav Ben Zion Abba Shaul explains further: "Even according to the *Beith Yosef*, women may say these blessings because they express praise and thanksgiving. The proof of this is that although many authorities exempt women from the obligation to recite the *birkhoth ha'shachar* (See note 26), the *Beith Yosef* explicitly states that they may recite the blessing *She'asani kirtzono.* It may be inferred then, that he would also permit women to say the other *birkhoth ha'shachar*, and so we must conclude that his ruling against women reciting blessings over time-bound *mitzvoth* does not apply to blessings of praise and thanksgiving. This was also the

Shema and Its Blessings

21. A woman's recitation of *Shema* proclaims her willingness to accept the Yoke of Heaven. Women are advised to say at least the first verse of this most important prayer.[39]

22. Many authorities rule that women are obligated to

---

halakhic decision of our revered teacher, HaGaon Rav Ezra Atiya, of Blessed Memory."

39. *Shulchan Arukh, Orach Chayim* 70:1, and *Mishnah Berurah.*

The *Mishnah, Berakhoth* 3:2, states, "Women are exempt from the *mitzvah* of reciting *Shema.*" The *Gemara (Berakhoth* 20b) explains that since the *mitzvah* to recite *Shema* is fulfilled *b'shakhb'kha u'v'kumekha* (when you lie down and when you rise up), it is time-bound, and women are exempt.

The *Mishnah Berurah* explains that although the *Shulchan Arukh* recommends that women recite at least the first verse of *Shema,* they are not obligated to do so, either by Torah or Rabbinic Law. The *Bach,* however, rules that there is a Rabbinic obligation for women to recite the first verse.

The *Kaf HaChayim, Orach Chayim* 70:5, cites the *Levush,* who adds that women should also recite *Barukh shem k'vod malkhutho l'olam va'ed* (Blessed is the name of the glory of His kingdom forever and ever.) because it appears from the *Shulchan Arukh, Orach Chayim* 66:1, that it completes the idea expressed in the first verse.

It is advisable for women to recite the entire *Shema* whenever possible (*Magen Giborim, Magen HaElef* 3). *Minchath Elazar,* Vol. 2, No. 28, points out that a woman who recites the entire *Shema* without a *minyan* of ten adult males should precede it with the words *keyl melkh ne'eman* (Almighty, faithful King), just as men do. The custom among Sephardim and some Chassidim is to say the final three words of the full *Shema, HaShem Elokeikhem emeth* (The Lord your God is true.), a second time when praying alone. (This repetition is made to bring the total number of words in *Shema* to 248, corresponding to the 248 parts of the human body counted by *Chazal.* In a congregation, the prayer leader repeats the last three words aloud on behalf of all the worshippers to reach this number of words.)

recite the blessing *Emeth v'yatziv*, which follows *Shema*.[40]
This is in order to fulfill the *mitzvah* of remembering the
Exodus from Egypt.[41]

23. Women may recite the two blessings, *Yotzer ohr*
(Former of light) and *Ahavah rabbah* (With unbounded

---

40. "True and firm," the seven-paragraph blessing which follows
Shema and joins it to *Shemoneh Esrey*.

41. "In order that you should remember the Exodus from Egypt all the
days of your life" (*Shemoth* 13:3). From this verse, *Chazal* derive
the obligation to mention *Y'tziath Mitzrayim* (the Exodus from
Egypt) twice daily, once during the day and once at night: " 'The
days of your life' would refer to the daytime; but *all* the days of
your life includes the nights as well" (Tractate *Berakhoth* 12b). The
blessing which follows *Shema, Emeth v'yatziv*, praises God for this
miracle and fulfills the commandment of remembrance.

The *Magen Avraham* 70:1, cited in the *Mishnah Berurah* 70:2 and
106:4, reasons that since the daytime *mitzvah* of remembrance can
be fulfilled the entire day, and the nighttime *mitzvah* the entire
night, remembering the Exodus is not a time-bound *mitzvah*, and it
is incumbent on women. While he does not explicitly discuss
whether women must recite the paragraph beginning *emeth
ve'emunah* (true and faithful) in the evening (the counterpart of
emeth v'yatziv in morning prayers), the *Mishnah Berurah* assumes
that he would definitely require it in order to fulfill the nighttime
mitzvah.

The *Sha'agath Aryeh*, No. 13, rejects this view, maintaining that
remembering the Exodus is a time-bound *mitzvah* since it includes
two parts, one of which can be fulfilled only during the day and the
other only at night.

Objections have also been raised to the *Magen Avraham*'s
insistence that specifically *Emeth v'yatziv* is required to fulfill this
mitzvah. *Be'er Avraham, Berakhoth*, p. 157, wonders why it is not
sufficient for women to recite the third paragraph of *Shema*, which
also mentions the Exodus.

See also *Orukh HaShulchan* 70:4; *Beith Yitzchak, Orach Chayim*
12:2; *Rabbi Akiva Eiger, Teshuvoth HaChadashoth*, No. 5.

love), preceding *Shema*.[42] Some Sephardic authorities rule that women should say these blessings without *shem* and *malkhuth*,[43] but the general custom is to rely on others who permit it.[44]

24. A woman who did not recite *Birkath HaTorah* before prayer should not recite it afterwards, provided that she included *Ahavah rabbah* and *Shema* in her sequence of prayers.[45]

25. The authorities who obligate women in the *mitzvah* of remembering the Exodus from Egypt[46] also obligate them to join the blessing *Ga'al Yisrael*[47] to the beginning of

---

42. *Mishnah Berurah* 70:2; *Pri Megadim, Eshel Avraham* 296:11; *Shulchan Arukh HaRav* 70:1; *Orukh HaShulchan* 70:1. Although the requirement to recite the blessings preceding *Shema* is time-bound, Ashkenazic women are still permitted to recite them, in accordance with the *Remah*'s decision, in *Orach Chayim* 17:2, that women may recite blessings for *mitzvoth* from which they are halakhically exempt.

   Further evidence that this practice is acceptable is found in the spiritual will of the *Tosafoth Yom Tov* who writes, "And also my daughters, be diligent to pray each morning, beginning with the blessing *Yotzer ohr* and concluding with *Shemoneh Esrey*."

43. *Yabiah Omer*, Vol. 2, *Orach Chayim*, No. 6. For a full discussion, see note 38.

44. Since these blessings do not include the word *v'tzivanu*. See note 38.

45. *Yeshuoth Yaacov, Orach Chayim* 47:8. *Chazal* state, in Tractate *Berakhoth* 11b, that a man who has not recited *Birkath HaTorah* may substitute *Ahavah rabbah*, provided he studies Torah immediately after morning prayers. A woman's recitation of *Shema* can be considered voluntary "study" because she is exempt from the *obligation* to recite it, and so *Ahavah rabbah* can substitute for *Birkath HaTorah* without any additional learning. In this case she should have in mind that the blessing *Ahavah rabbah* is serving as a substitute for *Birkath HaTorah*.

46. See note 41.

47. "Who has redeemed Israel." This is the concluding blessing of

Shemoneh Esrey with no interruption between the two.[48]

Time Limits for Morning Prayers

26. Women need not be particular to read even the first verse of *Shema* in its prescribed time,[49] but the blessings preceding *Shema* should not be recited after the first third of the day has passed.[50]

27. The *Shacharith Shemoneh Esrey* should be recited within the first third of the daylight hours.[51] A woman who was unable to pray within this time may still recite *Shemoneh Esrey* until midday.[52]

If midday is approaching, and she will not be able to recite *Shemoneh Esrey* before it passes, she should recite those sections of the morning service for which she has time, in accordance with the order of priority described in paragraph 3.

The law for one who has failed to recite *Shemoneh Esrey*

Emeth v'yatziv and precedes *Shemoneh Esrey.*

48. This practice is known as *s'mikhath ge'ulah l'tefillah* (joining redemption to prayer) and connects the two *mitzvoth.* See the *Mishnah Berurah* 70:2, citing *Magen Giborim.*
49. *Eshel Avraham* (Butchach) 70. A man must recite *Shema* within the first quarter of the daylight hours. This is determined by calculating the length of the day from sunrise to sunset and dividing it by four. The earliest time for its recitation is when there is enough daylight to recognize a casual acquaintance at a distance of four cubits. (See Chapter 2, note 21.)
50. *Shulchan Arukh, Orach Chayim* 58:6, and *Mishnah Berurah.* After this time, *Shema* should be recited without the blessings. The *Biur Halakhah* adds that if it was not possible to recite them earlier, the blessings may be recited until midday.
51. The *Shacharith Shemoneh Esrey* should not be recited before sunrise except in a case of pressing need, in which case it can be said any time after dawn.
52. *Shulchan Arukh, Orach Chayim* 89:1; *Machazeh Eliyahu,* No. 19.

before midday is discussed in paragraph 35.

The Remainder of the Morning Service

28. It is questionable whether women are obligated to say *Tachanun*. The general practice is to omit it.[53] Women who do recite *Tachanun* must omit the Thirteen Attributes of Mercy except when they are praying with a congregation.

29. Women are not required to recite the second *Ashrey*,[54] *U'Vah l'Tziyon*[55] or the Psalm of the Day,[56] all of which are found near the end of the morning service. They

---

53. *Machazeh Eliyahu*, No. 20.

   The argument for exempting women is based on a statement of the *Tur*, citing Rav Natrunai Gaon's ruling that *Tachanun* is voluntary, giving it a status similar to *Ma'ariv*. Since women as a group have not accepted the obligation to recite either of these prayers, they remain voluntary for them. (See paragraph 31.)

54. *Ashrey*, Psalm 145, is recited once in *P'sukey D'zimrah*, once in the concluding portion of the morning service, and once to open the afternoon service.

55. *U'Vah l'Tziyon* ([The redeemer] shall come to Zion) introduces the section known as *Kedushah D'Sidrah*. This section was introduced to accommodate people who came to the synagogue too late to say the *Kedushah* during the repetition of *Shemoneh Esrey*.

   Machazeh Eliyahu, No. 20, explains that a woman's exemption from *U'Vah l'Tziyon* stems from *Rashi*'s comment on Tractate *Sotah* 49a, linking this prayer to the *mitzvah* of studying Torah. Since women are exempt from Torah study, they need not recite this prayer. In practice, many women do recite *Ashrey* and *U'Vah l'Tziyon* in light of the Talmudic saying, "All who recite *Ashrey* three times daily are guaranteed a special place in the World to Come" (Tractate *Berakhoth* 4a).

56. These Psalms are connected to the daily sacrifices, as explained in Tractate *Sofrim* 18:1. Women, who took no part in these sacrifices (See note 36.), likewise need not recite them. Nevertheless, many do so voluntarily.

should recite *Aleinu l'shabei'ach*[57] and are advised to say *Ein K'Elokeinu*[08] and *Pitum ha'k'toreth,*[59] in communities where men customarily say them.

Afternoon and Evening Prayers

30. Most authorities require women to recite the *Minchah Shemoneh Esrey*. Women who only recite a short prayer in the morning should make every effort to recite the entire *Minchah Shemoneh Esrey* in the afternoon.[60]

31. In accordance with the Talmudic ruling that the evening *Shemoneh Esrey* is voluntary, most women do not recite it. Although men have accepted *Ma'ariv* as an obligatory prayer, women have not done so.[61] Nevertheless, some authorities do require women to recite it.[62]

---

57. "It is our obligation to praise," *Machazeh Eliyahu, Ibid.*
58. "There is none like our God," a popular hymn of praise recited by Ashkenazim outside of Israel only on *Shabbath* and *Yom Tov*. It is recited daily by most Ashkenazim in Israel and by Sephardim and Chassidim in all parts of the world. The *Kaf HaChayim* 132:18 notes the *Zohar*'s emphasis on the importance of this prayer.
59. "The composition of the incense." This passage from Tractate *Kerithoth* 6a contains the recipe for the incense offered in the *Beith HaMikdash* and instructions for its preparation. It follows *Ein K'Elokeinu* and is only said in those places where *Ein K'Elokeinu* is said.
60. Even if she could not find sufficient time to recite *Shemoneh Esrey* in the morning, it is often easier to find time in the afternoon. See *Y'chaveh Da'ath*, Vol. 3, No. 7.
61. *Mishnah Berurah* 106:4 and 299:37. The *Mishnah Berurah* cites the *Magen Avraham*, who reports that women are not accustomed to recite *Ma'ariv*, even on *motzo'ei Shabbath*. The *Pri Megadim, Mishbetzoth Zahav* 271:1, further notes that women have also not accepted the obligation to recite *Ma'ariv* on *Shabbath* or *Yom Tov*.
62. The *Orukh HaShulchan* 106:7 writes, "It is difficult to explain why women are not particular to pray three times daily." See also

32. Some authorities require women to recite *Emeth ve'emunah*[63] and *Hashkiveinu*,[64] the two blessings that follow *Shema* in the evening service. If they wish, they may recite the entire service.[65]

Some Sephardic authorities rule that the blessings that precede *Shema* should be said without *shem* and *malkhuth*; it is customary to rely on contrary authorities.[66]

33. A woman may begin the evening service with the blessings *Emeth ve'emunah* and *Hashkiveinu*. She may then proceed to *Shemoneh Esrey*.[67]

Correcting Errors in Shemoneh Esrey

34. A woman who forgets to include *v'theyn tal u'matar*

Sha'agath Aryeh, No. 14. The *Kaf HaChayim* 299:62 writes, "Nowadays, women have the custom to pray *Shacharith, Minchah* and *Ma'ariv*." See also *Iggereth HaTeshuvah* of Rabbenu Yonah, *HaDrash HaSh'lishi* 79, with the notes of HaRav Binyamin Zilber.

63. "True and faithful", the prayer which follows the last paragraph of *Shema* in the evening. See note 41 for the opinions of the *Magen Avraham* and the *Sha'agath Aryeh* concerning a women's obligation in the *mitzvah* of remembering the Exodus from Egypt. Women who do not recite *Emeth ve'emunah* rely on the view of the *Sha'agath Aryeh*, which exempts them from this *mitzvah*.

64. "Cause us to lie down." This is the second of the two prayers that follow *Shema* in the evening and is considered an extension of *Emeth ve'emunah*. See the *Mishnah Berurah* 70:2.

65. See note 42.

66. See note 38.

67. The blessing *Barukh HaShem le'olam* (Blessed be the Lord forever), recited in many communities after *Hashkiveinu*, is not connected to the *mitzvah* of remembering the Exodus from Egypt and may be omitted when not reciting the entire evening service according to all opinions.

livrakhah[68] during the winter, or *Ya'aleh v'yavoh*[69] on *Rosh Chodesh* or *Chol HaMoed*, should repeat the entire *Shemoneh Esrey*.[70] She should note to herself that she may not be obligated, and that if this is the case, her repetition

---

68. "And bestow dew and rain for blessing," a phrase inserted into the ninth blessing of *Shemoneh Esrey, Ba'reikh aleinu* (Bless for us), during the winter months. In Israel, the phrase is inserted from *Ma'ariv* on the seventh of *Cheshvan* until the first day of *Pessach*. Outside of Israel, it is inserted beginning with *Ma'ariv* on December 4 (or 5th in a civil leap year), regardless of when that falls in the Hebrew calendar.

    If a woman realizes, before finishing *Shemoneh Esrey,* that she did not insert *v'theyn tal u'matar* in its proper place, she may add it to the blessing *Shema koleinu* (Hear our voice), prior to the words *ki atah shomey'ah* (for You hearken). Details of this provision may be found in the *Shulchan Arukh, Orach Chayim* 117:5, and *Kitzur Shulchan Arukh* 19:6.

    A person who omits *mashiv ha'ruach* (Who causes the wind to blow), the phrase inserted into the second blessing of *Shemoneh Esrey* in winter (from *Mussaf* on *Sh'mini Atzereth* through *Shacharith* on the first day of *Pessach*), must repeat *Shemoneh Esrey*. One who has the custom to recite the words *morid ha'tal* (Who brings the dew) during the summer months and mistakenly says these words instead of *mashiv ha'ruach*, does not repeat *Shemoneh Esrey*. See *Shulchan Arukh, Orach Chayim* 114, and *Kitzur Shulchan Arukh* 19:1.

69. "May there ascend and come." This special prayer for *Rosh Chodesh* and *Chol HaMoed* is inserted into the seventeenth blessing of *Shemoneh Esrey, R'tzey* (Be pleased). If *Ya'aleh v'yavoh* was omitted from *Ma'ariv* of *Rosh Chodesh, Shemoneh Esrey* is not repeated by women or men.

70. A woman who normally recites *Shemoneh Esrey* is required to observe all the laws relevant to it. See *Machazeh Eliyahu*, No. 24; *Magen Giborim* 106:3; *Yabiah Omer*, Vol. 6, *Orach Chayim*, No. 18. *Yabiah Omer* decides that this ruling applies even to women who recite *Shemoneh Esrey* only occasionally.

    Birur Halakhah, Vol. 2, No. 259, rules that a woman who regularly recites *Ma'ariv* must repeat *Shemoneh Esrey* in the same situations in which a man must repeat it.

should be considered a *tefillath n'davah* (voluntary prayer).[71]

A woman who does not regularly recite *Shemoneh Esrey* need not repeat it if these insertions are omitted.[72]

Compensating for a Missed Prayer

35. A woman who normally recites *Shemoneh Esrey*, but who neglects to do so due to forgetfulness or pressing circumstances, may compensate for the missed prayer by reciting a second *Shemoneh Esrey* at the following service.[73]

An omitted *Shacharith Shemoneh Esrey* is made up at Minchah by first reciting *Minchah* and then an additional *Shemoneh Esrey*. A woman who omitted *Minchah* should compensate for it by reciting two *Shemoneh Esrey*s at *Ma'ariv*, even if she does not usually say *Ma'ariv*.[74]

If a woman recalls in the morning that she omitted

---

71. *Yabiah Omer, Ibid.* Whatever was omitted from the first *Shemoneh Esrey* is counted as the *chiddush* (special request or praise normally needed in a voluntary prayer — see note 76) during the second, complete recitation.

72. *Machazeh Eliyahu, Ibid.*, contrary to the ruling of *Yabiah Omer* cited in note 70.

73. The second *Shemoneh Esrey* must be identical to the first. Thus, if *Minchah* on *Erev Shabbath* was omitted, the *Ma'ariv Shemoneh Esrey* of *Shabbath* is said twice that evening. The halakhic details of the compensatory *Shemoneh Esrey* are discussed in the *Shulchan Arukh, Orach Chayim* 108, and *Kitzur Shulchan Arukh* 21.

74. This ruling is based on a Responsa written by HaGaon Rav Shlomo Zalman Auerbach and is supported by the *Mishnah Berurah* 263:43's discussion of a woman who did not have time to recite *Minchah* before candle-lighting on *Erev Shabbath*. The *Mishnah Berurah* concludes that rather than say *Minchah* after lighting the *Shabbath* candles, she should recite *Ma'ariv* twice, and the wording indicates that this procedure should be followed even if she does not usually say *Ma'ariv*.

Minchah the previous day, she may not make it up.[75] Technically, she may recite a voluntary prayer with the missed *Minchah* in mind providing she adds a special request or praise (*chiddush*).[76] In general, however, voluntary prayer is discouraged.[77]

Mussaf

36. Authorities disagree as to whether women are obligated to recite *Mussaf*, the prayer which takes the place of the additional sacrifices offered on *Shabbath, Rosh Chodesh, Yom Tov* and *Chol HaMoed.*[78] Even if exempt,

---

75. A missed *Shemoneh Esrey* may be made up only during the next service. HaGaon Rav Auerbach explains that although women are not obligated to recite *Ma'ariv*, it provides the only opportunity to make up an omitted *Minchah*. Even women who do not regularly recite *Ma'ariv* should do so in this situation in order to make up *Minchah*.

    HaGaon Rav Auerbach has further ruled that a woman who regularly recites *Ma'ariv* need not make it up if she omits it one evening. He explains: "Since most women have not accepted *Ma'ariv* as an obligation, she is exempt from compensating for it. If she wishes, however, she may do so without adding a *chiddush*. This is not considered a voluntary prayer because it is being said in place of a missed prayer." (HaGaon Rav Auerbach's Responsa has been published in *Midresheth El-HaMekoroth*, Jerusalem, Ellul, 5740.)

76. The *Shulchan Arukh, Orach Chayim* 107, explains that the special request must be for something that the worshipper is not accustomed to ask for every day, and it must be included in at least one of the middle thirteen blessings.

77. Says the *Shulchan Arukh*: "One who wishes to recite a voluntary prayer must be...diligent to maintain proper devotion from beginning to end. If he is unable to devote himself properly, God says of him, 'Why do I need all your sacrifices' (*Yeshay'ahu* 1:11)? Would it be that he should properly devote himself during the three obligatory prayers."

78. The *Mishnah Berurah* 106:4 cites the *Tzlach*, who exempts women from reciting *Mussaf*, and the *Magen Giborim*, who obligates them.

women are permitted to recite *Mussaf* with *shem* and *malkhuth*,[79] a practice also accepted by the Sephardim.[80]

In his commentary on Tractate *Berakhoth* 20b, the *Tzlach* bases his argument on the view of the *Ramban*, cited above in note 1, who maintains that *Chazal* obligated women to recite *Shemoneh Esrey* because women are in need of God's mercy as much as men are. *Mussaf*, however, was enacted strictly to commemorate the additional sacrifice offered on special Holy Days. Since there are no personal requests in *Mussaf*, there is no special reason for women to say it, reasons the *Tzlach*. The general principle of exempting women from time-bound *mitzvoth* applies here. Rabbi Akiva Eiger finds an additional reason in the Responsa of *B'samim Rosh*, No. 89. He explains that the animals offered as communal sacrifices were purchased with the half-shekel funds given each year to the *Beith HaMikdash* by every Jewish male. The exemption of women from this *mitzvah* means that they were not expected to contribute toward the cost of animals used for communal sacrifices. Therefore, they are exempt from *Mussaf*, which is purely a commemoration of these sacrifices.

The authorities who maintain that women are required to recite *Mussaf* cite the Talmudic ruling that women are included in the *mitzvah* of *Kiddush*, inferring that any *mitzvah* related to the sanctity of a particular day is incumbent upon women and is not treated as a regular time-bound obligation. See Responsa of Rabbi Akiva Eiger, No. 9, and his glosses to the *Shulchan Arukh, Orach Chayim* 106; *Maharm Shick, Orach Chayim*, No. 90; *Shevet HaLevi*, Vol. 4, *Orach Chayim*, No. 12:2.

79. The *Tzlach* decides that although women are exempt from *Mussaf*, they may recite it voluntarily with *shem* and *malkhuth*. He explains that this does not conflict with the *Beith Yosef*'s ruling forbidding women to recite blessings over *mitzvoth* from which they are exempt since, according to the *Tzlach*, the *Beith Yosef* means only those blessings that contain the word *v'tzivanu*. *Mussaf* does not contain the word *v'tzivanu*, and so it may be said even by those women who follow the rulings of the *Beith Yosef*. See note 38.

80. Lengthy discussions of this issue are found in *Tzitz Eliezer*, Vol. 9, No. 2, and *Machazeh Eliyahu*, No. 23. It should be noted that the *Mishnah Berurah* appears to favor the view of the *Magen Giborim*, which does require women to recite *Mussaf*.

Nevertheless, there are some Sephardic authorities who rule that it is preferable for women to come to the synagogue and listen to the *Chazan*'s recitation rather than recite *Mussaf* themselves.[81]

37. Women *are* required to recite *Mussaf* on the High Holy Days. They are also required to recite *Ne'ilah* on *Yom Kippur*.[82]

38. The preferred time to recite *Mussaf* is no later than half an hour after midday — but if one does recite *Mussaf* later in the day, the *mitzvah* is fulfilled.[83]

Hallel

39. Women are exempt from reciting *Hallel* on *Rosh Chodesh* and *Yom Tov*.[84] They are, however, required to recite it at the *Pessach Seder*.[85] Ashkenazic authorities permit women to say the complete blessings — before and after *Hallel* even on *Rosh Chodesh*.[86]

---

81. *Yabiah Omer*, Vol. 2, *Orach Chayim*, No. 6. See note 38.
82. *Yabiah Omer, Ibid.*, explains that since we ask mercy from God in these prayers, women are obligated to recite them. See also *Moadim Uz'manim*, Vol. 1, No. 9, which adds that on these days a woman should not fulfill her obligation with a short prayer but should recite the entire *Shemoneh Esrey* and, if possible, the entire service.
83. *Shulchan Arukh, Orach Chayim* 286:1, and *Biur Halakhah*. If *Mussaf* is recited in the afternoon, it should be preceded by *Minchah*.
84. The *Biur Halakhah* 422, beginning *Hallel*, based on Tractate *Sukkah* 38a and the *Magen Avraham* 422:5, exempts women because *Hallel* is a time-bound *mitzvah*.
85. *Biur Halakhah, Ibid. Hallel* at the *Seder* commemorates the Exodus from Egypt, and since women benefited from this miracle as much as men did, they are required to recite *Hallel*. For women living outside of *Eretz Yisrael, Hallel* at the second *Seder* is likewise obligatory.
86. *Chazal* point out that the recitation of half-*Hallel* on *Rosh Chodesh*

Saying Shema at Bedtime

40. Women should recite *Shema* before retiring for the night. They should also say the blessing *HaMapil.*[87] It is customary for married women to say the blessing with their hair covered.

is a custom (*minhag*). The Ashkenazic practice is for men to say the blessing over *Hallel* even when its recitation is not strictly required by Law. Sephardic men and some Chassidim, following the view of the *Beith Yosef,* do not recite a blessing in performance of a *minhag.* The *Biur Halakhah* specifies that Ashkenazic women are permitted to recite the blessing over the *minhag* of *Hallel* on *Rosh Chodesh.* The *Yeshuoth Yaacov* 422:6, however, argues with this ruling, reasoning that since women are exempt from saying *Hallel* even when it is obligatory for men, they should not recite the blessing on days when it is only a *minhag.*

The *Biur Halakhah* suggests that because there is no actual obligation to recite *Hallel* on *Rosh Chodesh,* a man's status might be considered equivalent to a woman's. If this is the case, argues the *Biur Halakhah,* she could recite the blessings and exempt both of them. The *Biur Halakhah* does not make a definitive ruling, however.

Sephardic women may also recite *Hallel* but should omit the blessings, even on *Yom Tov,* following the view of the *Beith Yosef* cited in note 38. See *Y'chaveh Da'ath,* Vol. 1, No. 78; *Yabiah Omer,* Vol. 6, *Orach Chayim,* No. 45; *Tzitz Eliezer,* Vol. 9, No. 2.

87. "Who causes [the fetters of sleep] to fall." This is the main prayer before retiring at night. It should be said within one-half hour of actually falling asleep, and one is not allowed to engage in conversation after saying it.

The *Magen Avraham* reports that in his day it was not customary for women to say this blessing because it is "bound" to the time of just before retiring. The *Machatzith HaShekel,* however, cites the *Eliyahu Rabbah,* who asserts that women should say *HaMapil* because it offers protection during sleep. The *Pri Megadim, Eshel Avraham* 239:2, states that in his day women did recite *HaMapil;* the *Kaf HaChayim* 239:3 and the *Orukh HaShulchan* make the same observation.

Many men omit *shem* and *malkhuth* from the blessing *HaMapil.* The *Ben Ish Chai, Parshath Pikudey* 12, reports this to have been the

Nussach

41. A woman, before her marriage, must retain the *nussach*[88] of prayer and all other customs of her father's family. A single woman[89] may not deviate from the *nussach* inherited by her father, even if he does not himself fulfill the *mitzvah* of prayer.[90]

---

custom of many Sephardim and most of the Chassidim of Jerusalem in the nineteenth century. The reason for the omission is the fear that one may converse after the blessing, thereby invalidating it. The *Ben Ish Chai* concludes, "It is proper for each person to follow the custom of his forefathers...but even those who do not include *shem* and *malkhuth* should bear them in mind at the appropriate point in the blessing."

88. The term *nussach* refers to the prescribed order and liturgical tradition of the prayers. There are several variant forms of *nussach ha'tefillah*. The most widely followed are *Nussach Ashkenaz*, *Nussach Sephard*, *Nussach Polin*, *Nussach Teman* and *Nussach HaAri*.

89. After marriage, a woman adopts all the customs and practices of her husband.

90. The *Mishnah Berurah* 68:4, citing *Sha'ar HaKavanoth*, explains that there are twelve gates in Heaven, corresponding to the twelve tribes of Israel. The prayers of each tribe can only ascend to Heaven through the particular gate that corresponds to its unique spiritual quality, and only by means of its specific *nussach*. The Talmud *Yerushalmi*, Tractate *Eruvin*, Chapter 3, states, "Although you have received the order of prayer [prescribed by the Sages], do not deviate from the customs of your forefathers."

It is said that deviating from one's own *nussach* constitutes a transgression of the admonition, "Forsake not the Law of your Mother" (*Mishley* 1:8). ("Mother" refers to the customs that have been adopted by the communities of Israel.) See *Pe'ath HaShulchan* 3:14 and *Sho'el U'meishiv, Mahadurah Sh'lishi*, Vol. 1, No. 247.

HaGaon Rav Ben Zion Abba Shaul rules that a Sephardic, single woman who moves to a community that follows a different *nussach* must maintain her father's *nussach*. If she has already changed her *nussach*, she should return to that of her father.

42. In a synagogue which follows a different *nussach*, a woman should say the silent *Shemoneh Esrey* in accordance with her own *nussach*. *Kedushah*[91] and other prayers recited aloud should be said in accordance with the *nussach* of the congregation.[92]

43. Hebrew is the preferred language of prayer. If a woman is unable to pray in Hebrew, she may pray in any language that she understands. The prayer itself should be the standard Hebrew prayer translated into the familiar language.[93] If possible, though, she should try to use the Hebrew words even if she does not understand their meaning.

Praying with a Congregation

44. A woman is not required to pray with a *minyan*,[94] and she is not counted as part of a *minyan*.[95] Nevertheless, it is meritorious for her to pray with a congregation in a synagogue.[96]

---

91. *Kadosh, kadosh, kadosh* (holy, holy, holy), the public proclamation of the holiness of God in the third blessing of *Shemoneh Esrey* as repeated by the leader.
92. *Iggeroth Moshe, Orach Chayim*, Vol. 2, No. 23, and *HaTefillah B'Tzibur*, Chapter 6.
93. *Mishnah Berurah* 101:8 and 62:3; *HaTefillah B'Tzibur, Ibid.*
94. *Shevuth Yaacov, Orach Chayim*, Vol. 3, No. 54; *Teshuvah MeAhavah*, Vol. 2, No. 229.
95. *Mishnah Berurah* 55:3, based on the verse, "And I will be sanctified in the midst of *b'ney Yisrael* (the sons of Israel)" (*VaYikra* 22:32). This verse is the source for the principle that certain prayers may only be recited in the presence of a *minyan* of ten *b'ney Yisrael*. Since the expression *b'ney Yisrael* refers to men and not to women, *Chazal* infer that women are not to be counted as part of a *minyan*.
96. The *Gemara, Sotah* 22a, relates that a certain widow would walk to the synagogue of R. Yochanan even though there was another synagogue closer to her home. This woman's practice was

45. Women are forbidden to pray in a synagogue that does not have a proper *mechitzah* (partition between men and women).[97] Even on *Rosh Hashanah* and *Yom Kippur*, it is better to pray at home than in a synagogue that contravenes this essential law.[98]

46. The requirement of *mechitzah* applies to all gatherings in a synagogue, including those whose purpose is other than prayer.[99]

Prayer When a Woman is a Niddah

47. When a woman is a *niddah*, she may enter the synagogue, pray, and recite all blessings.[100]

---

considered so significant that the *Magen Avraham* 90:22 cites it as the source for the idea that a person receives greater reward for attending a distant synagogue than one closer to home. See also *Yalkut Shimoni, Parshath Ekev* 871.

97. *Mechitzah* is a requirement of Torah Law. The partition should be at least as high as the shoulders of those standing on either side of it. Preferably, one should not be able to see the head of someone standing on the other side. See *Iggeroth Moshe, Orach Chayim*, Vol. 1, No. 39, and Vol. 3, No. 23.

   Shevet HaLevi, Vol. 1, No. 29, points out that children should be trained in the importance of *mechitzah*; boys and girls should not be allowed to sit in the same synagogue without a proper *mechitzah*.

98. *Menachem Meishiv, Orach Chayim*, No. 9, citing *Machaneh Chayim*, Vol. 3, *Orach Chayim*, No. 1.

99. *Iggeroth Moshe*, Vol. 1, *Orach Chayim*, No. 39. In *Teshuvoth U'Biurim*, 5743, the Lubavitcher Rebbe cites many sources which indicate that it is permissible to hold a gathering for women in the men's section of the synagogue providing that no men are present.

100. The *Remah, Orach Chayim* 88:1, cites two opinions concerning a woman entering the synagogue, reciting blessings and praying during her menstrual period. Although he agrees with the opinion that permits it, he reports that the practice in his community was to follow the stringent view. He specifies that even in places where

Strong objection should be made to those who mistakenly assume that a woman should not enter the synagogue for forty days after the birth of a son or eighty days after the birth of a daughter. This practice has no basis in Jewish Law.[101]

48. When a woman is a *niddah*, she is permitted to pray at the *Kothel HaMa'aravi* (Western Wall).[102]

Torah Reading

49. Some authorities rule that women are obligated to listen to *K'riath HaTorah* (Torah reading) on *Shabbath*.[103]

---

women are stringent in this matter, they may attend synagogue services during the High Holy Days. (The *Mishnah Berurah* explains that these days begin from the first day of *Selichoth*.)

The *Mishnah Berurah* 88:6 states that the consensus of the later authorities obligates women to pray and recite all blessings during the menstrual period. "Moreover," he concludes, "in our countries the practice is for these women to attend synagogue services as well. It is customary, however, for them not to look at the *Sefer Torah* when it is raised before the congregation." (See paragraphs 51 and 52 with their notes.) *Y'chaveh Da'ath*, Vol. 3, No. 8, adds that while a woman is allowed to act stringently and absent herself from synagogue services, under no circumstances should she neglect to pray or recite blessings.

Although a woman has the halakhic status of a *niddah* until she purifies herself in a *mikvah*, the above stringencies only apply during her actual menstrual period.

101. *Mishnah Berurah* 88:5.
102. *Yabiah Omer*, Vol. 5, *Yoreh De'ah*, No. 27.
103. *Magen Avraham* 282:6, citing Tractate *Sofrim*. The *Magen Avraham* likens *K'riath HaTorah* to the *mitzvah* of *Hakhel* (Gathering of the People), a *mitzvah* that was fulfilled every seven years when all Jews — men, women and children — came to the *Beith HaMikdash* to hear the King read the Torah during the *Sukkoth* holiday.

The *Birkey Yosef, Orach Chayim* 282:7, finds support for the *Magen Avraham*'s view in the *Tur*'s (*Orach Chayim* 417) explanation

Generally, however, women are not particular in this regard.[104] Accordingly, a woman who comes late to the synagogue on *Shabbath* may recite the *Shacharith Shemoneh Esrey* during *K'riath HaTorah*.[105]

50. All authorities agree that a woman may not read the Torah for the congregation or be called for an *aliyah*.[106]

51. When the *Sefer Torah* is raised[107] before the congregation, both men and women must look at it, bow and say, "This is the Torah that Moshe placed before the Children of Israel..."[108]

---

that a fourth *aliyah* is added on *Rosh Chodesh* because women refrain from certain types of work on that day. This implies that *K'riath HaTorah* is relevant to them.

The *Orukh HaShulchan* 282:11 criticizes the *Magen Avraham*'s comparison of *K'riath HaTorah* to *Hakhel*. Since women are exempt from studying Torah and since *K'riath HaTorah* is time-bound, he finds no reason to obligate them.

104. *Mishnah Berurah* 282:12. The *Mishnah Berurah* reports that it was common in many places for women to leave the synagogue during *K'riath HaTorah*, in contradiction to the view of the *Magen Avraham*.

HaGaon Rav Yosef Sholom Eliashiv states that since today's women are often capable of understanding the Torah reading, it is highly recommended that they remain in the synagogue and listen to *K'riath HaTorah*.

105. This is based on a ruling of HaGaon Rav Yosef Sholom Eliashiv that it is better for a woman to miss *K'riath HaTorah* than miss the time for prayer.

106. *Shulchan Arukh, Orach Chayim* 282:3, based on Tractate *Megillah* 23a.

107. In Sephardic and in some Chassidic congregations, this takes place before *K'riath HaTorah*, in Ashkenazic congregations, after the reading. See *Shulchan Arukh, Orach Chayim* 134:2.

108. *Shulchan Arukh, Orach Chayim, Ibid.* The *Mishnah Berurah* 134:11 adds that it is meritorious to see the letters of the *Sefer Torah* themselves.

52. It is customary for a woman who is a *niddah* to refrain from looking at the Torah when it is raised.[109]

53. It is customary to bring young children to the synagogue so that they may kiss the *Sefer Torah*[110] and learn to love *mitzvoth*.

54. We conclude this chapter with a quotation from Rabbenu Yonah in *Iggereth HaTeshuvah*:

"At the end of her prayers, her main supplication should be for the welfare of her children — that they be God-fearing and successful in the study of Torah. A woman's greatest merit in the World to Come is when her children serve God, fulfill His Will and fear Him. When she is in the World to Come, and her children are God-fearing and diligent in *mitzvoth*, it is as if she is still alive and performing all the command-ments."[111]

---

109. *Mishnah Berurah* 88:7. As explained in note 100, this only applies to a woman during her menstrual period. Otherwise, even if she has not yet purified herself in a *mikvah*, she may look at the *Sefer Torah*.
110. *Remah, Orach Chayim* 149.
111. See also the *Mishnah Berurah* 47:10.

CHAPTER 3
Mitzvoth of the Meal

Netilath Yadayim

1. Both men and women are required to perform the *mitzvah* of *Netilath Yadayim* before eating bread.[1] One who does not know how to recite *Birkath HaMazon* is nevertheless obligated to perform the *mitzvah* of washing.

Children should be trained to fulfill this *mitzvah* at an early age.[2]

---

1. The *mitzvah* of washing the hands before eating bread is not considered time-bound, and so women are not exempt. It is fulfilled by pouring water twice over each hand from a utensil that contains at least a *revi'ith*. A *revi'ith* is measured as 150 cubic centimeters (5.3 fluid ounces), according to the *Chazon Ish*, and 86 cubic centimeters (3 fluid ounces), according to HaRav Chaim Naeh.

   The procedure for *netilath yadayim* before eating bread differs from washing the hands to remove *ruach ra* (See Chapter 1.) in that water is not poured alternately over each hand, but twice over the right hand and then twice over the left hand. Other details of this *mitzvah* are found in *Shulchan Arukh, Orach Chayim* 158-165.

2. *Ben Ish Chai, Shanah Rishonah, Parshath Sh'mini* 2.

2. The *mitzvah* of *Netilath Yadayim* is fulfilled only if there is nothing to prevent the water from touching every part of the hand, i.e., if there is no *chatzitzah* (separation) between the hand and the water.[3]

3. Nail polish does not constitute a *chatzitzah* unless it is chipped.[4]

4. If a woman removes her rings on certain occasions, she must also remove them for *Netilath Yadayim*.[5] This rule applies even if they are loose-fitting.[6] It is better to avoid holding rings between the teeth while washing.[7]

If she forgets to remove loose-fitting rings, she need not wash again, providing a full *revi'ith* of water was poured over the hand.[8]

5. Some authorities rule that a *niddah* should not pour water for *Netilath Yadayim* over another person's hands.[9]

---

3. *Shulchan Arukh, Orach Chayim* 161:1. In unavoidable circumstances, a *chatzitzah* is permissible above the knuckles joining the fingers to the hand.
4. A substance that covers a small part of the hand and that one is never particular to remove is not a *chatzitzah*. Nail polish is considered a *chatzitzah* only if it is chipped, because then women are particular to remove it. See *Shulchan Arukh, Orach Chayim* 161:2.
5. *Shulchan Arukh, Orach Chayim* 161:3, and *Mishnah Berurah*. Since she sometimes removes the rings, they constitute a *chatzitzah*. This rule also applies to men's rings.
6. *Remah, Orach Chayim* 161:3.
7. According to the *Shulchan Arukh, Orach Chayim* 172:2, one is forbidden to recite a blessing with something in the mouth. If she keeps rings in her mouth while washing, she may forget to remove them before reciting the blessing.
8. *Mishnah Berurah* 161:18. The amount of water that is called a *revi'ith* is discussed in note 1.
9. *Shulchan Arukh, Orach Chayim* 159:11, and *Mishnah Berurah*. The

More recent authorities report that this stringency is not generally observed.[10]

Mayim Acharonim

6. The requirement of *mayim acharonim* (washing the hands before *Birkath HaMazon*) applies to both men and women.[11] The custom of many women, however, is not to wash *mayim acharonim*.[12]

---

reason given is that a woman in a state of *tum'ah*, ritual impurity, who lifts the water, renders it also *tom'ey*, ritually impure; such water should not be used in a purification process.

10. *Chazon Ish, Orach Chayim* 83:8. The *Mishnah Berurah, Ibid.*, explains that, in our times, we are all assumed to be *tom'ey meith*, ritually impure from contact with dead bodies or from entering cemeteries. This *tum'ah* can only be removed through a purification process involving the ashes of the Red Heifer. (See *BaMidbar* 19.) Since it is transmitted to water if a *tom'ey* person raises the container, anyone — a man or a woman, even when she is not a *niddah* — would, in any case, make the water *tom'ey* today.

11. This is based on a ruling of HaGaon Rav Shlomo Zalman Auerbach. He explains that one reason why many women have not accepted this practice is a story in Tractate *Yoma* 83b, where the requirement of *mayim acharonim* indirectly resulted in a woman's death. Nevertheless, in his opinion, there is no valid exemption from this requirement for women. HaGaon Rav Yosef Chayim Sonnenfeld, of Blessed Memory, also maintained that women should wash *mayim acharonim*. See *Salmath Chayim*, Vol. 4, No. 3:2.

12. HaGaon Rav Shmuel HaLevi Wossner writes in *Shevet HaLevi*, Vol. 4, *Orach Chayim*, No. 23, that the basis for women not washing *mayim acharonim* is found in the *Shulchan Arukh, Orach Chayim* 181:10. *Chazal* explain that in Talmudic days a certain type of salt, called *melach s'domith* (salt from Sodom) was commonly used, and that it could cause blindness if it came in contact with the eyes. The original purpose of *mayim acharonim* was to rinse the *melach s'domith* off the hands. The *Shulchan Arukh* states that since this salt is no longer in use, the obligation of *mayim acharonim* no longer applies. Although many men follow the view of other

Birkath HaMazon

7. Women are obligated to recite *Birkath HaMazon*.[13] Although they are halakhically exempt from saying the words *v'al briskhah shechasamta bivsareynu, v'al toraskha shelimadtanu*,[14] most women do say them.[15]

8. It is not clear whether a woman's obligation to recite *Birkath HaMazon* is a Torah or a Rabbinic requirement.[16]

---

authorities who maintain that the *mitzvah* does apply today, women commonly follow the view of the *Shulchan Arukh*.

HaGaon Rav Yonah Merzbach reports that in many German communities, before the Second World War, women omitted *mayim acharonim* and that this practice was common even in households extremely scrupulous in the performance of *mitzvoth*.

13. *Shulchan Arukh, Orach Chayim* 186:1. *Birkath HaMazon* is not considered a time-bound *mitzvah*.

14. "And [we thank you] also for Your convenant that You sealed in our flesh, as well as for Your Torah which You taught us."

15. The *Remah, Orach Chayim* 187:3, states that women should not recite these words since they refer to *brith milah* and Torah study, and they are not obligated in these *mitzvoth*. The *Mishnah Berurah* 187:9 states, however: "Today, women are accustomed to say these words, having in mind that through the merit of the *mitzvoth* of *brith milah* and Torah study all Jews come to inherit *Eretz Yisrael*. Moreover, women do have the obligation to study those sections of Torah that are relevant to them."

16. *Shulchan Arukh, Orach Chayim* 186:1, and *Mishnah Berurah*.

The question of a woman's obligation to recite *Birkath HaMazon* is discussed in Tractate *Berakhoth* 20b. Most early authorities maintain that the Talmudic discussion remains unresolved.

At first it appears that women should be obligated by Torah Law to fulfill the *mitzvah* of *Birkath HaMazon* since it is not time-bound. Two explanations are offered for the Talmudic suggestion that a woman's obligation is only Rabbinic. *Rashi* reasons as follows: The Torah characterizes this *mitzvah* as an obligation to "Bless the Lord your God for the good Land that He has given to you" (*Devarim* 8:10). Since women were not granted individual portions in *Eretz Yisrael*, they may be exempt. *Tosafoth* rejects this argument,

Therefore, she may not recite *Birkath HaMazon* and thereby *motzie* (exempt) a man who has eaten a *shiur sevi'ah*, an amount of bread that "satisfies" his hunger. When a man eats a *shiur sevi'ah*, he is definitely obligated by the Torah to recite *Birkath HaMazon*,[17] and a woman, whose obligation may only be Rabbinic, cannot discharge his Torah obligation for him.[18]

Situations of Doubt

9. Some authorities maintain that a woman who has eaten a *shiur sevi'ah* of bread and forgotten whether or not

---

pointing out that *cohanim* and *levi'im* were also not granted individual portions in the Land, yet they are definitely included in the *mitzvah*. *Tosafoth*'s argument may be countered with the fact that *cohanim* and *levi'im* were given various residential cities, which could be considered their portion in the Land. (See *BaMidbar* 35:1-8.)

Tosafoth postulates that women might be exempt from the Torah requirement because of the Talmudic ruling, "Anyone who fails to mention *brith milah* and Torah study in *Birkath HaMazon* has not fulfilled his obligation" (Tractate *Berakhoth* 49a). The apparent connection between *Birkath HaMazon* and the *mitzvoth* of *brith milah* and Torah study (from which women are excluded) may be the basis for exempting them from the Torah requirement to recite *Birkath HaMazon*.

17. *Chazal* explain that according to Torah Law a man is obligated to recite *Birkath HaMazon* only if he has eaten enough bread to satisfy him. This *shiur sevi'ah* is not a fixed amount, but depends on the individual. If other foods are eaten with the bread, they contribute to the *shiur sevi'ah*. If other foods are eaten separately, they do not, in which case the obligation of Torah Law is calculated only by the amount of bread eaten.

Chazal decreed, however, that *Birkath HaMazon* should be recited if a man ate only an amount of bread equivalent to the volume of an olive — a *k'zayith*. A *k'zayith* is a dry volume measurement equivalent to approximately 28 cubic centimeters (1 ounce).

18. *Mishnah Berurah* 186:3; *Shulchan Arukh HaRav* 186:3.

she has said *Birkath HaMazon* should nevertheless say it. Other authorities reach the opposite conclusion.[19] One is permitted to act stringently and say *Birkath HaMazon.*[20]

If the woman washes her hands a second time, recites the blessing *Ha'motzie lechem min ha'aretz,*[21] and eats a *k'zayith* of bread, according to both opinions she can recite *Birkath HaMazon* with the intention that it also cover the first meal. Another solution is to ask someone else who is reciting *Birkath HaMazon* to include her.[22]

Exempting Oneself by Listening

10. The *mitzvah* of *Birkath HaMazon* may be fulfilled by listening to another's recitation, even if the listener does

---

19. The *Mishnah Berurah* 186:3 cites the *Chaye Adam, Magen Giborim* and *Sha'arey Ephrayim*, who maintain that in a case of doubt a woman is obligated to recite *Birkath HaMazon*. Rabbi Akiva Eiger, *Birkey Yosef*, and the *Pri Megadim* are among the authorities who exempt women from reciting *Birkath HaMazon* in this situation.

   The authorities who require a woman to say *Birkath HaMazon* cite the general rule that in cases of doubt one must be stringent with respect to Torah obligations. The dissenting authorities argue that a woman may act leniently because the obligation may be Rabbinic. Clearly, this dispute applies only when a *shiur sevi'ah* has been eaten. If not, the obligation of *Birkath HaMazon* is definitely Rabbinic, and in practice we are lenient with all Rabbinic obligations in situations of doubt.

20. This is based on the conclusion of the *Mishnah Berurah, Ibid.* Some authorities maintain that the question posed in Tractate *Berakhoth* 20b (See note 16.) was resolved, and a woman's obligation to recite *Birkath HaMazon* is, in fact, a Torah Law; in a situation of doubt, she may rely on these authorities and recite *Birkath HaMazon*.

21. "Who brings forth bread from the earth", the blessing recited before eating bread.

22. *Kaf HaChayim* 184:25. The *Mishnah Berurah* 184:15 recommends this solution to both men and women who are uncertain whether they have already recited *Birkath HaMazon*.

not know how to say *Birkath HaMazon* herself.[23] It is preferable, however, for the listener to repeat each word silently.[24]

11. Many authorities maintain that the listener fulfills the *mitzvah* even if she does not understand the meaning of the words. Since some authorities do insist that a person who is only listening must understand the meaning of the words, the listener should try to be particular to repeat each word silently to herself; with this repetition, all agree that the *mitzvah* is fulfilled, with or without comprehension.[25]

12. A woman who has eaten a *k'zayith* of bread may *motzie* another woman who has eaten a *shiur sevi'ah.*[26]

---

23. *Shulchan Arukh, Orach Chayim* 193:1; *Remah, Orach Chayim* 199:7; *Mishnah Berurah* 193:5. If the listener is capable of reciting *Birkath HaMazon* herself, it is preferred, since it is difficult to listen with concentration to every word of someone else's recitation. Also see *Mishnah Berurah* 183:27.

    For one person to include another in her recitation of *Birkath HaMazon,* she must intend to include the listener, and the listener must have intention to discharge her obligation in this way.

24. *Mishnah Berurah* 193:5 and 199:19.

25. *Mishnah Berurah, Ibid.*

26. Responsa of Rabbi Akiva Eiger, No. 7, and Glosses of Rabbi Akiva Eiger to *Shulchan Arukh, Orach Chayim* 271:2, refuting the view of the *Tzlach* in his commentary on *Berakhoth* 20b.

    A man who has eaten a *k'zayith* of bread may *motzie* another man who has eaten a *shiur sevi'ah*, although the one reciting *Birkath HaMazon* is only obligated by Rabbinic Law, and the other is obligated by Torah Law. This is an application of the general principle of *arvuth* (mutual responsibility), which enables a man to recite a *birkath ha'mitzvah* (blessing over the fulfillment of a *mitzvah*) for another man even if he himself is not fulfilling the *mitzvah* at that time. *Chazal* have established that *arvuth* may be

13. A woman who has eaten a *shiur sevi'ah* may *motzie* a man who is in doubt whether he has said *Birkath HaMazon*, even if he has eaten a *shiur sevi'ah*.[27]

14. A woman may *motzie* a child who has eaten any amount of bread,[28] but a child may not *motzie* a woman who has eaten a *shiur sevi'ah*.[29]

A man who has eaten a *k'zayith* may *motzie* a woman who has eaten a *shiur sevi'ah*.[30]

---

applied to *Birkath HaMazon* only if the person reciting the blessing has eaten at least a *k'zayith*, as explained in Tractate *Berakhoth* 48a. While the *Tzlach* asserts that the principle of *arvuth* does not apply to women and that a woman may not *motzie* another woman unless they are equally obligated in the *mitzvah* at the same time, Rabbi Akiva Eiger insists that the principle of *arvuth* applies to women no less than to men.

27. Glosses of Rabbi Akiva Eiger to *Shulchan Arukh, Orach Chayim* 186:1. The *K'thav Sofer* accepts this ruling only in the case where the man is in doubt whether he has actually eaten a *shiur sevi'ah*.

28. *Shulchan Arukh HaRav* 186:3. It appears that a woman who has only eaten a *k'zayith* may even *motzie* a child who has eaten a *shiur sevi'ah*.

29. A child who has reached an age at which he has begun performing *mitzvoth* is obligated by Rabbinic Law to recite *Birkath HaMazon*. Accordingly, he may *motzie* a man or woman who has eaten less than a *shiur sevi'ah*, in which case the adult's obligation is also only Rabbinic.

30. *Shulchan Arukh HaRav* 186:2. This decision follows the view of Rabbi Akiva Eiger, cited in note 26, that the principle of *arvuth* applies equally to men and women.

A woman who has eaten a *shiur sevi'ah* may not *motzie* a man who has eaten a *shiur sevi'ah*, since for *arvuth* to apply the essential obligation of the person reciting must be at least equal to that of the person listening. Since a woman's essential obligation may be Rabbinic, she may not *motzie* a man, who definitely has a Torah obligation.

Additions on Shabbath and Yom Tov

15. On *Shabbath*, the paragraph that begins with the words *r'tzey v'hachalitzeinu* (may it please You to strengthen us) is added to *Birkath HaMazon* just before the words *u'v'nei Yerushalayim* (rebuild Jerusalem).

On *Yom Tov, Rosh Chodesh* and *Chol HaMoed*, the paragraph beginning with the words *Elokeinu...ya'aleh v'yavoh* (our God...may there ascend and come) is added at the same place.

16. If a woman realizes that she has omitted *R'tzey* from *Birkath HaMazon*, either at the Friday night or *Shabbath* morning meal, she should follow these rules:

a) If she has begun the paragraph following *U'v'nei Yerushalayim*, beginning with *baruch...Hakeil avinu*, she must repeat the entire *Birkath HaMazon*.[31]

b) If she has not yet spoken God's Name in the blessing *Bonei Yerushalayim*, she must stop immediately, return to *R'tzey*, and proceed from there.

c) If she has spoken God's Name in the blessing *Bonei Yerushalayim*, but has not begun the following

---

31. Responsa of Rabbi Akiva Eiger, No. 1. *Chazal* explain, in Tractate *Berakhoth* 49b, that when one fails to mark a special occasion in *Birkath HaMazon*, it must be repeated only if there is an obligation to eat bread at that meal. Women are obligated to eat three meals on *Shabbath*, although the *mitzvah* of eating three meals is time-bound. Their obligation is deduced from the tradition that God uttered *zakhor* (remember [the *Shabbath*]) and *shamor* (guard [the *Shabbath*]) simultaneously in order to teach us that everyone included in guarding the negative commandments of *Shabbath* is also included in performing the positive ones. Thus, women, like men, are obligated to eat three meals on *Shabbath*, the first two of which definitely require bread. (See note 33.) Also see *Y'chaveh Da'ath*, Vol. 4, No. 20.

paragraph, a special blessing is inserted after the conclusion of *Bonei Yerushalayim.*[32]

Neither men nor women should repeat *Birkath HaMazon* if they omit *R'tzey* at the third *Shabbath* meal.[33]

17. If a woman omits *Ya'aleh v'yavoh* from *Birkath HaMazon*, she repeats *Birkath HaMazon* only if the omission occurs on the first night of *Pessach* (the first two nights in the Diaspora).[34] On other *Yamim Tovim*, a woman does not repeat *Birkath HaMazon* if this paragraph is omitted.

Some authorities maintain that if *Ya'aleh v'yavoh* is omitted on any of the *Yamim Tovim, Birkath HaMazon* must be repeated,[35] but all agree that it is not repeated — by men or women — on *Rosh Chodesh* or *Chol HaMoed.*

---

32. These special blessings are found in many editions of the *siddur.* Their laws are detailed in the *Shulchan Arukh, Orach Chayim* 189:6-8. If the blessing is unavailable, follow rule a).

33. Authorities disagree whether there is an obligation to eat bread at the third *Shabbath* meal. The obligation to repeat *Birkath HaMazon* in this case is therefore questionable, and so we do not.

34. Responsa of Rabbi Akiva Eiger, *Ibid.*, and Glosses of Rabbi Akiva Eiger to *Shulchan Arukh, Orach Chayim* 188:6. Rabbi Akiva Eiger cites the view of *Tosafoth,* in Tractate *Kiddushin* 34a, that women are exempt from the positive *mitzvoth* of *Yom Tov*, including the eating of a festive meal with bread. Just as men who omit *Ya'aleh v'yavoh* on *Rosh Chodesh* or *Chol HaMoed* do not repeat *Birkath HaMazon* (since they are not obligated to eat bread on these days), women who omit *Ya'aleh v'yavoh* on *Yom Tov* do not repeat it. An exception is the *Pessach Seder*, at which women are obligated to eat at least a *k'zayith* of *matzah.* In this case, if *Ya'aleh v'yavoh* is omitted, *Birkath HaMazon* must be repeated. (If she has not yet begun the paragraph following *Bonei Yerushalayim*, rules b) and c) in paragraph 16 should be followed.)

35. *Pithchey Teshuvah* of *Mahariyah* of Vilna, No. 188, and *She'ilath Shmuel* disagree with this ruling of Rabbi Akiva Eiger. Moreover, no reference is found in the *Shulchan Arukh* or any of its

Zimun and Sheva Berakhoth

18. A woman is not counted as one of the three people needed to form a *zimun*,[36] even if she is eating with her husband and children.[37]

Three women who have eaten bread together may form their own *zimun*.[38]

If ten women have eaten bread together, the additional word *Elokeinu* should not be said.[39]

19. Three women who have eaten bread with three men are permitted to form their own separate *zimun*. If there are ten men present, the women may not form their own *zimun*.[40]

---

commentaries to warrant a distinction between men and women on *Yamim Tovim. Zecher Simchah*, No. 27, concludes that in practice it is still best for women not to repeat *Birkath HaMazon*, except at the *Pessach Seder*.

36. This refers to the introductory sentences of *Birkath HaMazon* when three people have eaten bread together. One person "invites" the others to recite *Birkath HaMazon* with him by beginning *rabothai n'vareikh*.

37. *Shulchan Arukh, Orach Chayim* 199:6, and *Mishnah Berurah; Chazon Ish, Orach Chayim* 30:8.

38. *Shulchan Arukh, Orach Chayim* 199:7. The *Biur Halakhah* explains that this is not an obligation. The *Ben Ish Chai, Shanah Rishonah, Parshath Korach* 13, however, advises men to instruct the women in their families to form a *zimun* when three or more of them eat together.

39. *Shulchan Arukh, Orach Chayim* 199:6, and *Mishnah Berurah*. God's Name may be said only when a *minyan* is present, and a *minyan* must consist of at least ten adult males. (See Chapter 2, note 95.) The *Shulchan Arukh HaRav* adds that even if there are nine men and one woman, the group is not permitted to add *Elokeinu*.

40. *Mishnah Berurah* 199:18, based on the *Shulchan Arukh HaRav*. If they separate themselves from the ten men, they will miss the opportunity to add *Elokeinu* to their *zimun*.

20. A woman who has eaten bread with three or more men is obligated to participate in the *zimun*. This means that she is required to respond to the invitation of the leader, but she may not assume the role of the leader.[41]

21. A father and his adult sons may leave the table in the middle of a meal to say *Birkath HaMazon* with *Sheva Berakhoth*[42] at a different place, even though the mother will be left without a *zimun*.[43]

22. At *Sheva Berakhoth* women cannot be counted as *panim chadashoth*,[44] the "new faces" necessary at a meal for *Sheva Berakhoth* to be recited. Similarly, a woman cannot be counted as one of the ten people who must be present when *Sheva Berakhoth* are said.[45]

Drinking From the Cup of Wine

23. When *Birkath HaMazon* is recited over wine, the leader of the *zimun* should recite the blessing *Borey pri*

---

41. *Shulchan Arukh, Orach Chayim* 199:7, and *Mishnah Berurah*.
42. The seven blessings added to *Birkath HaMazon* in honor of a newly-married couple during their first week of marriage; a *minyan* is required for *Sheva Berakhoth*.
43. *Shevet HaLevi*, Vol. 1, No. 38, states, "One may rely on the view of the *Bach*, cited in the *Magen Avraham* 200:2, that members of the *zimun* may leave the table before the meal is completed even though there will no longer be a *zimun*." The *Mishnah Berurah* 200:5 comments that in a time of necessity one may rely on the *Bach*'s viewpoint.
44. In order to recite *Sheva Berakhoth*, there must be a "new face" present at the meal — a person who attended neither the wedding nor a previous *Sheva Berakhoth*.
45. *Pitchey Teshuva, Evven HaEzer* 62:14. The *Shittah M'kubetzeth*, on Tractate *Kethuboth* 7a, explains that the person fulfilling the requirement of *panim chadashoth* must be someone who may be

ha'gafen[46] and drink from the cup, after concluding *Birkath HaMazon.* If the host led the *zimun,* he should pass the cup to his wife, who also drinks from it,[47] even if she did not eat with her husband.[48]

If a guest is given the honor of leading the *zimun,* he should drink and return the cup to the host, who also drinks. It is questionable whether the host should now pass the cup to his wife.[49]

A man is not permitted to pass the wine to his wife if she is a *niddah.*[50]

---

counted for the *minyan.* See, however, *Chiddushey Chatham Sofer, Kethuboth* 7a.

46. "Who creates the fruit of the vine," the blessing recited before drinking wine.

47. *Shulchan Arukh, Orach Chayim* 183:4, based on Tractate *Berakhoth* 51b, where it indicates that this practice brings blessings to a woman. *Gilyoney HaShas* shows that only the wife should drink from the cup and that she should not pass it on to anyone else at the table.

48. *Mishnah Berurah* 183:19, based on the *Magen Avraham.*

49. *Ibid.*

50. *Shulchan Arukh, Yoreh De'ah* 195:13; *Pithchey Teshuvah, Yoreh De'ah* 195:14.

CHAPTER 4
Modesty

Introduction

1. *Chazal* tell us that the sanctity of the home, the foundation of Jewish life, is maintained primarily through the laws of *tzniuth* (modesty). *Tzniuth* creates an atmosphere of holiness and wholesomeness that permeates family life. Laws on this subject are considered so important that in certain situations a man is actually required to divorce his wife if she insists on disobeying them.

The laws of *tzniuth* are derived from two sources and are classified accordingly: *Dath Moshe* requirements are those specified in the Torah itself; *Dath Yehudith* refers to those traditions that have defined the practice of Jewish women through the generations. Although these are distinct categories, both are binding on Jewish women today.[1]

---

1. *Shulchan Arukh, Evven HaEzer* 115:4.

Covering the Body

2. The *Mishnah* in Tractate *Kethuboth*,[2] in discussing *tzniuth*, observes that it was a custom of Jewish women not to weave in the marketplace, thereby identifying this as a restriction derived from *Dath Yehudith*. The *Gemara*[3] explains that this prohibition arose because the motions of weaving inevitably cause a woman to expose her upper arms in public, and this immodesty is a violation of *Dath Moshe*. Here, the secondary *Dath Yehudith* restriction is a "fence" around a more serious infraction against the Torah, *Dath Moshe*. This Talmudic discussion is the direct and indirect source of many of the laws of modest dress.

3. It is a serious transgression for a woman to dress immodestly.[4] By ignoring the laws of modest dress, a woman not only violates the Torah herself, but causes

---

2. *Kethuboth* 7:3.
3. *Kethuboth* 72b.
4. *Iggeroth Moshe, Yoreh De'ah*, Vol. 1, No. 81; *Y'chaveh Da'ath*, Vol. 3, No. 67.

There are numerous prohibitions against wearing immodest clothing. *Iggeroth Moshe* states that one who wears immodest clothing is said to be "walking in the way of the gentile," which involves a violation of the Torah injunction, "You shall not walk in their ways" (*VaYikra* 18:3).

Y'chaveh Da'ath adds that a woman who dresses immodestly violates the biblical prohibition, "You shall not set up a stumbling block in front of a blind person" (*VaYikra* 19:14), since by ignoring the laws of *tzniuth*, a woman causes men to violate the law forbidding them to view the parts of a woman's body that should be covered. The author continues that immodest dress violates the prohibition, "And you shall guard yourself from any evil thing" (*Devarim* 23:10), and that immodesty causes the *Shechinah* (Divine Presence) to depart from Israel, as it is written, "He shall not see any eroticism in your midst, for then He will turn away from you" (*Devarim* 23:15).

others who see her to transgress. Jewish Law not only prohibits a woman from dressing immodestly, but also forbids men to look at someone who is so dressed.[5]

Parts of the Body Which Must be Covered

4. Jewish Law requires that the following parts of a married or unmarried woman's body be covered in public:
   a) The neck (below and including the collarbone[6])
   b) The arms (the upper arms,[7] including the elbow[8])

---

5. *Shulchan Arukh, Evven HaEzer* 21:1; *Mishnah Berurah* 75:7; *Iggeroth Moshe, Orach Chayim*, No. 40, and *Evven HaEzer*, No. 56. This prohibition applies even where no sexual desire is involved.
6. The *Mishnah Berurah* 75:2, clearly states that the area above the collarbone may be exposed. Also see *Kuntres Malbushey Nashim*, p. 12.
7. *Mishnah Berurah* 75:2 and 75:7; *Chaye Adam* 7:2; *Kaf HaChayim* 75:2 and 75:3.
   The *Gemara, Kethuboth* 72b, explains that the *Mishnah* confirms the *Dath Yehudith* prohibition against a woman weaving in the marketplace because she will invariably expose her *z'roah* (arm) in public. The *Mishnah, Ohaloth* 1:5, defines *z'roah* as the bone extending from the shoulder to the elbow.
   The *Chazon Ish, Orach Chayim* 16:8, raises the possibility that the *lower* arm may also be considered *z'roah*. He concludes that it is possible that the entire arm should be covered to the wrist. The *Ben Ish Chai, Shanah Rishonah, Parshath Bo* 11, and the *Kaf HaChayim* 75:2 cite the *Zohar*, which states that only the hands should be exposed, but most later authorities accept the view of the *Mishnah Berurah* that only the upper arm and elbow need be covered. Also see *Yabiah Omer*, Vol. 6, *Orach Chayim* 14:3.
   It should be noted that in a community where the accepted practice of observant Jewish women is to dress in a more stringent manner, a visitor should adopt the prevailing custom so as not to appear conspicuous.
8. The elbows are covered because, if they were not, the upper arms would often be exposed as the woman raised her arms. See *Kuntres*

c) The legs (the thighs, including the knees[9])

A woman is required to wear a dress or skirt which is long enough to cover her knees whether she is standing or sitting,[10] and this is necessary even if she wears non-transparent stockings.[11] Some authorities maintain that the dress must be ankle-length, but this is not the generally-accepted practice. It is, however, the general practice of women in many Jewish communities to wear stockings.[12]

Malbushey Nashim, p. 8-9, which explains that the prohibition against exposing the upper arms applies even if it is done occasionally or unintentionally.

9. *Mishnah Berurah* 75:2, quoting Tractate *Berakhoth* 24a: "The exposed *shoke* (thigh) of a woman constitutes *ervah* (an erotic stimulus)."

10. *Kuntres Malbushey Nashim*, p. 10, suggests that, in order to ensure that the thigh will always be covered, a dress should reach approximately ten centimeters (four inches) below the knee.

11. HaGaon Rav Shlomo Zalman Auerbach and HaGaon Rav Yosef Sholom Eliashiv write in the journal *Bam'silah* (5730, p. 97): "The *shoke* must be covered when the woman is sitting or standing. Under no circumstances should one rely on stockings as a covering." In *Kuntres Malbushey Nashim*, p. 11, HaRav Binyamin Zilber writes that covering the knee with non-transparent stockings might satisfy the *Dath Moshe* requirement of covering the *shoke*, but the traditionally-accepted practice of Jewish women, *Dath Yehudith*, mandates that the dress itself cover the knees.

12. *Shulchan Arukh HaRav* 75:1; *Orukh HaShulchan* 75:3; *Chaye Adam* 14:2; *Ben Ish Chai, Shanah Rishonah, Parshath Bo* 11-12; *Kaf HaChayim* 75:2.

The two opinions cited in the text on the required length of a woman's dress are based on different definitions of *shoke*. The *Mishnah Berurah* 75:2 states that the area below the knee is not *shoke*, consequently, the obligation to cover this area is not *Dath Moshe*, but depends on the accepted practice of observant Jewish women in a particular community. The *Chaye Adam*, however, maintains that only the feet are excluded from *Dath Moshe* and that the calf is part of the *shoke*. This view reflects the definition of

5. Some women mistakenly believe that they may expose up to a *tefach* (four inches) of parts of the body which require covering. This is not correct; they must be completely covered.[13]

---

shoke in the *Mishnah, Ohaloth* 1:8. *Shevet HaLevi, Orach Chayim,* Vol. 1, No. 1, brings additional support from a Responsa of Rabbi Akiva Eiger. HaRav Yehoshua Neuwirth, writing in the journal *Sh'matin,* No. 11, says that this opinion is the same as the *Bach, Shulchan Arukh HaRav* and the *Orukh HaShulchan.* The *Chazon Ish, Orach Chayim* 16:8, also finds it difficult to agree with the *Mishnah Berurah.* HaGaon Rav Binyamin Zilber, in *Kuntres Malbushey Nashim,* p. 10, writes that after corresponding with the *Chazon Ish,* he, too, is unable to agree with the *Mishnah Berurah* on this question. Clearly, many opinions require a woman's dress to be ankle-length.

In spite of the weight of so many contrary views, most Jewish communities today have adopted the more lenient definition of the *Mishnah Berurah.* It *is,* however, a widely accepted practice to wear non-transparent stockings, and a woman is obligated to do so in a community which follows this practice.

Minchath Yitzchak, Vol. 6, No. 10, rules that a woman should wear stockings at home because strangers or visitors may come at any time. Nevertheless, HaGaon Rav Shlomo Zalman Aurbach writes, "According to the letter of the Law, a woman is not required to wear stockings in her husband's presence, yet she is still required to wear a dress that accords with the minimum standards of modesty." According to *Shevet HaLevi,* Vol. 5, No. 77, a woman who wears an ankle-length dress need not wear stockings.

HaGaon Rav Yosef Sholom Eliashiv rules that in communities where it is the accepted practice for women to wear stockings, a man is forbidden to recite *Shema,* blessings or study Torah in the presence of his wife if she is not wearing them. This is based on the principle that a man may not recite prayers or study Torah in the presence of any woman, including his wife, if any normally-covered part of her body is exposed. This principle is discussed at length in paragraphs 6-11.

13. *Iggeroth Moshe, Evven HaEzer,* No. 58, based on the *Remah, Orach Chayim* 75:1. This ruling concerns areas of flesh, not the hair. For a discussion of the amount of hair that a married woman may leave

Prayer and Torah Study

6. A man may recite *devarim shebikdushah* (words pertaining to holiness) — prayers, *Shema*, words of Torah and blessings — in the presence of a woman only if she is modestly dressed. He is forbidden to do so in the presence of a woman, even his wife, if any normally-covered part of her body is exposed.[14] This prohibition applies even if the man is not looking at her.[15] Areas of the body covered by transparent clothing are considered exposed.[16]

7. In communities where observant Jewish women do not cover their calves and forearms, a man may recite

---

exposed, see Chapter 5, paragraph 9.

The mistake is based on a misunderstanding of the *Beith Yosef*'s view in *Orach Chayim* 75:1, permitting a *man* to recite prayers and blessings in the presence of a woman if less than a *tefach* is exposed. But the *Beith Yosef* does not mean to imply that such exposure is permissible for the *woman*. Also see *Chazon Ish, Orach Chayim* 16:7; *Lev HaIvri*, p. 65; *Mishnah Berurah* 75:7.

14. *Shulchan Arukh, Orach Chayim* 75:1 and *Mishnah Berurah*; *Minchath Yitzchak*, Vol. 2, No. 84; *Sh'arim Metzuyanim BeHalakha* 5:9; *Yabiah Omer*, Vol. 6, *Orach Chaim*, No. 12.

Following this rule, a man should not recite *devarim shebikdushah* while facing his wife when she is nursing a baby unless she covers herself. See *Chaye Adam* 4:7.

Salmath Chayim, Vol. 4, No. 4, states that these rules also apply when a man wishes to write words of Torah in the woman's presence.

15. The *Mishnah Berurah*, 75:1, 75:7 and 75:29-30, points out that if the man turns his entire body away and faces the opposite direction, he may recite *devarim shebikdushah* even though the woman is in the same room. When there is no alternative, the *Mishnah Berurah* even permits him to close his eyes and recite *devarim shebikdushah* without turning away. The *Chazon Ish, Orach Chayim* 16:7-8, concurs with this decision. Also see *Y'chaveh Da'ath*, Vol. 4, No. 6.

16. *Magen Avraham* 75:1, based on Tractate *Berakhoth* 25a.

devarim shebikdushah in their presence,[17] but he is forbidden to recite *devarim shebikdushah* in the presence of a woman who exposes any part of her upper arms or thighs, even in communities where women normally appear this way.[18]

8. Many authorities maintain that the prohibition against reciting *devarim shebikdushah* applies even if *less* than a *tefach* is exposed of parts of a woman's body normally-covered in that community.[19] If the woman is his wife, *devarim shebikdushah* is only forbidden if a full *tefach* is exposed.

If any part of a woman's *shoke* is exposed, many authorities rule that it is forbidden for a man to recite *devarim shebikdushah* at all — even if she is his wife and less than a *tefach* is exposed.[20]

---

17. If the accepted practice of a community is to cover the calves and forearms, a man is forbidden to recite *devarim shebikdushah* in the presence of a woman who does not adhere to these standards.
18. *Mishnah Berurah* 75:2 and 75:7. See paragraph 8, note 20.
19. *Iggeroth Moshe, Evven HaEzer*, No. 58, in accord with the view of the *Remah, Orach Chayim* 75:1. The *Tur, Orach Chayim* 75, and the *Chaye Adam* 4:2, conclude that even if the woman is not his wife, he may say *devarim shebikdushah* if less than a *tefach* is exposed. This is also the view of the *Beith Yosef* cited in note 12.
20. *Mishnah Berurah* 75:7. The *Chazon Ish, Orach Chayim* 16:8, maintains that *devarim shebikdushah* are permitted if less than a *tefach* of his wife's *shoke* is exposed. See note 12, where the definitions of *shoke* are discussed.

    The laws discussed in paragraphs 7 and 8 are based on a discussion in Tractate *Berakhoth* 24a: "Rabbi Yitzchak said: 'An exposed *tefach* of a woman's body constitutes *ervah* (erotic stimulus)...[This is the limit] for reciting *Shema* if [the woman] is his wife...but for other women, even if less than a *tefach* is exposed [a man may not recite the *Shema* in her presence]'...Said Rav Chisda, 'A woman's exposed *shoke* constitutes *ervah*...' "

    The commentators are troubled by the seeming redundancy of

9. A woman may recite *devarim shebikdushah* in the presence of a partially-dressed woman,[21] but she is forbidden to recite *devarim shebikdushah* if her or the other woman's genital area is exposed.[22]

Rav Chisda's statement. If an exposed *tefach* of any part of a woman's body constitutes *ervah*, then obviously an exposed *shoke*, such as an entire thigh, would be *ervah* as well. Talmudic commentators deduce from this apparent redundancy that Jewish Law recognizes two dimensions of modesty in dress — one subjective, the other objective.

The Law of *Tefach* defines the parameters of the subjective dimension of *tzniuth*. If observant Jewish women in a particular community are accustomed to covering a certain part of the body, it becomes *ervah* and must be covered even though not required by *Dath Moshe*. The Law of *Shoke* defines an objective standard of modesty. Even if all the women of a society appear in public with part of their *shoke* exposed, that part of the body is still intrinsically *ervah*, since it is outside the minimal level of modesty required by the Torah (*Dath Moshe*). Thus, in paragraph 7, a distinction is drawn between calves and forearms, which are regulated by the Law of *Tefach*, and thighs and upper arms, which are regulated by the Law of *Shoke*. These two levels of *tzniuth* also explain the reason why many authorities treat a woman's exposed *shoke* with greater severity than an exposed *tefach* elsewhere on the body, i.e., if any part of the *shoke* is exposed, *devarim shebikdushah* are forbidden, even if the woman is his wife and the area is less than a *tefach*.

It should be noted that the area below the collarbone is included with the upper arm and thigh in the definition of *shoke*.

21. *Mishnah Berurah* 75:8, citing the *Pri Chadash, Eliyahu Rabbah* and the Vilna Gaon. It was explained above that a man may not recite *devarim shebikdushah* in the presence of a woman if any normally-covered part of her body is exposed. The *Rosh* and the *Rashba* disagree about whether this principle also applies to a woman in the presence of another woman. Although the *Remah* takes the stricter position, the *Mishnah Berurah* reports that most later authorities are lenient.

22. The *Remah, Orach Chayim* 75, rules that the woman herself may recite *devarim shebikdushah* even if she is naked. The *Mishnah*

10. A woman may recite *devarim shebikdushah* even if there is nothing to separate her heart and genital area. Nevertheless, she is advised to make such a separation.[23]

Berurah cites the *Pri Megadim* and the *Chaye Adam* who explain that this leniency only applies when the woman is sitting, since her genital area would be covered. If she is standing, neither she nor another woman may recite *devarim shebikdushah.*

Based on this ruling, the *Mishnah Berurah* 74:16 states: "A naked woman may recite the blessing before immersion in a *mikvah* only when she is already standing in the water. Even though the water is clear, it covers the genital area." The *Shakh* expands this concept in *Yoreh De'ah* 200:1: "Our women, if not themselves prophets, have certainly descended from prophets, for they intuitively understand that the blessing before immersion must be said while standing in the water with their eyes above the surface. This is consistent with the requirements of the Torah."

The *Mishnah Berurah* concludes: "It is preferable for her heart to be above the surface of the water. Otherwise, she should hug herself below the heart in order to create a separation between the heart and the genital area...If there are other naked women in the *mikvah* room, she must turn away from them when reciting the blessing."

The above solution follows the Ashkenazic custom. Sephardic women follow the decision of the *Beith Yosef*, in *Shulchan Arukh, Yoreh De'ah* 220, and say the blessing while the body is still covered, before entering the water.

23. A man is forbidden to recite *devarim shebikdushah* unless a separation between his heart and the genitals is made. The *Shulchan Arukh, Orach Chayim* 75:4, rules, "Women may recite blessings and pray when wearing a long robe even though the heart 'sees' the genital area." The *Mishnah Berurah* explains that since the genital area of a woman is lower on the body than a man's, her heart cannot actually "see" it, even though no separation is made. The *Bach*, however, requires women to make a separation, and the *Mishnah Berurah* therefore recommends that a woman should make a separation between the upper and lower parts of her body if possible. The ramifications of this ruling as it effects the blessing over immersion in a *mikvah* have been discussed in note 22. Also see *Chazon Ish, Orach Chayim* 16:10.

11. A woman may recite *devarim shebikdushah* in the presence of a man, even if normally-covered parts of his body are exposed.[24]

Children's Clothing

12. A girl should be dressed modestly in public beginning at the age of three.[25]

Some authorities[26] maintain that as long as she is not regarded as a "young lady", the standards of modest dress need not be strictly observed.[27]

13. A girl must dress modestly in her father's presence from the age of eleven.[28]

14. A girl under the age of six may wear a short skirt if she wears socks or tights that cover the rest of her legs.[29]

---

24. The *Orukh HaShulchan, Orach Chayim* 75:5, infers from Tractate *Kethuboth* 64b that men are more prone to erotic thoughts than are women.
25. *Biur Halakhah* 75, beginning *Tefach m'gulah*. Also see *Kuntres Malbushey Nashim*, p. 13-14. Although the *Biur Halakhah* actually discusses whether a man is permitted to recite *devarim shebikdushah* in the young girl's presence, his conclusion also establishes general requirements for her mode of dress.
26. *Chazon Ish, Orach Chayim* 16:8.
27. Although some commentators maintain that the *Chazon Ish*'s leniency relates only to *devarim shebikdushah*, most agree that it also applies to a young girl's general mode of dress. It is understood that a girl of six or seven is considered a "young lady" according to the *Chazon Ish*'s ruling.
28. *Biur Halakhah, Ibid.*, based on the *Rambam, Hilkhoth Kriath Shema* 3:19 and Tractate *Berakhoth* 24a. Also see *Da'ath Sofer, Orach Chayim*, No. 14.
29. *Kuntres Malbushey Nashim*, p. 14. Even though *Dath Yehudith* requires that the dress itself cover the knees (See notes 10 and 11.), one may be lenient in the case of a small child. After the age of six,

Even if the child wears a long skirt, it is still proper for her to wear socks or tights.[30]

Bringing Girls to the Synagogue

15. Some authorities rule that a man may recite *devarim shebikdushah* in the presence of very young girls even in communities which are not accustomed to dress them modestly.[31] It is not, however, proper to bring them to the synagogue dressed immodestly.[32]

Once girls have reached the age at which they are required to dress modestly,[33] it is certainly forbidden for a man to recite *devarim shebikdushah* in their presence if they are immodestly dressed.

16. If the majority of a congregation wishes to adopt the lenient ruling as to the age at which modest dress is required (cited in paragraph 12),[34] the minority cannot object.[35]

---

girls should wear dresses that cover the knees, because at that age they are old enough to be trained in the performance of *mitzvoth*, and *Dath Yehudith* is considered a *mitzvah*.

30. *Salmath Chayim*, Vol. 4, No. 1 and No. 17. A parent need not be as particular with this detail of *Dath Yehudith* as with explicit requirements of *Dath Moshe*.

31. *Chelek HaLevi*, No. 36; *Sh'arim Metzuyanim BeHalakha*, Vol. 1, p. 21.

32. *Ben Ish Chai, Shanah Rishonah, Parshath Bo* 8; *Teshuvah MeAhavah*, Vol. 2, No. 229:1; *Yabiah Omer*, Vol. 6, *Orach Chayim*, No. 14.

33. The dispute between the *Mishnah Berurah* and the *Chazon Ish* cited in notes 25 and 26 concerns the definition of this age.

34. The view of the *Chazon Ish*, which considers a girl to be a "young lady" at the age of six or seven.

35. This based on HaGaon Rav Yosef Sholom Eliashiv's Responsa to the community of Azata-Netivot, Israel, dated *Erev Shabbath Parshath Balak*, 5735: "If the majority of a community wishes to adopt the view of the *Chazon Ish* regarding the age at which a girl

79

17. Once a child reaches the age at which she is required to dress modestly, she should not be brought to the synagogue in a short skirt even if she is wearing tights.[36]

Owning and Selling Immodest Clothing

18. A woman who owns immodest garments that cannot be modified or worn with other garments may sell or give them only to a non-Jew who will either wear them or sell them to other non-Jews. If this is not possible, the garments should be disposed of, even if it involves a great loss.[37]

19. We conclude this chapter with a quotation from the *Midrash Rabbah, Bereshith* 18:13:

" 'God built (*va'yiven*) the rib that He took from the man [and fashioned it] into a woman.' R. Yehoshua of Skinin said in the name of R. Levy, 'The word *va'yiven* also signifies that He considered from what part [of

---

must be modestly dressed in order for a man to say *devarim shebikdushah* in her presence, the minority may not stand in their way."

36. HaGaon Rav Eliashiv comments in the Responsa cited in the previous note: "One should refrain from bringing a young girl who is wearing a short skirt and tights to the synagogue once she has reached the age at which she is required to wear a long skirt. This depends, however, on her physical appearance and whether she draws attention to herself (in accordance with the view of the *Chazon Ish*)."

37. *Y'chaveh Da'ath*, Vol. 3, No. 67, based on the prohibition against setting up a stumbling block before a blind person, which forbids one from causing another to transgress Jewish Law. In a letter to *Midresheth El-Hamekoroth*, reprinted in the journal *HaMidrashah, Kislev*, 5743, HaGaon Rav Ovadiah Yosef adds that this ruling also applies to forbidden reading materials, which should be destroyed even if they are extremely valuable.

Adam's body] He would create her. He said, 'I will not create her from Adam's head, lest she be swell-headed, or from his eye, lest she be a coquette...but from the modest part of man, for even when he stands naked that part is covered.' And as He created each limb, He said to her, 'Be a modest woman.' "

CHAPTER 5
A Woman's Hair

Covering the Hair

1. The Torah forbids[1] a married woman to appear in public with her hair uncovered.[2] *Dath Yehudith* mandates

1. It is explained in Tractate *Kethuboth* 72a that *Dath Moshe* prohibits a married woman from appearing in public with her hair uncovered. This prohibition is inferred from the discussion of the laws of *sotah* found in *BaMidbar* 5. A *sotah* is a woman whose husband suspects her of infidelity. If, after being warned by her husband against any private meetings with a particular man, she ignores his warning and is seen with the man, she can either clear her name by drinking the "bitter waters", or she can accept a divorce and forfeit her *kethubah* (alimony settlement). The procedure of drinking the "bitter waters" was only carried out in the *Beith HaMikdash.*

   The ordeal of drinking the "bitter waters", described in detail in *BaMidbar* 5:11-31, includes an element of public humiliation — uncovering the woman's hair. From the fact that the Torah considers uncovering the *sotah*'s hair a degradation, *Chazal* infer that modest Jewish women do cover their hair in public. See *Rashi*'s commentary on *Kethuboth* 72a.

2. *Shulchan Arukh, Orach Chayim* 75:2, and *Evven HaEzer* 21:2, based on the *Mishnah, Kethuboth* 7:3.

that she also cover her hair in a semi-public place, even if men are not usually found there.[3]

2. Women of later generations have taken it upon themselves to cover their hair in the privacy of their homes.[4]

3. Some women who are extremely scrupulous regarding modest behavior do not expose any hair, even when alone in their room. But this is not a requirement of *Dath Moshe* or of *Dath Yehudith* in most communities.[5]

---

3. *Shulchan Arukh, Ibid. Dath Moshe* only forbids appearing publicly with the hair uncovered. It is *Dath Yehudith* that requires covering the hair in a courtyard, even where there usually are no men present.

4. *Biur Halakhah* 75, beginning *Chutz l'tzamathan*, based on the *Bach, Evven HaEzer* 115: "The prevailing custom in all places is for women to cover their hair, even in the privacy of their homes." After citing the various sources, the *Biur Halakhah* concludes, "It is written in *Teshuvoth Chatham Sofer, Orach Chayim*, No. 36, that since our ancestors, in all localities, have adopted this practice, it has taken on the full status of Jewish Law [and is obligatory]...as stated in the *Magen Avraham* 551:17..."

5. *Darkey Moshe, Evven HaEzer* 115:4. In Tractate *Yoma* 47a, *Chazal* relate that a certain woman by the name of Kimchith was particular that "the walls of her house should not see the hairs of her head." She was rewarded with seven sons who served as High Priests.

The *Mishnah Berurah* 75:14 cites the *Zohar*, which also emphasizes the great reward reserved for a woman who maintains this high level of modesty. But in *Iggeroth Moshe, Evven HaEzer*, Vol. 1, No. 58, HaGaon Rav Moshe Feinstein explains that praiseworthy as this practice is, it is not required. HaGaon Rav Feinstein emphasizes that a woman who does not wish to conform to this standard is transgressing neither *Dath Moshe* nor *Dath Yehudith*, and that a man should not refrain from marrying such a woman if she is of fine character, God-fearing and diligent in all other matters.

4. Some authorities rule that a husband is forbidden to see his wife's hair when she is a *niddah*. Other authorities disagree with this ruling.[6]

5. The custom for married women to cover their hair when praying or reciting blessings, even when no other

---

It has become the practice in certain communities for married women to shave their heads, either immediately after the wedding ceremony or on the following day. This custom is not based on any requirement of the Torah. According to all early authorities, the obligation is to *cover* the hair, not to cut it off. *Minchath Yitzchak*, Vol. 7, No. 3, elaborates on three possible reasons for this custom. First, since it is virtually impossible to cover the head so that *no* hairs will be visible, it ensures that no part of the hair will ever be exposed in public. Second, there is a worry that when a woman immerses in the *mikvah,* her hair may float on top of the water, invalidating the immersion, since absolutely every part of her body, including the hair must be under water. Finally, if a woman's head is shaved, the "walls of her house" will certainly "not see the hairs of her head," and she will thereby merit righteous children. But *Iggeroth Moshe, Evven HaEzer*, Vol. 1, No. 59, and *Yabiah Omer*, Vol. 4, *Yoreh De'ah*, No. 1, maintain that a husband may object to his wife adopting this practice. They point out that one need not fear invalid immersion, since there is always another woman supervising. Moreover, *Chazal* have cautioned women against appearing unattractive to their husbands.

6. HaGaon Rav Yosef Sholom Eliashiv equates a married woman's hair with other normally-covered parts of her body, and it is explicitly stated, in *Shulchan Arukh, Yoreh De'ah* 195:7, and *Evven HaEzer* 21:4, that a husband is forbidden to look at normally-covered parts of his wife's body when she is a *niddah*. The same ruling is found in *Pardes Simchah* 195, in the commentary *Ma'ayan Tahor*, par. 30.

HaGaon Rav Moshe Feinstein, however, in *Iggeroth Moshe, Yoreh De'ah*, Vol. 2, No. 77, writes that there is a distinction between hair and other normally-covered parts of the body, ruling that the *Shulchan Arukh*'s prohibition does not extend to the hair. In HaGaon Rav Feinstein's opinion, one who is stringent in this matter is to be praised, but it is not required.

person is present, is not strictly required by Jewish Law.[7]
It is the Sephardic custom for women to recite the
blessing over immersion in the *mikvah* with the head and
body covered, before actually entering the water. The
Ashkenazic practice is to recite the blessing while standing
in the water with the head covered.[8]

Women Obligated to Cover Their Hair

6. The Torah obligates a woman who is married or was
married to cover her hair.[9]

_____

7. This is a ruling of HaGaon Rav Yosef Sholom Eliashiv.
8. *Shulchan Arukh, Yoreh Deah* 220, and commentaries; *Chokhmath
   Adam* 121:14; *Ben Ish Chai, Shanah Rishonah, Parshath Sh'mini.* See
   Chapter 4, note 22.
9. *Beith Shmuel, Evven HaEzer* 21:5; *Ba'er Heytev* and *Pithchey
   Teshuvah, Evven HaEzer* 21:5, based on the *Prishah.*

   HaGaon Rav Shlomo Zalman Auerbach rules that a divorcee who
   is returning to Judaism and is studying in an institution for *ba'aley
   teshuvah* should be instructed to cover her hair. But if she is still in
   the process of committing herself to *mitzvah* observance, a man
   may say *devarim shebikdushah* in her presence, even if her hair is
   exposed.

   HaGaon Rav Moshe Feinstein, in *Iggeroth Moshe, Evven HaEzer,*
   Vol. 1, No. 57, permits a widow in extreme circumstances to accept
   a job in which she will not be able to cover her hair. He allows this
   only in situations where the job is absolutely necessary for the
   support of her family.

   HaGaon Rav Chaim Pinchus Sheinberg takes the following
   position: "Concerning the lenient ruling found in *Iggeroth Moshe*
   permitting a widow to uncover her hair if it is essential for her
   livelihood, I feel that there is no reason to search for leniencies
   when it is possible to avoid the problem by wearing a wig. In any
   case, one must be stringent on the street, where *Dath Moshe* clearly
   forbids even a widow from appearing without headcovering.
   Perhaps in the office she may rely on *Iggeroth Moshe*, when there is
   absolutely no alternative, and there are no men present." See also
   Machazeh Eliyahu, No. 118.

7. Single women may appear in public without a head covering.[10] Some authorities maintain that they should braid their hair rather than wear it loose,[11] but most of them are lenient in this.[12]

Some Sephardic authorities require single women to cover their heads during *Shemoneh Esrey* and *Birkath HaMazon.*[13] Today, most Sephardic women are not particular to do so.[14]

8. In some communities, it is customary for brides to cover their hair before the wedding ceremony to ensure

---

10. *Shulchan Arukh, Orach Chayim* 75:2, and *Mishnah Berurah; Beith Shmuel, Evven HaEzer* 21:5; *Chazon Ish, Orach Chayim* 16:8.

    The *Mishnah Berurah* rules that a single woman who has had sexual relations is required to cover her hair. This ruling is contrary to the *Pithchey Teshuvah*'s understanding of the *Beith Shmuel*, and the *Mishnah Berurah* himself adds that if she is unwilling to cover her hair, she should not be coerced.

11. *Magen Avraham* 75:3, cited in the *Mishnah Berurah* 75:12.

12. *Machatzith HaShekel* and *Magen Giborim*, cited in the *Mishnah Berurah, Ibid.* If a woman does wear her hair loose, she must be careful never to appear provocative.

13. *Yaskil Avdi*, Vol. 6, No. 1, is quite stringent in this matter. *Yabiah Omer,* Vol. 6, *Orach Chayim,* No. 15, states: "Since, according to the *Maharshal, Pri Chadash* and the *Vilna Gaon*, it is only a custom for men to cover their heads when reciting blessings, one should not insist that girls do so. I discussed this issue with HaGaon Rav Yosef Sholom Eliashiv, who agreed that one can be lenient since pious women are not accustomed to cover their heads when reciting blessings. Nevertheless, it is my opinion that single women should wear a headcovering during *Shemoneh Esrey* in order to satisfy the opinion of those authorities who require it. This should be communicated in a pleasant manner, so that it will be acceptable to them."

14. *Tzitz Eliezer*, Vol. 12, No. 13, cites numerous reasons why most women are lenient. See also the *Responsa of Rabbi Ezriel Hildesheimer*, No. 8 and the journal, *Ohr Torah*, Adar-Sivan 5732.

that it will be covered at the moment of marriage.[15]
Elsewhere, brides cover their hair after *yichud* (the time
following the wedding ceremony when the bride and
groom are first permitted to be alone together).[16] Still
others wait until the following day to cover their hair.[17]

Coverings

9. A woman is required to wear a head-covering that
hides all her hair from view.[18] It is proper to ensure that no
hair protrudes from it.[19]

---

15. *Mishnah Berurah* 75:11; *Chavoth Ya'ir* 196; *Rabbi Akiva Eiger,Tinyana*, No. 179. Some authorities maintain that an *aruthah* (betrothed woman) is also required to cover her hair. Today, the betrothal is performed under the wedding canopy, and the hair should be covered at this time. See *Az Nidb'ru*, Vol. 8, No. 65.

16. *Otzar HaPoskim, Evven HaEzer* 21:21.The *Remah, Evven HaEzer* 21:27, maintains that *yichud* is the most important part of the wedding ceremony. According to this view, the bride is required to cover her hair only after *yichud*.

    Y'chaveh Da'ath, Vol. 5, No. 62, suggests that, according to the Ashkenazic practice of having *yichud* immediately after the *chupah*, a woman should cover her hair after *yichud*. The Sephardic practice is to have *yichud* after the wedding meal, and those who follow this practice may leave the hair uncovered during the meal. See also *Yabiah Omer*, Vol. 1, *Evven HaEzer*, No. 8.

17. These communities rely on the view of the *Ba'er Heytev, Evven HaEzer* 21:5, and the *Chatham Sofer, Yoreh De'ah*, No. 195, who maintain that even after the wedding ceremony the bride need not cover her hair until she has had relations with her husband.

18. *Iggeroth Moshe, Evven HaEzer*, Vol. 1, No. 58; *Yabiah Omer*, Vol. 4, *Evven HaEzer*, No. 3:3; *Dath V'Halakhah*, p. 12. See also *Chatham Sofer, Orach Chayim*, No. 36; *Teshuvah MeAhavah*, No. 40; *Salmath Chayim*, Vol. 4, No. 10:5.

19. The *Mishnah Berurah* ascribes the obligation to cover the entire top of the head so that no hair will protrude to *Dath Yehudith*. *Iggeroth Moshe* further states that even if the accepted practice is to cover

10. In communities where it is the accepted practice, a wig may be worn even if it is made from the wearer's own hair.[20] There are authorities who prohibit wigs made from the wearer's own hair, but permit all other wigs.[21]

Some authorities forbid the use of wigs altogether, on the grounds that they often are mistaken for natural hair.[22] Where the community practice is not to wear wigs, one

---

the entire head, less than a *tefach* of hair may be allowed to protrude — meaning that an area one-half *tefach* in width by two *tefachim* in length may be exposed. (A *tefach* is eight centimeters, about three inches, according to Rav Chaim Naeh, or ten centimeters, four inches, according to the *Chazon Ish.*)

Many authorities maintain, however, that Jewish Law strictly forbids women to allow any hair at all to protrude from the covering. This opinion, expressed in the *Zohar*, is cited by the *Magen Avraham* 75:4. Certain authorities even go so far as to say that if any part of the hair is exposed, *Dath Moshe* has been violated. See *Dovev Meysharim*, Vol. 1, No. 124; *Taharath Yom Tov*, Vol. 14, p. 75. HaRav Moshe Sternbuch, in *Dath V'halakhah*, p. 20, writes that this was the opinion of the *Chazon Ish.* See also *Otzar HaPoskim* 21:24.

20. *Remah, Orach Chayim* 75:2, and *Mishnah Berurah*, based on the *Pri Megadim*, who maintains that Jewish Law only forbids a married woman to expose hair which is attached to her head. Additional sources on this subject: *Shiltey HaGiborim, Shabbath* 29a; *Shulchan Arukh HaRav, Orach Chayim* 75:4; *Kaf HaChayim, Orach Chayim* 75:19; *Ba'er Heytev, Evven HaEzer* 155:10.

21. *Magen Giborim*, cited in the *Mishnah Berurah, Ibid.*

22. *Mishnah Berurah, Ibid.*, citing *Be'er Sheva* and *Yeshuoth Yaacov; She'ilath Ya'avetz*, Vol. 1, No. 9, and Vol. 2, No. 7-8; Glosses of *Chatham Sofer* to *Shulchan Arukh, Orach Chayim* 75:2. See also *Sdeh Chemed, Ma'arekheth Daled*, par. 3; *Otzar HaPoskim* 21:24; Responsa of *Maharil Diskin, Kuntres Acharon*, No. 23; *Tiffereth Yisrael*, commentary on the *Mishnah, Shabbath* 6:5.

Citing numerous Sephardic authorities who forbid the use of wigs, HaGaon Rav Ovadiah Yosef writes in *Yabiah Omer*, Vol. 5, No. 5, and in Vol. 4, No. 3:3, that Sephardic women should not

must abide by it. In such places, a man is forbidden to say *devarim shebikdushah* in the presence of a woman who is wearing a wig.[23]

All authorities agree that a wig is permissible with a headcovering over it, even if the wig can be seen.[24]

Prayer and Torah Study

11. A man may not recite *devarim shebikdushah* in the presence of a Jewish woman who is required to cover her hair if her hair is uncovered. This prohibition applies to his wife, mother, daughter or any woman who does not observe the requirement.[25]

He may recite *devarim shebikdushah* if he turns away completely. When this is not possible, he may say *devarim shebikdushah* if he closes his eyes.[26]

---

wear them in public. Other Sephardic authorities permit them, however.

In *Dath V'Halakhah*, HaRav Moshe Sternbuch maintains that today there is no prohibition against wearing a wig — for Ashkenazic, Sephardic or Yemenite women — providing that the wig is not provocative.

HaGaon Rav Moshe Feinstein writes in *Iggeroth Moshe, Evven HaEzer*, Vol. 2, No. 12, that a husband may not prevent his wife from wearing a wig. Since she is acting in accordance with the decision of the majority of halakhic authorities, he may not impose his own stringent view on her.

23. *Pri Megadim*, cited in the *Mishnah Berurah, Ibid.*
24. *Otzar HaPoskim* 21:24; *She'ilath Ya'avetz*, Vol. 1, No. 9; Responsa of *Maharatz Chayeth*, No. 53. Some women wear wigs with small coverings on them. The source of this custom is found in the Responsa of *Maharam Chagiz*, No. 262, which requires a recognizable covering, in addition to the wig, in order to conform to *Dath Yehudith*.
25. *Shulchan Arukh, Orach Chayim* 75:2; *Mishnah Berurah* 75:10, 75:12 and 76:2; *Chazon Ish, Orach Chayim* 16:8.
26. *Mishnah Berurah* 75:5. See Chapter 4, note 15.

12. A man may recite *devarim shebikdushah* in the presence of a married gentile woman who does not normally cover her hair.[27]

13. A woman is permitted to recite *devarim shebikdushah* in the presence of a married woman whose hair is uncovered.[28]

14. In recent generations, many married women have become lax in covering their hair. In light of this unfortunate situation, some authorities maintain that, today, a man is permitted to recite *devarim shebikdushah* in the presence of a married woman whose hair is uncovered. A number of contemporary authorities rule to the contrary, that the prohibition remains in effect.[29]

---

27. *Iggeroth Moshe, Orach Chayim*, Vol. 4, No. 15:1; *Yabiah Omer*, Vol. 6, *Orach Chayim*, No. 13:5.

28. *Mahari Shteiff*, No. 102. See Chapter 4, paragraph 9.

29. The *Orukh HaShulchan, Orach Chayim* 75:3, states: "Let us now decry the tragic circumstances that have befallen us in our generation....Jewish women have become lax and now appear in public with their hair uncovered...Woe us that this has occurred in our time...Nevertheless, according to the Law, it appears to me that it is now permissible for a man to recite *devarim shebikdushah* in their presence. Since it is common practice for women not to cover their hair, it has become a normally-exposed part of the body..."

HaGaon Rav Moshe Feinstein, in *Iggeroth Moshe, Orach Chayim,* Vol. 1, No. 44, cites these words of the *Orukh HaShulchan* and brings evidence from Talmudic sources to support his view. HaGaon Rav Feinstein concludes, "The *Orukh HaShulchan*'s view may be relied on in pressing circumstances, but a God-fearing person should be stringent and turn away...or, if this is not possible, he should close his eyes..." The *Ben Ish Chai, Shanah Rishonah, Parshath Bo* 12, arrives at the same conclusion. See also *Yabiah Omer*, Vol. 4, No. 33.

The leniency of the *Orukh HaShulchan* can be understood in light of the framework for defining *ervah* that was presented in Chapter 4, note 20. Thus, the *Orukh HaShulchan* equates a woman's hair with other normally-covered parts of her body, which are regulated by the Law of *Tefach* — meaning that its status as *ervah* depends on the norms of a particular community. The more stringent authorities maintain that hair falls within the category of *shoke*, in which case it is intrinsically *ervah*, unaffected by the norms of the community. As explained in Chapter 4, note 20, *shoke* is considered to be *ervah*, even in a community where it is customarily exposed.

CHAPTER 6
A Woman's Voice

The Prohibition

1. A man is forbidden to listen to a woman sing.[1] According to some authorities, this is a Torah prohibition.[2] To others it is Rabbinic.[3] So as not to cause men to transgress this prohibition, women should not sing in their presence.

---

1. *Shulchan Arukh, Evven HaEzer* 21:1, based on Tractate *Berakhoth* 24a: "A woman's voice constitutes *ervah*." HaGaon Rav Shlomo Zalman Auerbach rules that boys nine years of age and older are prohibited from listening to women sing.

   HaRav Shaul Vagshall, writing in *Taharath Am Yisrael*, p. 53, raises the possibility that it may be permissible for a man to listen to his sister sing, whether or not she is married. He bases his suggestion on the numerous instances in which the laws regulating intimacy are more lenient between brother and sister than between men and women not so closely related. He notes, however, that the *Chazon Ish* clearly forbade it. See paragraph 11 for a discussion of *Shabbath Zemiroth*.

2. *Sdeh Chemed, Ma'arekheth Kaf*, No. 42, citing the *Pri Megadim* in *Shoshanath Ha'amakim*, Rule 9; *Divrey Chafetz Chayim*, p. 136.

3. *Nishmath Adam* 4:1, cited in the *Mishnah Berurah* 75:17.

2. A man may listen to his wife sing if she is not a *niddah*[4] and if he is not reciting *devarim shebikdushah.*[5] There are differing opinions as to whether a man may listen to his wife sing when she is a *niddah.*[6]

3. A woman may listen to men sing, whether or not they are relatives, even if she is reciting *devarim shebikdushah* at the time.[7]

4. A man may listen to the singing of an unmarried girl who is not a *niddah,*[8] on the condition that he not intend to become sexually stimulated by her singing.[9]

---

4. *Beith Shmuel, Evven HaEzer* 21:4, and *Ba'er Heytev.*
5. If he is reciting *devarim shebikdushah,* see paragraphs 9 and 10.
6. The *Pithchey Teshuvah, Yoreh De'ah* 195, remains undecided on whether a man may listen to his wife sing when she is a *niddah.* HaGaon Rav Moshe Feinstein concludes in *Iggeroth Moshe, Yoreh De'ah,* Vol. 2, No. 75, that it is proper to act stringently in this situation. *Yabiah Omer,* Vol. 1, No. 15, rules that a man *may* listen to his wife sing when she is a *niddah.*

   The *Ben Ish Chai, Shanah Rishonah, Parshath Tzav,* concludes: "A man may not listen to his wife sing when she is a *niddah.* Since in many communities it is normal for a woman to sing her children to sleep or to comfort them by singing, she should be careful not to do so in her husband's presence when she is a *niddah.* If a child is agitated, and a song will have a soothing effect, she may be lenient." See also *Minchath Yitzchak,* Vol. 7, No. 7.
7. *Yabiah Omer,* Vol. 1 *Orach Chayim,* No. 65. This is contrary to the view of *Sefer Chassidim,* No. 616, which advises women not to listen to men sing.
8. He is still forbidden to recite *devarim shebikdushah* when she is singing, as explained in paragraphs 9 and 10.
9. *Prishah, Evven HaEzer* 21:4, citing the *Maharshal; Pri Megadim, Mishbetzoth Zahav, Orach Chayim* 75.

   The *Ba'er Heytev, Evven HaEzer* 21:4, however, cites the *Be'er Sheva*'s dissenting opinion, which allows a man to listen only to his wife's singing and only when he is not reciting *devarim*

Today, all girls over eleven are assumed to have the halakhic status of *niddah*, and so men are forbidden to listen to them sing.[10]

5. When necessary, a man may listen to girls who are under the age of eleven sing, even if he enjoys listening to them.[11]

6. Girls over the age of eleven who are studying in school or gathered for other purposes should be careful not to sing when they can be heard by people in the street.[12]

---

shebikdushah. Iggeroth Moshe, Orach Chayim, Vol. 1, No. 26, argues that the *Ba'er Heytev* is only citing the view of the *Be'er Sheva* and does not necessarily agree with it. See also *Api Zutri* 21:8 and the journal *Ohel Torah*, Vol. 5, No. 1.

10. *Mishnah Berurah* 75:17. Since it is not the custom today for unmarried women to purify themselves in a *mikvah*, they have the halakhic status of *niddah* from the onset of puberty, which is assumed to occur at approximately eleven years of age. See also the *Pri Megadim, Ibid.*, and the *Chatham Sofer, Choshen Mishpat*, No. 190.

11. HaGaon Rav Moshe Feinstein explains in *Iggeroth Moshe, Orach Chayim*, Vol. 1, No. 26, that the purpose of the prohibition against listening to women sing is to remove a possible stimulus of erotic thoughts. Since the singing of young children does not normally stimulate erotic thoughts, he permits parents to attend a choral performance of schoolgirls under eleven years of age. HaGaon Rav Feinstein adds, however, that it is praiseworthy to be stringent in this matter.

12. *Beith Avi, Orach Chayim*, Vol. 3, No. 32.

HaGaon Rav Shlomo Zalman Auerbach instructs girls who are traveling on a bus with a male Jewish driver to refrain from singing during the journey in order not to cause the bus driver to transgress. He adds that there is room for leniency if the girls are in the back of a pick-up truck, and the driver sits in a separate compartment from which he cannot see them as they sing.

7. A man is forbidden to listen to a female gentile sing, even a child.[13]

8. Some authorities rule that a man should refrain from listening to a woman singing on the radio or on a recording, even if he does not know her.[14]

Prayer and Torah Study

9. A man should avoid hearing any woman sing, including his wife,[15] while he is reciting *devarim shebikdushah.*[16]

---

13. *Pri Megadim*, cited in the *Mishnah Berurah* 75:12; *Iggeroth Moshe, Orach Chayim*, Vol. 4, No. 15:2. See also the journal *Ohel Torah*, 5693, Vol. 1.

14. *Chelkath Yaacov*, Vol. 1, No. 163; *Pri HaSadeh*, Vol. 3, No. 32; *Shevet HaLevi*, Vol. 3, *Evven HaEzer*, No. 181; *Yaskil Avdi*, Vol. 5, *Orach Chayim*, No. 12; *Az Nidb'ru*, Vol. 19, No. 59.

   Tzitz Eliezer, Vol. 5, No. 2, cites authorities who rule that it is permissible for a man to listen to a woman sing over the radio or on a recording since he does not hear her true voice. Other authorities permit it on the condition that the listener has never seen the woman who is singing. See also *Otzar HaPoskim* 21:20; *Me'ah Shearim, Orach Chayim*, No. 33; *Yabiah Omer*, Vol. 1, *Orach Chayim*, No. 6.

   Yabiah Omer cautions men against watching a woman sing on television since it will invariably lead to erotic thoughts.

15. *Birur Halakhah*, Vol. 1, p. 158, cites some *Rishonim* (early commentators) who rule that it is permissible for a husband to say *devarim shebikdushah* while his wife is singing, as long as she is not a *niddah*. The author concludes that a man may rely on these authorities rather than take time from Torah study in order to avoid saying *devarim shebikdushah* while his wife is singing. Thus, in the extenuating circumstance of his wife entertaining a group of children at home, for example, he may study Torah there even though he can hear her sing.

16. *Shulchan Arukh, Orach Chayim* 75:3; *Mishnah Berurah* 75:17, and 76:2. The *Ben Ish Chai, Shanah Rishonah, Parshath Bo*, writes that

If he does hear a woman sing while reciting *Shema,* he should repeat it without any of its preparatory or concluding blessings.[17]

10. If a man finds himself in a situation in which he cannot avoid hearing women sing, he may say *devarim shebikdushah,* but he should make every effort to concentrate on his prayers and ignore the singing.[18] This ruling also applies if the woman's singing is coming from a radio.[19]

Zemiroth

11. The laws discussed in the preceding paragraphs also apply to songs at the *Shabbath* table (*Shabbath Zemiroth*) and communal prayers.[20] Therefore, a husband

---

one need not refrain from *devarim shebikdushah* if he hears girls younger than six years old singing.

17. *Mishnah Berurah* 75:16, citing the *Pri Megadim* and *Biur HaGra.*
18. *Chaye Adam* 4:6, cited in the *Mishnah Berurah* 75:17.
19. *Yabiah Omer,* Vol. 1, *Orach Chayim,* No. 6, adds that, if possible, he should request that the radio be turned off. See also *Mahari Shteiff,* No. 102.
20. *Be'er Sheva, Kuntres Be'er Mayim Chayim,* par. 3, states: "It is proper for every God-fearing woman to refrain from singing *Shabbath Zemiroth*...whenever she is in the company of men...A modest woman should move her lips without singing aloud." See also *Az Nidb'ru,* Vol. 3, No. 71, and Vol. 9, No. 59.

   Menachem Meishiv, No. 26, cites the *Chok Yaacov* 479:6, who states that women should not sing those parts of *Hallel* that are often recited in song at the *Pessach Seder.*

   S'ridey Aish, Vol. 2, No. 8, concludes that one *may* rely on lenient authorities who permit boys and girls to sing *Zemiroth* together when their intentions are noble. This Responsa, however, was specifically addressed to the leader of the Yeshurun youth group in France, immediately after the Holocaust. A competent halakhic authority must be consulted to determine in which circumstances

and wife may sing together as long as they do not sing scriptural verses or pronounce the Name of God.[21]

12. A man is forbidden to listen to men and women singing together. Similarly, he is forbidden to listen to a group of women singing together.[22]

---

this leniency may be applied today.

HaGaon Rav Yosef Sholom Eliashiv interprets the *Biur Halakhah* 75 to say that a man may not listen to his daughter sing if she is older than eleven. HaGaon Rav Chaim Pinchus Sheinberg, however, attempts to justify the prevailing practice in many God-fearing homes of allowing girls to sing *Shabbath Zemiroth* at the family table. He cites the *Remah*'s ruling, in *Orach Chayim* 75:3, that if a man is accustomed to hear a particular woman's voice, her voice will not induce erotic thoughts in him. He points out that although the *Mishnah Berurah* maintains that the *Remah* is referring to a woman's speaking voice, since it has become accepted practice for girls to sing *Zemiroth* at the family table, their singing may also be included under the *Remah*'s category. HaGaon Rav Sheinberg emphasizes, however, that this ruling only applies when the girl is the man's daughter, and only at the *Shabbath* table during the singing of *Zemiroth*.

21. In such a situation, he would find himself reciting *devarim shebikdushah* while listening to a woman's singing. For a discussion of whether this is permissible when his wife is a *niddah*, see paragraph 2.

22. *Be'er Sheva, Kuntres Be'er Mayim Chayim; Be'er Yehudah*, commentary on *Sefer Chassidim, Lo Ta'aseh*, Chapter 3.

The *Chathan Sofer, Orach Chayim, Sha'ar Taharath Yadayim*, No. 14, rejects the *Be'er Sheva*'s ruling. He argues that the verse in *Shoftim* 5, "And Devorah the Prophetess sang with Barak the son of Avinoam," indicates that the prohibition against listening to a woman sing does not apply to a man and woman singing together. *Devash LePhi*, written by the *Chiddah*, however, offers an alternative explanation of that verse.

Female Speakers and Musicians

13. A man may listen to a woman speak in public.[23] He may also attend a woman's instrumental performance.[24]

---

23. *Shulchan Arukh, Orach Chayim* 75:3, and *Mishnah Berurah*; *Shevet HaLevi*, Vol. 4, *Orach Chayim*, No. 14; *Otzar HaPoskim* 22:10; *Kaf HaChayim, Orach Chayim* 689:13. All these authorities emphasize that there is no difference between listening to a woman speak privately and listening to her speak publicly. Of course, a man is forbidden to intend to become sexually stimulated by listening to her speak. Indeed, it is even forbidden to look at her clothing with this intention.

24. *Orukh HaShulchan* 75:8. *Mishneh Halakhoth*, Vol. 6, states that a man should not sit next to his wife while she is playing a musical instrument if she is a *niddah*. This ruling comes under the special restrictions that apply to a man and his wife when she is a *niddah*.

CHAPTER 7
Miscellaneous
Laws of Modesty

Clothing and Make-Up

1. In general, clothing that is fashionable in non-Jewish society may be worn only if it conforms to Jewish standards of modesty. If this clothing oversteps propriety in even the smallest detail, it is a violation of the Torah injunction, "You shall not walk in their statutes" (*VaYikra* 18:3).[1]

2. A woman may not wear clothes that have been manufactured specifically for men, even if she wears them with clothes that are clearly and exclusively made for women.[2]

---

1. *Maharik*, No. 88, cited in the *Beith Yosef, Yoreh De'ah* 178; *Divrey Chayim*, Vol. 1, *Yoreh De'ah*, No. 3; *Chatham Sofer, Orach Chayim*, No. 159; *Minchath Chinukh* 251; *Iggeroth Moshe, Yoreh De'ah*, Vol. 1, No. 81.
2. *Shulchan Arukh, Yoreh De'ah* 182, with *Taz, Shakh*, and *Darkey Teshuvah*; *Chokhmath Adam* 90:1. Also see *Shevet HaLevi, Yoreh De'ah*, No. 63; *Yabiah Omer*, Vol. 5, *Yoreh De'ah*, No. 14:3, and

Some authorities allow women to wear men's garments for protection against rain or cold, provided that they are only worn temporarily.[3]

3. There is no prohibition against women wearing male undergarments that cannot be seen. For example, a girl may wear her father's undershirt, or even pajamas, provided that she wears a woman's garment over them.[4]

4. Women may wear garments manufactured for both men and women, provided the garments are not immodest.[5] If a garment is manufactured in different styles, one for men and another for women, a woman may not

---

Vol. 6, No. 14:5. This prohibition is based on the Torah's command, "A man's garment shall not be worn by a woman" (*Devarim* 22:5). Some authorities apply this prohibition even to clothing worn in jest, for example, as a Purim disguise or to gladden a bride and groom at their wedding. Although the *Remah* permits women to wear men's garments as part of Purim merrymaking, HaGaon Rav Yosef Sholom Eliashiv has ruled that it is better not to rely on this leniency.

3. *Bach, Yoreh De'ah* 182; *Taz, Yoreh De'ah* 182:14; *Yabiah Omer, Ibid.*

4. This is based on a ruling of HaGaon Rav Yosef Sholom Eliashiv.

5. *Birkey Yosef, Yoreh De'ah* 182:14; *Lev Chayim*, Vol. 3, No. 26; *Sdeh Chemed*, Vol. 4, *Ma'arekheth Lamed* 116. The *Gemara* relates in *Nedarim* 49b how Rabbi Yehudah and his wife shared the same jacket because of their extreme poverty. The *Maharsha* comments that no transgression was involved since the jacket was made for both of them.

   In light of the above, HaGaon Rav Yosef Sholom Eliashiv has ruled that wearing thick, warm socks in the winter does not involve the prohibition against wearing men's garments. The propriety of wearing socks instead of stockings depends on the accepted practice of modest Jewish women in that community. (See Chapter 4, paragraph 4.) Similarly, HaGaon Rav Eliashiv has ruled that women may wear ties or headgear similar to men's in places where it is customary.

wear the man's style (or vice versa).[6]

5. Women are forbidden to wear pants.[7] If the pants have been manufactured specifically for women, they may be worn for protection from the cold, provided they are worn under a skirt.[8]

6. Men's pants may never be worn by women, even when alone in the house. A woman may wear women's pants for exercising if no men are present.[9]

6. This is based on a ruling of HaGaon Rav Yosef Sholom Eliashiv. An example of "different styles" is the placement of buttons on a garment, i.e., if the male version buttons to the right, and the female version buttons to the left, women may not wear the former.

7. The issue of women wearing pants is discussed at length in *Minchath Yitzchak*, Vol. 2, No. 108. The author concludes that pants are forbidden for two reasons: they are immodest because they outline the lower half of a woman's body; and, they are considered a male garment. According to *Minchath Yitzchak*, pants may not be worn under *any* circumstances, and even pants specifically manufactured for women are "men's clothing". See also *Tzitz Eliezer*, Vol. 11, No. 62; *Shevet HaLevi, Yoreh De'ah*, No. 63; *Sdeh Chemed*, Vol. 4, *Ma'arekheth Lamed* 116; *Yaskil Avdi*, Vol. 5, *Yoreh De'ah*, No. 14:7.

A number of contemporary authorities take issue with *Minchath Yitzchak*, maintaining that the injunction against wearing male garments does not apply if the pants were specifically manufactured for women; the only reason for prohibiting them is that they outline the lower half of the body. According to these authorities, who include HaGaon Rav Yosef Sholom Eliashiv and HaGaon Rav Chaim Pinchus Sheinberg, women's pants may be worn where there is no issue of modesty — for example, in a gym where there are no men present. See paragraph 6.

8. *Kuntres Malbushey Nashim*, p. 14, explains that this is permitted because the outline of her body is hidden by the skirt. The skirt should conform to the normal criteria of modesty. See Chapter 4, paragraph 4.

9. See the discussion of *Minchath Yitzchak* and other contemporary authorities, in note 7.

7. Women may not wear a male hairstyle.[10]

8. Bright, red clothing is considered immodest.[11] Tight-fitted clothing is also considered immodest because it outlines the body.[12]

9. Women may not wear strong perfume in public.[13]

10. Although it is proper for a woman to make herself up attractively when she is alone with her husband,[14] she

---

10. *Shulchan Arukh, Yoreh De'ah* 182:5; *Chokhmath Adam* 90:1, based on the *Rambam, Hilkhoth Avodath Kokhavim* 12:10.

11. *Shulchan Arukh, Yoreh De'ah* 178:1. This is based on the prohibition against adopting pagan practices, especially those which are associated with licentious behavior. The *Sifri* on *Devarim* 9 states, "You should not say that just as [the pagans] go out in purple, so I will go out in purple." The *Shakh, Yoreh De'ah* 178:3, adds that it is not the manner of modest women to wear red clothing. See also *Rashi*'s commentary on *Bereshith* 49:11: "Their clothes have the color of wine...and are worn by women to entice." A further reason for this prohibition is presented by Rabbenu Bechaya in his commentary on *Shemoth* 28:15, where he writes, "Red is a color associated with arrogance."
      According to HaGaon Rav Yosef Sholom Eliashiv, this prohibition only applies to bright red. Darker shades, such as burgundy, are acceptable.

12. The sources for this are dealt with at length by HaGaon Rav Binyamin Zilber, in *Sefer HaHistakluth*, p. 62. See also *Kuntres Malbushey Nashim*, p. 12 and 15.

13. *Midrash Rabbah, Eicha* 4; Tractate *Shabbath* 62b. See also *Shulchan Arukh, Orach Chayim* 217:4, and *Mishnah Berurah; Shulchan Arukh, Evven HaEzer* 21:1; *Otzar HaPoskim* 21:9. The *Mishnah Berurah* forbids a man to smell perfume worn by a woman who is not his wife.

14. Tractate *Bava Kama* 82a. One of Ezra's Ten Enactments was, "Spice and cosmetics peddlars should travel from city to city so that women may make themselves attractive to their husbands."

should not exaggerate when going out in public.[15]

Modesty in the Presence of Holy Books

11. A woman may not stand naked in front of *sifrey kodesh* (holy books) unless they are covered.[16]

12. It is best not to leave a child undressed in front of *sifrey kodesh* for an extended period of time.[17]

13. It is permitted to change a baby's diaper where there are *sifrey kodesh*. A receptacle into which the child relieves himself may also be left in the room.

Nevertheless, it is praiseworthy to be stringent in this matter, especially if there are many *sifrey kodesh* in the room. When possible, it is preferable that the baby be changed and the receptacle be placed in another room.[18]

Orchoth Chayim, Hilkhoth Kethuboth, No. 27, explains, "A Torah scholar must encourage his wife to appear attractive, even when she is in mourning, in order that she not be disagreeable in his eyes." *Sdeh Chemed, Ma'arekheth Shin*, No. 31, cites authorities who maintain that Torah Law forbids a woman to dress in a way unattractive to her husband. The *Shulchan Arukh, Yoreh De'ah* 195:9, refers to this idea: "The Sages reluctantly allowed a woman to beautify herself when she is a *niddah* because the Torah does not want her to become disagreeable in her husband's eyes."

15. *Iggereth HaTeshuvah* of Rabbenu Yonah 78; *Geder Olam* 4:8. It states in the *Midrash Tanchumah Yashan, VaYishlach* 10, "Ornaments are only given to women to beautify themselves *at home*."

16. *Magen Avraham* 45:2, based on the *Shulchan Arukh, Yoreh De'ah*, 286:2. The *Taz, Yoreh De'ah* 286:5, rules that a transparent covering is sufficient. In the room where husband and wife sleep, a non-transparent covering should be used.

17. *Machazeh Eliyahu*, No. 5:9-11.

18. *Ibid.*, No. 5:8. The author concludes that if there is a sign on which God's Name is printed hanging in the room, the child should be

Prayer and Torah Study

14. Some authorities permit the recitation of *devarim shebikdushah* in the presence of a child whose genitals are exposed.[19] They also allow a person to recite *devarim shebikdushah* where a child is relieving himself into a receptacle. The child's clothes must cover the receptacle, and there should not be an offensive odor.

It is preferable to follow the more stringent view, which forbids the recitation of *devarim shebikdushah* in the presence of a child whose genitals are exposed.[20]

15. One may recite *devarim shebikdushah* in a room in which there are clean diapers.[21]

Visiting a Hairdresser

16. It is recommended that women not patronize male

---

instructed to relieve himself with his back to the sign. This is sufficient to be considered praiseworthy.

Mishneh Halakhoth, Vol. 6, No. 24, states that although it is preferable not to change a baby in the presence of *sifrey kodesh*, it is only a *middath chassiduth* (an expression of piety) and not an obligation.

19. The *Mishnah Berurah* 75:23, and the *Magen Avraham* 75:8, define "child" as nine years old for a boy and three years old for a girl. But the Vilna Gaon maintains that boys are considered children for these purposes until they are twelve and girls until eleven.

20. The *Mishnah Berurah* 75:21 states that even though it is preferable to act stringently in this matter, if a man did recite *Shema* in the presence of a child whose genitals were exposed, he need not repeat it.

21. *Iggeroth Moshe, Orach Chayim*, Vol. 4, No. 106:2. *Rivevoth Ephrayim*, Vol. 1, No. 70, cites a Responsa of Hagaon Rav Moshe Feinstein which specifies that this ruling applies to diapers which have been laundered and not merely soaked in water.

hairdressers although it is not actually forbidden.[22]

Visiting a Doctor

17. A woman is advised to select a female doctor if she will receive the same quality of treatment as offered by a male doctor.[23] A male doctor may, however, carry out any

---

22. The *Shakh* and *Kreysi U'Pleysi, Yoreh De'ah* 195, maintain that if the man does not have erotic thoughts when involved in his profession, this service may be performed by him. Nevertheless, HaGaon Rav Chaim Pinchus Sheinberg recommends that both single and married women should avoid these situations whenever possible.

23. HaGaon Rav Shmuel Wossner deplores the fact that many women do not search for competent female doctors and considers this behavior to be inconsistent with the high standards of modesty expected from God-fearing Jewish women. HaGaon Rav Chaim Pinchus Sheinberg adds, "Considering the loose mores of contemporary society, where immoral behavior is not uncommon even in a professional context, it may be actually forbidden for women to visit male doctors." *Minchath Yitzchak*, Vol. 7, No. 73, concludes: "Where there is no danger to life, it is certainly preferable for a woman to visit a female doctor. If this is not possible, she should, at the very least, see a religious Jewish doctor."

Shevet HaLevi, Vol. 4, No. 167, lists ten general instructions for women who must see a doctor:
1. If possible, select a female doctor.
2. If the patient feels that a particular male doctor is more competent than the female doctor, she may see him.
3. Avoid visiting a male gynecologist unless it is absolutely necessary.
4. Never visit a doctor reputed to have loose morals.
5. Make an appointment only during regular visiting hours, when it is usual for other patients to be in the waiting room.
6. If the visit must take place outside normal visiting hours, her husband or another woman should accompany her.
7. If there are immodestly-dressed women in the waiting room, her husband should not accompany her.

medically necessary examinations.[24]

Physical Contact

18. A parent may kiss children of the opposite sex[25] even after they are married.[26] A grandparent may kiss a grandchild of the opposite sex.[27] According to most

---

8. Keep the door to the examination room open, according to the laws of *yichud*. If this is not possible, make sure it is unlocked. (Details of the laws of *yichud* may be found in Chapter 8.)

9. Check any advice given concerning birth control with a competent halakhic authority.

10. Refrain from engaging the doctor in any unnecessary discussion. Conversation should be limited to professional matters pertaining to the visit.

24. Medical procedures are not considered to have erotic overtones. Since the doctor is presumed to be involved with his work, there is no fear that he will have erotic thoughts.

25. *Shulchan Arukh, Evven HaEzer* 21:7; *Chokhmath Adam* 125:6. It is absolutely forbidden for a man to kiss his niece, whether she is his brother's or his sister's daughter. See *Iggeroth Moshe, Yoreh De'ah*, Vol. 2, No. 137.

26. *Beith Shmuel, Evven HaEzer* 21:14-15, and *Ba'er Heytev* 21:16; *Az Nidb'ru*, Vol. 3, No. 70; *M'kor Halakhah*, Vol. 2, No. 17.

   B'tzeyl HaChokhmah, Vol. 3, *Evven HaEzer*, No. 12, adds that a father may kiss his daughter when she is a *niddah*, and a son may kiss his mother when she is a *niddah*. *Ba'er Heytev, Orach Chayim* 262:2, reports that in many communities it is customary for a boy to kiss his mother's hands on Friday night. This practice is also cited in *Ben Ish Chai, Shanah Sh'niah, Parshath Bereshith* 29.

27. *Beith Shmuel, Evven HaEzer* 21:14; *Ba'er Heytev* 21:14; *Chokhmath Adam* 125:6; *Pithchey Teshuvah, Evven HaEzer* 21:5; *Otzar HaPoskim* 21:52.

   Iggeroth Moshe, Evven HaEzer, Vol. 1, No. 60, questions this decision and concludes that a God-fearing person should be stringent. *Mishneh Halakhoth*, Vol. 4, No. 173-174, rules to the contrary and approves it. Neither authority makes a distinction between a son's daughter and a daughter's daughter.

authorities, it is even permitted if the grandchild is married.[28]

19. A woman is forbidden to kiss any male over the age of nine other than her husband, father, grandfather, son or grandson.[29] She must do all she can to avoid situations where it will be difficult to avoid transgressing this law. She should be particularly careful at joyous occasions and family gatherings.[30]

---

28. *Beith Shmuel, Ibid.* Some authorities advise men not to kiss their married granddaughters. See *Be'er Moshe*, Vol. 4, No. 145, and *Iggeroth Moshe, Ibid.*

29. *Shulchan Arukh, Evven HaEzer* 22:1 and *Beith Shmuel* 66:14. Nine years old is given by HaGaon Rav Yosef Sholom Eliashiv as the age at which a woman must refrain from engaging in physical contact with a young boy.

    Be'er Moshe, Vol. 4, No. 145, notes that a man should refrain from kissing a girl over the age of three. HaGaon Rav Eliashiv points out that this is true even according to the *Chazon Ish*'s view cited in Chapter 4, paragraph 12, and notes 26 and 27. Although he is lenient concerning a young girl's mode of dress, the *Chazon Ish* would agree that physical contact should be avoided once she has reached the age of three.

    If the man is not a relation, both the man and the woman violate Torah Law when they kiss. Torah Law, however, does not forbid kissing between blood relations who are forbidden to marry. For example, a woman may, according to Torah Law, kiss her brother or nephew since it is abnormal for one to have erotic thoughts concerning these relations. It is Rabbinic Law that forbids women to kiss these men, as a safeguard against kissing men who are in fact forbidden to her by the Torah.

30. It often helps if a woman explains in advance that she is observing a *mitzvah* of the Torah and does not mean to slight anybody. A friendly, "I'm sorry, but I can't kiss you," is almost always sufficient.

    In Tractate *Sotah* 22a, it is related how Rabbi Yochanan observed a young maiden fall on her face and pray: "Master of the Universe! You have created *Gan Eden* and *Gehinom*. You have created the righteous and the wicked. May it be your will that no man transgress on my account!"

20. A girl who has reached puberty should avoid kissing or engaging in any physical contact with brothers who have also reached puberty.[31] Nevertheless, she is not obligated to stop a brother from kissing her or holding her hand if doing so will create friction in the family.[32]

21. A woman may not shake a man's hand,[33] even if she is wearing gloves.[34] In situations in which a woman will

---

31. *Rambam, Hilkhoth Issurey Bi'ah* 21:6: "A man who hugs or kisses a forbidden relation, even a blood relative to whom there is no sexual attraction, such as his pubescent sister or his mother's sister...is committing a degrading, forbidden and foolish act. One should not draw close to any forbidden relation, old or young. The only exceptions are a mother to her son or a father to his daughter." These words are cited in the *Shulchan Arukh, Evven HaEzer* 21:7.

32. *Sefer Taharath Am Yisrael*, p. 44, states that a man may be lenient and shake hands with a sister, since we find other leniencies concerning brother and sister. Certainly, if the brother takes the initiative, and her role is solely passive, she need not stop him.

33. *Sha'arey Teshuvah* of Rabbenu Yonah, *Sha'ar Sh'lishi* 80:138; *Darkey Teshuvah, Yoreh De'ah* 183:15; *Sdeh Chemed*, Vol. 5, *Ma'arekheth Kaf* 7, and Vol. 7, *Ma'arekheth Chathan V'Kallah* 12; *D'var Halakhah*, Vol. 1, No. 113; *Az Nidb'ru*, Vol. 2, No. 73; *Otzar Haposkim* 20. These sources explain that even if intimacy is not the intention, a Rabbinic prohibition is still involved.

In *Iggeroth Moshe, Evven HaEzer*, Vol. 1, No. 56, HaGaon Rav Moshe Feinstein examines the argument of those who rule leniently in the case when a man who is ignorant of Jewish Law offers his hand to a woman. He explains that these authorities wave the Rabbinic prohibition in order to avoid embarrassing a person, which is a Torah prohibition. Although certain German Rabbis did make this argument, HaGaon Rav Feinstein rules that one should not rely on it. The woman should explain politely that she is acting in this manner out of respect for Jewish Law and that no personal insult is intended.

34. *Sefer Chassidim* 1090 states: "A Jewish man should not shake the hand of a gentile woman...even if she is wearing gloves. This is a safeguard against sexual transgression."

almost certainly be expected to shake hands with men, such as family gatherings, she is advised to carry a glass or plate of food in her right hand. King Solomon describes a God-fearing woman as one whose "mouth opens in wisdom" (*Mishley* 31:26). In most cases, a woman can ward off potential problems with a polite explanation without offending anyone.[35]

Sitting Next to a Stranger

22. A woman seated on a bus need not change her seat if a man sits next to her. She is even permitted to take a seat next to a stranger,[36] but some women do their best to avoid this.

A man may sit next to a woman when there are no other empty seats.[37] Some authorities, however, forbid this.[38]

---

35. *Orukh HaShulchan, Evven HaEzer* 21:7 adds, "In general, a woman with foresight will not stumble...but one who pays no attention [to her deeds] will surely fall into the net of the *yetzer hara* (evil inclination), for it is much stronger than she is."

    A woman's own manner can do much to prevent any tension while scrupulously observing laws of physical contact with family and friends, particularly those who may be ignorant of the Torah's requirements. "I'm sorry, but I'm not allowed to shake hands," if coupled with a genuine greeting, should not be taken amiss. If a woman's observance of these laws does produce a negative or angry response, she will eventually be respected for her commitment to the principles of her faith.

36. This ruling is based on a Responsa of HaGaon Rav Shlomo Zalman Auerbach. It makes no difference which side of the seat she sits on and whether or not there are other available seats on the bus.

37. *Iggeroth Moshe, Evven HaEzer*, Vol. 2, No. 14, explains that this is permitted on the assumption that the man has no erotic intention. One who feels that he cannot avoid erotic thoughts in such a situation must refrain from sitting next to a woman, even when there are no other empty seats.

Dancing

23. Women may not dance in the presence of men, for by doing so they cause men to transgress.[39] This applies even to women who are dancing among themselves. Mixed dancing is strictly forbidden.[40]

---

38. *Shevet HaLevi*, Vol. 4, No. 136, forbids a man to sit next to a woman if he is able to stand. The author also rules that it is modest for a woman to sit in the back seat when traveling alone in a taxi.

39. When women dance in front of men, they cause them to have erotic thoughts. Singing often accompanies the dancing, in which case the men would be transgressing the prohibition of hearing a female voice. (See Chapter 6.)

   The *Ben Ish Chai, Shanah Rishonah, Parshath Shoftim* 18, states: "It is forbidden for women to dance by themselves in the presence of men, for this will arouse the *yetzer hara* in the men who observe them. Contemporary authorities strongly support this view, stating unequivocally that such activity is not permitted, even for the *mitzvah* of gladdening a bride and groom."

   Shulchan HaEzer 9:2, and *Shevet Mussar* 24 add that a woman may not participate in a dance group or drama group if there is a male musician involved.

40. This law is explicitly cited in the *Shulchan Arukh, Orach Chayim* 529:4, and the *Mishnah Berurah* 529:21. It can also be found in the following commentaries: *Kol Bo* 66, citing Rabbi Meir of Rothenberg; *Yosef Ometz*, No. 97; *Binyamin Ze'ev*, Vol. 2, No. 303-305; *Yam Shel Shlomo*, Novellae to Tractate *Gittin*, Chapter 1, No. 18. See also *Kitzur Shulchan Arukh* 152:13; *Orukh HaShulchan, Orach Chayim* 529:7; *Ben Ish Chai, Shanah Rishonah, Parshath Shoftim* 18.

   Iggeroth Moshe, Evven HaEzer, Vol. 1, No. 97, and Vol. 2, No. 13, and *Minchath Yitzchak*, Vol. 5, No. 99, and Vol. 3, No. 109, emphasize the seriousness of this sexually-related prohibition, a prohibition so severe that one is required to sacrifice one's life rather than violate it. *Yabiah Omer*, Vol. 1, *Orach Chayim* 30:15, and Vol. 6, *Yoreh De'ah*, No. 15, arrives at the identical conclusion, that dancing for and with men belong to this category of transgressions.

   HaRav Binyamin Zilber, writing in *M'kor Halakhoth*, comments:

Modesty at the Beach

24. Women should not swim where it is likely that men will pass by.[41] According to some, it is forbidden for a woman to visit a beach where men are bathing, even if she is modestly dressed.[42]

25. It is best for women's beaches to have female lifeguards. A woman is allowed to swim at a beach with a male lifeguard, but she should wear a shirt over her bathing

---

"Some people are extremely scrupulous in regard to Jewish dietary laws, rules pertaining to *Shabbath* and the like, yet this prohibition [against mixed dancing] has become meaningless in their eyes...What distinction can be made between the prohibition against pork and the prohibition against mixed dancing?"

Minchath Yitzchak, Ibid., prohibits girls from studying in a dance class if there is a likelihood that it will later lead to dancing in places where men are present.

Answering the question whether a woman may attend a wedding at which there will be mixed dancing, HaGaon Rav Ben Zion Abba Shaul rules that she may attend, unless she might be invited to join in the dancing and will be unable to refuse. He concludes: "She must be made aware of the fact that it is entirely forbidden for her to dance there, even with other women, if she will be seen by men. She is advised only to remain for the wedding ceremony."

41. By bathing there she causes men to look at her.

Y'chaveh Da'ath, Vol. 5, No. 63, concludes that it is strictly forbidden for a man to bathe at a mixed beach, even for health reasons.

42. *Rivevoth Ephrayim, Orach Chayim*, Vol. 2, No. 197:25. This possible prohibition is because of *mar'ith ayin* (acting in a suspicious manner), since it might appear to others that she plans to swim there.

Female camp counselors should be cautioned not to accompany boys to the beach, even if it is a men's beach.

Yabiah Omer, Vol. 1, No. 20, citing *Sefer Chassidim* 614, adds that a woman should refrain from viewing men in bathing suits, even though it is not actually prohibited.

suit. She may remove the shirt just before entering the water as long as she puts it back on immediately after leaving the water.[43]

26. A mother is advised not to bring a son over the age of three to a woman's beach. A father may bring a daughter to a men's beach until she is five or six years old.[44]

Visiting the Sick and Comforting Mourners

27. A woman may visit a sick man provided the laws of *yichud* are observed.[45]

---

43. *Az Nidb'ru*, Vol. 3, No. 24; *Iggeroth Moshe, Evven HaEzer*, Vol. 1, No. 57. Some authorities permit men to be lifeguards at mixed beaches, based upon the argument in Tractate *Sotah* 21b: "Who is foolish in his piety? One who sees a woman drowning and turns away, saying it would not be modest to look at her." They also suggest that the male lifeguard qualifies as someone "pre-occupied" with his job and will therefore not have erotic thoughts. Other authorities argue, pointing out that the statement in *Sotah* does not provide a rationale for women to place themselves in situations where there is only a man to protect them in case of danger. Since the lifeguard sits for long periods watching all the swimmers, he is not exempted as someone "pre-occupied" with his work. It is also likely that the lifeguard's friends will visit him at the beach, and they will not be there to work at all.

44. HaGaon Rav Shlomo Zalman Auerbach writes: "It is advisable to refrain from bringing a boy to a woman's beach after he has reached the age of three. One may be more lenient with a girl who is accompanied by her father." It is emphasized that the girl must be dressed modestly, especially if one of the men wishes to recite *devarim shebikdushah*. See Chapter 4, paragraph 15.

   Imrey Yosher, discussing whether a woman may take her son to the seashore, cites the opinion of the *Chazon Ish* that she should not take him if he is old enough to remember the experience.

45. *Orukh HaShulchan, Yoreh De'ah* 335:11. The Laws of *Yichud* are discussed in Chapter 8.

A woman may assist a sick man, help him to stand, sit and attend to all his needs, provided it is not done in an intimate manner.[46]

28. A woman may make a condolence call to a male mourner provided the laws of *yichud* are observed.[47]

Teaching and Counseling

29. A woman may teach or be a camp counselor for boys under the age of nine.[48]

---

46. This ruling applies especially to doctors and nurses working in hospitals or other public institutions. See *Shulchan Arukh, Yoreh De'ah* 335:10; *Orukh HaShulchan, Evven HaEzer* 21:9; *Yaskil Avdi*, Vol. 2, *Evven HaEzer*, No. 23.

    If a woman feels that her actions might overstep the bounds of propriety, or give men erotic thoughts, she should consult a competent halakhic authority, particularly if she is taking a course or working in a profession which necessitates this kind of physical contact with men.

    The *Shulchan Arukh, Yoreh De'ah* 195:15, rules that a woman who is a *niddah* may tend to the needs of her ailing husband if no other person is available, and he is too weak to care for himself. But she is forbidden to bathe him. This leniency only applies when the husband is ill and not when the wife is ill. A husband may not assist his wife when she is a *niddah* unless it is a possible life-threatening situation, and no other person is available. See *Pardes Simcha, Yoreh De'ah* 195.

47. *Sh'arim Metzuyanim BeHalakhah* 207:1; *Chelkath Yaacov*, Vol. 3, No. 98; *Be'er Moshe*, Vol. 4, No. 117.

48. This ruling is based on a decision of HaGaon Rav Shlomo Zalman Auerbach. He adds that one should be more stringent regarding private lessons. The actual age of the boy depends on his physical maturity and whether other boys will also attend the lesson.

    There is another problem which may arise when a woman teaches youngsters, discussed in the *Shulchan Arukh, Yoreh De'ah* 245:21. The *Shulchan Arukh* states that a woman should not teach

Plastic Surgery

30. There is a dispute among authorities as to whether a woman may undergo plastic surgery for cosmetic reasons.[49]

Media

31. A woman should not watch any activity or event that is inconsistent with the moral standards of *Dath Yehudith*. She should not even look at a picture that depicts such behavior, or read about it in books, magazines or newspapers.[50]

---

children because she may violate the laws of *yichud* when their father comes to pick them up. The *Api Zutri* commentary on *Shulchan Arukh, Evven HaEzer* 22:33, comments, "The prevailing custom is that women teach youngsters, boys or girls...and we should allow them to do so..."

HaGaon Rav Yosef Sholom Eliashiv concludes that this restriction is no longer relevant because today women usually teach in institutions with people constantly coming and going.

49. *Tzitz Eliezer*, Vol. 11, No. 41, explains that a person who is not sick or in pain should not undergo unnecessary medical treatment that may involve even the slightest danger to life. The author bases this decision on the *Ramban* in *Sefer Torath HaAdam*. See also *Chelkath Yaacov*, Vol. 3, No. 11; *Noam*, Vol. 13, p. 311, and Vol. 6, p. 273.

50. *Iggeroth Moshe, Evven HaEzer*, Vol. 1, No. 67; *Yabiah Omer*, Vol. 1, No. 6:5. Books and journals that contain obscene or blasphemous material are discussed in the *Shulchan Arukh, Orach Chayim* 307:16. The *Chafetz Chayim* and other leaders of the past generation emphasized the great spiritual danger involved in reading or keeping such literature in the home.

CHAPTER 8
Yichud

1. *Yichud* is the term applied to situations where any man and woman — other than husband and wife — are alone in any place where there is no chaperon and where they are not likely to be disturbed.[1] Such situations are prohibited by Jewish Law.[2] Exceptions and exclusions will be discussed below.

---

1. *Shulchan Arukh, Evven HaEzer* 22; *Otzar HaPoskim* 22:1. This includes forests, fields, and beaches if there are no other people present.

   Situations of *yichud* can arise when least expected, such as when a woman finds herself alone in the house with a repairman, a salesman, or a male guest. An office secretary must be especially careful to avoid *yichud* with a male boss since most of the exclusions described below do not apply to her.

2. The following commentators note that certain categories of *yichud* are prohibited by Torah Law: *Tosafoth, Shabbath* 13a; *Me'iri, Kiddushin* 80a; *Sefer HaChinukh* 188; *Teshuvoth HaRashba* 587. This also appears to be the view of the *Tur*. They explain that Torah

Age

2. *Yichud* is permitted between children.[3] Therefore, if the girl is younger than twelve and the boy is younger than thirteen, they are exempt from these prohibitions.

3. Once a girl reaches the age of twelve, *yichud* is permitted only with boys younger than nine. When a boy reaches the age of thirteen, *yichud* is forbidden between him and girls over the age of three.[4]

Baby-sitting arrangements must take *yichud* into consideration. A girl over the age of twelve may not baby-sit for a boy over the age of nine, if *yichud* will be unavoidable.[5] Likewise, it is forbidden to leave a girl over the age of three in the charge of a male baby-sitter over the age of thirteen, except under the conditions detailed below.[6]

Law only prohibits *yichud* situations between two people who are forbidden to marry, or where the woman is a *niddah*. All other prohibitions of *yichud* are Rabbinic. Because today's unmarried women do not purify themselves in a *mikvah*, they have the status of *niddah*; *yichud* is forbidden to them by Torah Law.

3. *Sefer D'var Halakhah* 2:8 cites the *Smag*, who explains that there is no requirement of *chinukh* (religious training) for children with respect to *yichud*.

4. *Shulchan Arukh, Evven HaEzer* 22:11. The prohibition against *yichud* between a man and a young girl who has not reached puberty is Rabbinic. See *Binath Adam*, commentary to *Chokhmath Adam* 126.

5. *Shulchan Arukh, Ibid.*; *Sefer D'var Halakhah* 1:10 and 2:7.

6. *Shulchan Arukh, Ibid.*; *Sefer D'var Halakhah, Ibid.* This is also cited in *Kuntres Yichud* (Tropper), p. 17, in the names of HaGaon Rav Yosef Sholom Eliashiv and HaGaon Rav Chaim Pinchus Sheinberg.

Between Family Members

4. *Yichud* is permitted between a woman and her grandfather, father, son,[7] grandson,[8] or brother.[9]

5. *Yichud* is forbidden between a woman and her father-in-law,[10] brother-in-law, son-in-law,[11] uncle, nephew, cousin, adopted son over age nine, or step-son over age nine.[12]

---

7. *Shulchan Arukh, Evven HaEzer* 22:1.
8. *Pithchey Teshuvah, Evven HaEzer* 22:2; *Ezer Mekudash,* commentary on *Shulchan Arukh, Evven HaEzer* 22:10. This leniency applies even if the grandson is married.
9. This is based on the statement of Rav Assi in Tractate *Kiddushin* 81a, which permits a brother and sister to live alone in the same house together on a "temporary basis". *Imrey Yosher* Vol. 2, No. 43, comments that "temporary" may be defined as any number of days "up to thirty". Accordingly, although *yichud* is permitted between a brother and sister, they may not live alone in the same house for more than thirty days.

   Imrey Yosher specifies that in a hotel where other guests do not know that the man and woman are siblings, they should not occupy the same quarters for even a short period of time. Some authorities discourage a man from being alone in a house with his sister for more than three nights.

   Tzitz Eliezer, Vol. 12, No. 68, discusses whether two brothers can live with their sister permanently. Relying on the principle cited by the *Remah, Evven HaEzer* 22:5, that two "moral" individuals may have *yichud* with a woman, the author concludes that it is permissible, since the two brothers are assumed to be "moral" with respect to their sister. *Tzitz Eliezer* concludes, however, that it would be praiseworthy to avoid this situation.

   For a discussion of the problem of *yichud* between siblings, and between parents and children, if one or both of them have converted to Judaism, see *Sefer D'var Halakhah* 7:19.
10. *Shulchan Arukh, Evven HaEzer* 22:1. See also *Otzar HaPoskim* 22.
11. *Yaskil Avdi,* Vol. 7, *Evven HaEzer,* No. 6; *Be'er Moshe,* Vol. 4, No. 145:2.
12. *Sefer D'var Halakhah* 7:20, note 19. *Yichud* is also forbidden

6. When a father visits his married son and stays in his home, there is no prohibition of *yichud* between him and his daughter-in-law as long as the son is in the same city. He must not, however, act in too familiar a fashion with his daughter-in-law. If his son is not in the city, he may remain in the house with his daughter-in-law during the day as long as the front door is left open or if the neighbors are given permission to enter unannounced.[13]

---

between a man and his adopted daughter who is over age three, even if she is unaware that he is not her natural father. The laws governing *yichud* between parents and adopted children are also discussed in *Kuntres Yichud* (Tropper), p. 7, citing HaGaon from Tshebin, HaGaon Rav Yaacov Kanievsky, HaGaon Rav Yosef Sholom Eliashiv, and HaGaon Rav Chaim Pinchus Sheinberg.

For further information concerning the problems that may develop when a couple contemplates adoption, see *Iggeroth Moshe, Yoreh De'ah*, Vol. 1, No. 162, and *Tzitz Eliezer*, Vol. 6, No. 49:21, and Vol. 7, No. 44-45.

Tzitz Eliezer attempts to find solutions to the problems of *yichud* with adopted children, but admits that many of his suggestions are difficult to practice. He concludes that parents should not adopt children unless they are confident that they will be capable of observing the laws of *yichud*. The Lubavitcher Rebbe, in the journal *Yagdil Torah*, Vol. 10, No. 143, decries the fact that adopting parents do not concern themselves sufficiently with questions of *yichud* and physical contact with their adopted children. He expresses amazement that well-meaning couples are lenient in this matter and do not clarify the issues with competent halakhic authorities. When adopting parents do familiarize themselves with the problems involved and act accordingly, their merit is equal to that of natural parents who raise their children completely according to the Torah. See the *Chokhmath Adam, Evven HaEzer* 1, who explains that one may fulfill the commandment to "be fruitful and multiply" by raising an adopted child.

13. This is based on a ruling of HaGaon Rav Shlomo Zalman Auerbach. See paragraph 14, which discusses the leniencies that apply when the spouse is in the city, and paragraph 8, which discusses the details of leaving the front door open.

With a Guest or Tenant

7. A female guest may sleep alone in a room with the door unlocked, even if there are men in the house.[14] A woman should not rent a room in a house where there is a male boarder unless one of their doors — his or hers — is normally kept locked to prevent entry.[15]

Excluding Circumstances
An Open Door

8. If a man and woman are in a room with a door open to the street, *yichud* is permitted as long as the door remains open and there are people on the street.[16] This

---

14. *Sefer D'var Halakhah* 11:7.
15. *Sefer D'var Halakhah* 11:3 and 11:6. See also *Otzar HaPoskim* 22:28. *Tzitz Eliezer*, Vol. 6, No. 40, Chapter 8:5, states that it does not matter whether it is the man's or the woman's door that is kept locked. *Sefer D'var Halakhah* 11:8 discusses the case of two rooms on the same corridor and concludes, based on the *Chazon Ish*, that a woman is permitted to rent such a room if the doors are kept locked and if the tenants do not spend time in the hallway.
16. *Shulchan Arukh, Evven HaEzer* 22:9, based on Rav Yosef's statement in Tractate *Kiddushin* 81a.

    If the door is closed but unlocked, *Beith Meir* and Rabbi Akiva Eiger (Responsa, No. 100) forbid *yichud*. *Teshuvoth HaRashba*, Vol. 1, No. 251, *Mabit*, Vol. 1, No. 287, *Radvaz* and *Ezer Mekudash*, permit *yichud* when the door is closed and unlocked. *Sefer D'var Halakhah* 3:6 also ascribes this more lenient view to the *Chazon Ish*. According to these authorities, a man and woman may be alone in a house with an unlocked front door, even at night, until the time when there are no more people on the street.

    In practice, *Kuntres Yichud* (Tropper), p. 19, cites the decisions of HaGaon Rav Yosef Sholom Eliashiv and HaGaon Rav Chaim Pinchus Sheinberg that if people could and do enter an unlocked front door without warning, it is equivalent to an open door. In a place where people would not enter unannounced, it is considered a "locked door", and *yichud* is prohibited.

    Rav Tropper cites another view of HaGaon Rav Eliashiv that

leniency applies even if the man has a reputation for immorality.[17]

9. If there are no passers-by, or it is late at night, *yichud* is prohibited even if the door to the street is open.[18]

10. A man and woman who are fond of each other are advised not to remain alone in a house, even if the door is open.[19]

---

when the front door is open, *yichud* is permitted in an inner room with a closed door, provided it is unlocked. He also cites the opposing view of HaGaon Rav Sheinberg, who rules that in this case *yichud* should be avoided unless the door to the room itself is left open.

The *Nodah BeYehudah, Kama, Evven HaEzer*, No. 71, considers a window, or any other opening through which passers-by can see into a house, to be an "open door" — but stipulates that every part of the room must be visible from the outside.

Sefer D'var Halakhah 3:6 states that if the entrance to an upper-floor apartment is on a stairway or hallway through which people pass freely, the door to the apartment has the same status as the front door of a house.

17. This is the conclusion of the *Pithchey Teshuvah, Evven HaEzer* 22:9, citing the *Birkey Yosef*. Support for this ruling is inferred from the *Rambam*, who maintains that for purposes of the laws of *yichud*, all men should consider themselves capable of immoral behavior; still, the *Rambam* does permit *yichud* when the front door is standing open to the street.

18. *Ba'er Heytev, Evven HaEzer* 22:9, citing *K'nesseth Hag'dolah; Pithchey Teshuvah, Evven HaEzer* 22:9. *Tzitz Eliezer*, Vol. 6, *Kuntres Yichud* 11:6, cites the *Radvaz* as the source of this law. *Tzitz Eliezer* interprets the *Radvaz* to maintain that during late-night hours *yichud* is forbidden, even if the door to the street is open and there are passers-by.

19. *Chelkath M'chokek* and *Beith Shmuel*, commentaries on *Shulchan Arukh, Evven HaEzer* 22:9. This law is inferred from the *T'rumoth HaDeshen*, who explains that once a husband has warned his wife not to seclude herself with a man, she is forbidden to be alone with that man even if the door to the street is left open.

11. A man and woman may be alone in an unlocked room if it is usual for the people in the house to enter that room without warning.[20]

Excluding Circumstances
A Chaperon

12. The prohibition of *yichud* is removed when one of the following individuals is present: the man's sister, daughter, mother, or grandmother;[21] the woman's father, son, grandfather, brother, mother-in-law, husband's sister,[22] or his step-daughter.[23]

13. The prohibition of *yichud* between two adults is removed when a girl between the ages of five and nine or a boy between the ages of nine and thirteen is also present.[24]

---

20. See note 16. *Dovev Meysharim*, No. 5, comments that if someone with a house key is able to enter without warning, the front door is considered an "open door", even if it is locked. Although this ruling is also quoted in the name of the *Chazon Ish, Sefer HaHalakhah BaMishpachah*, p. 74, advises that it be utilized only when absolutely necessary or when there are additional factors that would permit *yichud*. Although the ruling of *Dovev Meysharim* assumes that an unlocked door cancels the prohibition of *yichud*, see note 16, which discusses the opinions of other authorities who forbid *yichud* when an unlocked door is closed.

21. *Beith Shlomo, Orach Chayim*, No. 148. See also *Sefer D'var Halakhah* 8:4 and 8:6, which explains that these individuals, because of their relationships, are likely to deter the couple from improprieties. *Kuntres Yichud* (Tropper), p. 26, notes that HaGaon Rav Moshe Feinstein and the *Chazon Ish* come to the same conclusion.

22. *Shulchan Arukh, Evven HaEzer* 22:2; *Rambam, Hilkhoth Ishuth*, Chapter 22.

23. Tractate *Kiddushin* 81b; *Shulchan Arukh, Ibid.*

24. *Shulchan Arukh, Ibid.; Pithchey Teshuvah, Evven HaEzer* 22:22. See also *Tzitz Eliezer*, Vol. 6, No. 40.

Some authorities rule that at night there must be *two* children present.[25]

Excluding Circumstances
A Spouse in the Same City

14.   *Yichud* is permitted when a woman's husband is in the same city. Some authorities insist on two additional conditions: the husband knows where his wife is; and, he could arrive there at any time.[26]

---

25. *HaHalakhah BaMishpachah*, p. 76, based on the *Remah, Evven HaEzer* 22:5, and *Beith Shmuel* commentary.

26. *Shulchan Arukh, Evven HaEzer* 22:8. This leniency is based on the premise that her husband's proximity will inhibit a woman from immoral behavior. Authorities conclude that under these circumstances *yichud* is permitted, even between a woman and a *parutz* (a person lax in any sexually-related matter).

   The *Pithchey Teshuvah, Evven HaEzer* 22:7, citing the *Binath Adam*, emphasizes that the leniency when the husband is present in the same city only applies if it is possible that he might appear unexpectedly. Therefore, argues the *Pithchey Teshuvah, yichud* is forbidden outside the home when the husband does not know where his wife is. *Otzar HaPoskim, Evven HaEzer* 31:2, however, cites the *Chiddah* and others, who do permit *yichud* in such a situation, and *Sefer D'var Halakhah* reports that this was the opinion of the *Chazon Ish*. They contend that a woman is naturally inhibited when her husband is in the same city, even if he does not know where she is.

   Those who follow the stringent authorities in this matter would find it difficult to permit a woman to visit a doctor who keeps the door of his examining room locked. If the examining room is not locked, and there are people in the waiting room, she may rely on those authorities who equate this situation to a door that is "open" to a public area. See paragraph 9. *Taharath Am Yisrael*, p. 49, suggests that a woman can avoid any possible transgression by having someone accompany her to the doctor's office.

   According to the *Chokhmath Adam* 126:6, *yichud* in the home is forbidden when the husband works a considerable distance away

Some maintain that when a husband gives his wife permission to be alone with a particular man, *yichud* with that man is no longer permitted, even if the husband is in the same city.[27]

Yichud with a man to whom a woman is attracted, especially a relative, is also prohibited whether her husband is in the same city or not.[28]

---

and would not be likely to arrive at any time; *yichud* is also forbidden during times of the day when he cannot leave his work. *Dovev Meysharim*, Vol. 1, No. 6, and the *Chazon Ish*, however, insist that a woman will be inhibited by her husband's being in the city even in these cases. *Ezer Mekudash* concurs and states that even in a large metropolis "like Antioch", the exemption of "a husband in the city" still applies.

If the husband is outside the city limits, *yichud* is forbidden even if he is in a neighboring town from which he could return in a relatively short time. *Sefer D'var Halakhah* cites the *Chazon Ish*, who rules that Tel Aviv and Ramat Gan, two adjoining cities in Israel, are not considered one city for purposes of *yichud*. According to the *Chazon Ish*'s definition, the husband is "in the city" only if he is in the same municipal jurisdiction as his wife.

HaGaon Rav Shlomo Zalman Auerbach rules that a woman who allows a man to enter her home is obligated to inform him that her husband is in the city. If she does not, the man is considered to have the intention of transgressing the prohibition of *yichud*. In Tractate *Nazir* 23a, *Chazal* teach us that a person who intends to eat pork and unintentionally eats lamb must still atone for his intended sin. This situation is similar in that the man has no knowledge of the special circumstances that permit him to enter the woman's house. As far as he knows, he is performing a forbidden act.

27. *Pithchey Teshuvah, Evven HaEzer* 22:7, citing the *Binath Adam* 126:6. When the husband gives his wife permission to have *yichud* with a particular man, the inhibiting factor of his presence in the vicinity is nullified. According to *Dovev Meysharim*, however, when the husband is in the same city, *yichud* is permitted even if he grants her permission to be alone with the man.

28. *Shulchan Arukh, Evven HaEzer* 22:8. The *Orukh HaShulchan* adds that this prohibition applies even when they meet in the course of business.

15. A man may be alone in his own home with a woman if his wife is in the same city and could possibly arrive at any moment.[29]

If a man comes into contact with women in the course of his profession,[30] he should not be alone with them unless his wife is present.[31]

A Woman and More Than One Man

16. Some authorities maintain that one woman may be alone with two or more men provided that the men are not *prutzim.*

A person is classified as a *parutz* if he is lax in any sexually-related matter.[32] Some rule that a man who is only suspected of transgressing such prohibitions is classified as a *parutz* for this purpose.[33]

---

29. The *Shulchan Arukh, Evven HaEzer* 22:3, explains that this is permitted because his wife becomes a chaperon. It appears from Tractate *Kiddushin* 80a and *Avodah Zarah* 25b that this leniency applies even if the man is a *parutz.*

   Imrey Yosher, Vol. 2, No. 9, stresses that the proximity of a man's wife is considered an inhibiting factor only if he is at home. If he is not in his home, the *Maharsham,* Vol. 4, No. 148, forbids *yichud* even when his wife is in the city. *Dovev Meysharim* goes further and advises men, even at home, not to rely on their wives' proximity — and to avoid being in a room with only one woman.
30. For example, a woman's tailor or hairdresser.
31. *Shulchan Arukh, Evven HaEzer* 22:7.
32. These include laxity in permitting physical contact between the sexes and in the regulations of *yichud* in addition to actual violations of the prohibitions against forbidden sexual relations.
33. *Remah, Evven HaEzer* 22:5. This definition of *parutz* is taken from *Sefer D'var Halakhah* 9. It is assumed that the average man is not a *parutz.* If any of the men are known to be *prutzim,* most authorities rule that *yichud* is forbidden, no matter how many are present.

   When only one of the men is a *parutz,* the *Maharshal,* writing in *Yam Shel Shlomo,* on Tractate *Kiddushin,* Chapter 4, No. 21, rules

17. In an unpopulated area, or in a city during late-night hours, there must be three men who are not *prutzim* with the woman.[34]

Sephardic authorities forbid one woman from being alone even with many men.[35]

18. Three women may be alone only with two or more men.[36]

In the Doctor's Office

19. *Yichud* is permitted with a male doctor in his office only under certain conditions: the door to the examining room must be unlocked; there must be people in the waiting room, *or* it must be usual for at least two other people, such as other doctors or nurses, to enter the examining room unannounced.[37]

---

that *yichud* is permitted, since the righteous man will restrain the *parutz*. The *Nodah BeYehudah, Kama, Evven HaEzer*, No. 69, and *Shev Yaacov*, No. 19, however, maintain that none of the men may be *prutzim*. It is proper to be stringent and to avoid *yichud* in such a situation.

34. *Remah, Ibid.* The *Biur HaGra* explains that the third man is required, because if only two were present and one left to relieve himself or go to sleep, the woman would be alone with the other man.

35. The *Shulchan Arukh, Evven HaEzer* 22:7, follows the view of the *Rambam*, who advises every man to consider himself a *parutz* in these matters. According to the Sephardic view, four women are needed for the presence of even one man to be allowed. See *Otzar HaPoskim* 22:26.

36. *Chokhmath Adam* 126:3; *Sefer D'var Halakhah* 9:11.

37. *Kuntres Yichud* (Tropper), p. 20, qualifies this exemption with the opinion of HaGaon Rav Yosef Sholom Eliashiv that the doctor and the two people who could walk in must be Jewish.

Minchath Yitzchak, Vol. 7, No. 73, arrives at the following conclusion concerning this issue: "When a woman needs to visit a

Some authorities rule that if the doctor's wife or some other person has a key to the examining room, *yichud* is permitted without other people present.[38]

20. If the doctor's office is at home, and his wife is in the house, the patient may enter the examining room even if the door will be locked.[39] Otherwise, the normal laws of *yichud* apply.

21. When a doctor makes a house call to a woman's home, if her husband is out of town and no other family members have a key to her house, the front door must be left open.[40]

In a Car

22. *Yichud* is not prohibited between a man and a woman traveling in a car through an area where there are

---

male doctor, her husband should accompany her and wait in an adjoining room. The connecting door should be left unlocked. If her husband cannot accompany her, she should ask one of the following women to accompany her: her mother-in-law, sister-in-law, daughter, or step-daughter. (See paragraph 12.) If this is not possible, she should be accompanied by another woman whose husband is in the same city. Both husbands should be aware of the visit. If she is thus accompanied, there is no problem of *yichud* even when the possibility exists that the doctor might act in an unbecoming manner. Ideally, the door should be left slightly ajar. If not, it should be left unlocked. It is best for an elderly woman to accompany her."

38. *Tzitz Eliezer*, Vol. 6, No. 40, Chapter 12:10; *Otzar HaPoskim* 22:35. Some authorities offer, as a reason for leniency, the doctor's concern for his reputation, which will deter him from acting improperly.
39. *Tzitz Eliezer, Ibid.*, par. 12.
40. *Sefer D'var Halakhah* 3:3 and 7:1.

passers-by. This leniency applies even at night if the streets are lighted.[41]

23. When traveling on a highway, or through an area without passers-by, two conditions must be satisfied: there must be at least one other man in the car; and, there must be minimal traffic (at least one passing car every five minutes).[42]

Some Sephardic authorities rule that a woman should refrain from traveling in a car, even with a group of men, unless three other women are present in the car.[43]

24. If a woman must travel alone at night in a taxi in order to fulfill a *mitzvah*, she may do so provided there are other cars on the road.[44]

With a Gentile

25. *Yichud* between a woman and a gentile man is forbidden, even if his wife is present.[45] Some authorities

---

41. *Otzar Haposkim* 22:35; *Shevet HaLevi*, Vol. 3, *Evven HaEzer*, No. 185.
42. Without these conditions, there must be three men in the car who are not *prutzim*. (See paragraph 17.) See also *Tzitz Eliezer*, Vol. 6, No. 40, 15:8, 15:10 and 15:12, and Vol. 7, No. 42.
43. This is the ruling of HaGaon Rav Ben Zion Abba Shaul, based on the Sephardic view cited in note 35.
44. *Iggeroth Moshe, Yore Deah*, Vol. 2, No. 83, explains that since there are other cars on the road and the taxi driver's livelihood might suffer if he acted improperly, one can act leniently in order to perform a *mitzvah* such as traveling to the *mikvah*, even if there is no one else in the cab. It would be preferable, however, for her husband to accompany her.
45. *Shulchan Arukh, Evven HaEzer* 22:3. *Taharath Am Yisrael*, p. 22,

maintain that *yichud* is permitted if the Jewish woman's husband is in the same city and knows where she is.[46]

26. A woman may travel through a populated area in a taxi driven by a gentile,[47] but she should refrain from doing so at night.[48]

In an Elevator

27. Some authorities maintain that the restrictions of *yichud* apply in an elevator.[49] Most, however, rule that it is permitted as long as the elevator can be stopped by someone who wishes to enter.[50]

---

comments: "One can only be amazed at the practice of many God-fearing Jews who send their daughters to gentile homes for music lessons, even when the doors to the homes are locked. It is clear from the sources that the presence of the gentile's wife does not remove this prohibition."

46. *Radvaz*, Vol. 3, No. 481. *Ezer Mekudash, Chokhmath Adam* and *Pithchey Teshuvah* (cited in *Sefer D'var Halakhah* 7:14) rely on this view in countries where rape is a punishable crime or where the gentile's business would suffer if he were to behave inappropriately.

Sefer D'var Halakhah cites the *Chazon Ish*, who rules that *yichud* is permitted only if the Jewish woman's husband is in the immediate vicinity, removing the fear of rape.

47. *Sefer D'var Halakhah* 15:2.

48. *Sh'arim Metzuyanim BeHalakhah* 152:3, in *Kuntres Acharon*.

49. *Noam*, Vol. 13, p. 44; *Minchath Yitzchak*, Vol. 4, No. 94. *Minchath Yitzchak* rules that it is permitted, when necessary. Also see *Chelkath Yaacov*, Vol. 2, No. 14, and *Shevet HaLevi*, Vol. 3, *Evven HaEzer*, No. 182, who emphasize that *yichud* is still forbidden when there is a possibility of intimate contact, even short of sexual relations.

50. *Chelkath Yaacov, Ibid.*; *Sefer D'var Halakhah* 15. This ruling is also cited in *Kuntres Yichud* (Tropper), p. 28, in the name of Hagaon Rav Yosef Sholom Eliashiv.

A Male Guest

28. A man is permitted to eat and sleep in the home of a divorcee, widow or single woman when she is not there.[51]

Between Spouses

29. A bride who becomes a *niddah* before having relations with her husband may not be alone with him except in the presence of a chaperon.[52] Once they have had relations, there is no further prohibition against *yichud* when the wife is a *niddah*.[53]

---

51. *Iggeroth Moshe, Evven HaEzer*, Vol. 1, No. 19, discusses the question of a *shochet* who travels in the course of his work. The author permits the man to eat breakfast and dinner at a woman's home, even when she is there.

52. *Shulchan Arukh, Yoreh De'ah* 192:4. The *Remah* adds that in this situation it is customary for a young boy to sleep in the room with the husband and a young girl with the bride. *Sefer D'var Halakhah* 11:5-6 points out that they may not be alone in the same house, even if the bride locks her door.

    This law applies even if it is the second marriage for one or both of them. But if a man remarries his former wife when she is a *niddah, yichud* is permitted. See *Sefer D'var Halakhah* 2:13.

53. *Shulchan Arukh, Yoreh De'ah* 195:1: "A man should not act flirtatiously with his wife when she is a *niddah*, lest they come to sin. Yet, *yichud* is permitted between them, for once they have had sexual relations their evil inclinations will not overpower them."

CHAPTER 9
Torah Study

A Woman's Obligation

1. While women are exempt from the *mitzvah* of *Talmud Torah* (Torah study),[1] they must understand the areas of the Written and Oral Torah that pertain to

---

1. *Shulchan Arukh, Yoreh De'ah* 246:6; *Shulchan Arukh HaRav, Hilkhoth Talmud Torah* 1:14.

It should be emphasized that this exemption applies only to the abstract and theoretical aspects of *Talmud Torah*. The obligation to receive and give education in practical *mitzvah* observance will be discussed in Chapter 10.

The *Gemara*, in Tractate *Kiddushin* 29a, derives the exemption of women from Torah study from the verse in *Shema*, "And you shall teach (*v'limadtem*) [the words of Torah] to your sons" (*Devarim* 11:19). Since the word *v'limadtem*, which means "to teach" can be read as *u'lemadtem*, meaning "to study", *Chazal* infer that only a child whom a parent is obligated to teach is himself obligated to study. Since the verse speaks of teaching male children, *Chazal* conclude that a parent is not required to teach a daughter and that she, in turn, is not required to study on her own. See also the *Sifri, Devarim* 46. The *Gemara* concludes that this exemption is threefold: from parental instruction, self-study, and teaching her children.

practical observance. Thus, they are required to study in order to fulfill their religious obligations properly, but not to study as a *mitzvah* in itself.[2] Some authorities take the requirement to be versed in practical halakhah as the basis

---

2. The *Beith HaLevi*, Vol. 1, No. 6, explains there are two distinct obligations: to study Torah, and to have knowledge of Torah. He finds support for this idea from *Tosafoth* in Tractate *Sotah* 21a, where the *mitzvah* of *Hakhel* (Gathering) is mentioned. *Hakhel* was observed every seven years by all Jews — men, women and children — who used to gather in the *Beith HaMikdash* to hear the king read the Book of *Devarim*. *Chazal* (Tractate *Chagigah* 3a) say, "Men came to learn, and women came to listen." *Tosafoth* explains that although women are exempt from the obligation to study Torah, they must still come to "listen", in order to learn the details of the commandments. The *Beith HaLevi* interprets *Tosafoth* to mean that women are only exempt from the first aspect of *Talmud Torah*, learning for learning's sake, but are obligated to learn how to perform *mitzvoth* properly.

The *Beith HaLevi*, in the introduction to his work, quotes another statement of *Chazal*: "When the Jewish people recited *na'aseh* (we will do) before *nishmah* (we will hear), 600,000 angels descended and crowned each Jew with two crowns." In explaining the significance of placing "we will do" before "we will hear", he comments that if the Israelites had said the reverse — we will hear and we will do — it would have implied that study ("hearing") is only a means to proper observance ("doing") and not a *mitzvah* to be performed for its own sake. *Na'aseh v'nishmah* (We will do and *then* we will hear.) implies learning for its own sake because the initial acceptance of doing, *na'aseh*, presupposes prior knowledge of what to do. The subsequent statement, "we will hear", indicates that even after we know how to perform *mitzvoth* properly, we will continue to study for its own sake.

The *Maharal*, in his *Exposition on the Torah (D'rush al HaTorah)*, gives another reason why only men are obligated to study Torah for its own sake. Men generally have aggressive tendencies and psychological constitutions incompatible with the peace and serenity of the World to Come. This condition can only be rectified through constant involvement in Torah study, which sublimates their aggressive drives and cultivates tranquility. Since women are

for a woman's obligation to recite *Birkath HaTorah* in the morning.[3]

2. Women must familiarize themselves with all negative precepts — both those forbidden by Torah and Rabbinic Law — as well as the positive precepts which they are obligated to perform.[4]

3. Women are required to study *Tanakh*,[5] the sayings of *Chazal*, and Jewish ethical works, all of which cultivate proper Jewish attitudes toward God and humanity.[6]

---

naturally disposed to peacefulness and serenity, they do not need to be constantly engaged in Torah study to merit the World to Come.

Additional sources that discuss the two aspects of *Talmud Torah* can be found in the works of the *Chiddah*. See *Yosef Ometz*, No. 67, and *Birkey Yosef, Orach Chayim* 47:7. See also *B'rith Olam*, commentary on *Sefer Chassidim* 313.

3. The *Shulchan Arukh, Orach Chayim* 47, obligates women to recite *Birkath HaTorah* each morning because "They are obligated to learn the laws of Torah that pertain to them." See Chapter 2, note 32, where this issue is discussed at length.

4. *Shulchan Arukh, Yoreh De'ah* 246:6, based on Tractate *Sotah* 21b; *Shulchan Arukh HaRav, Hilkhoth Talmud Torah* 1:14; *Sefer Chassidim* 313. See also the *Mishnah Berurah* 187:19.

The *Shulchan Arukh HaRav* specifies that women are obligated to study all laws specifically relevant to them, such as the laws of *niddah*, immersion, salting meat, and the prohibition against *yichud*, as well as all positive *mitzvoth* not bound by time.

See also *Iggeroth Moshe, Yoreh De'ah*, Vol. 1, No. 139, and Vol. 2, No. 109.

5. The *Chumash* (Five Books of Moses), the *Nevi'im* (Prophets), and the *Kethuvim* (Holy Writings).

6. The *Chafetz Chayim*, writing in *Chomath HaDath*, cautions, "Nowadays, women must be taught the Written Torah and Jewish ethical works so that our holy faith may be clarified for them." In the same vein, the *Chatham Sofer* is said to have studied the Aggadic sections of the Talmud with his daughters. The Vilna Gaon, in a letter to his wife and mother written during his

4. Some authorities maintain that a father is obligated to teach his daughter all areas of Torah that apply to her.[7]

5. A husband is responsible for ensuring that his wife has adequate knowledge in all areas of Torah Law relevant to her obligations. Spouses should regularly caution one another, through word and example, not to transgress the prohibitions of slander, anger and strife.[8] If one partner is lax in these areas, the other should offer gentle corrections.

6. A husband and wife should establish a regular time to study practical aspects of Jewish Law, especially those that are frequently applied and require periodic review.[9]

---

attempted journey to *Eretz Yisrael*, instructs them to spend *Shabbath* studying works of Jewish ethics. For further discussion, see paragraph 7.

7. *Sefer Chassidim* 313 asserts that a man is obligated to instruct his daughter in her obligations, explaining that the Talmudic exemption from and admonition against teaching Torah to women (See paragraph 7.) only applies to the complexities of Talmudic logic. He demonstrates that in the days of King Chizkiyah, during the first Temple period, women were familiar with the laws of sacrifices and ritual purity.

The *Maharil*, No. 199, takes a contrary view, maintaining that the Talmudic admonition against teaching women Torah applies to all areas of study; their training should be limited to practical applications, and they should be taught only by their mothers or other women. In the days of Chizkiyah, he argues, men studied the theoretical aspects of ritual purity and sacrifices, but women learned only the practicalities.

See paragraph 7, where it is explained that, in any case, the Talmudic admonition does not fully apply today.

8. *Iggereth HaGra.* See also *Mitzvoth HaBayith*, p. 94-97.

9. *Amuda D'nihora*, p. 13, relates how HaGaon Rav Yosef Chayim Sonnenfeld, of Sainted Memory, was particular to study a section of *Orach Chayim* with his wife for half an hour each day.

It is also recommended that a few laws of *Shabbath* be discussed at each *Shabbath* meal.

Torah Education for Women

7. In the days of *Chazal*, it was forbidden to instruct women in the Oral Law *(Torah Sheb'al Peh)*.[10] In addition,

---

10. *Shulchan Arukh, Yoreh De'ah* 246:6; *Taz, Yoreh De'ah* 246:4. This is based on the *Mishnah, Sotah* 3:4: "Rabbi Eliezer said that he who teaches his daughter Torah is considered to have taught her *tifluth*." There are several interpretations of the term *tifluth*. The *Rambam*, in *Hilkhoth Talmud Torah* 1:13, writes that the *Mishnah* refers to the teaching of *Torah Sheb'al Peh* and notes that since women are not generally free to dedicate themselves to long-term, intensive Torah study, their knowledge will be superficial. Without a thorough and sophisticated understanding of Torah, which can only be developed through years of intensive, time-consuming study, the Torah might, God forbid, appear trivial and irrelevant to them. According to this interpretation, *tifluth* is related to the root *tafel*, which appears in the verse, "Can that which is tasteless *(tafel)* be eaten without salt" *(Iyov* 6:6)? See HaRav Moshe Meiselman's work, *Jewish Woman in Jewish Law*, p. 34 -36, for a discussion of the *Rambam*'s words.

HaRav Meiselman also cites a second interpretation of *tifluth*, that of the *Remah*, relating the term to immorality. HaRav Meiselman explains that not only is superficial knowledge a "tasteless" dish, but it can also be easily misdirected. For example, in one of the major areas of Jewish Law, family purity, a man relies heavily on his wife's judgement. This makes it necessary for her to be thoroughly familiar with the practical applications of halakhah in this area. A woman with superficial knowledge of the theory of these laws might make incorrect halakhic decisions, causing herself and her husband to transgress.

Yet another interpretation of R. Eliezer's statement may be found in the *Torah Temimah, Devarim* 11:15, which bases the prohibition against teaching women *Torah Sheb'al Peh* on another Talmudic saying: "God has placed greater understanding in women than in men" *(Niddah* 45b). The implication here is that women might rely on their intuitive understanding before acquiring a firm foundation in Torah logic and thereby distort the intention of the law. *Chazal* address this danger by saying, "Without knowledge, there is no understanding" *(Avoth* 3:17).

it was considered proper to refrain from instructing them in the Written Law (*Torah Shebikhthav*), but such instruction was not actually forbidden.[11]

Today it is common practice for women to study *Tanakh*,[12] and some even permit them to learn *Torah*

---

11. *Shulchan Arukh, Ibid.* See also *Atereth Z'keinim*, commentary on the *Shulchan Arukh, Orach Chayim* 47:14; *Taz, Yoreh De'ah* 246:4; *Shulchan Arukh HaRav, Hilkhoth Talmud Torah* 1:16.

12. A landmark decision was rendered by the *Chafetz Chayim* in *Likutey Halakhoth, Sotah* 21b: " '...as if he taught her *tifluth*.' It appears that this principle was only valid in earlier generations when the traditions of our forefathers were clear and strongly upheld in every Jewish household...Then one could truly rely on the dictum, 'Ask your father, and he will instruct you.' Of those times it could be said that girls were better not taught Torah, but should learn its practical applications from their parents.

   "In this generation, due to our multitude of sins, the chain of tradition has been severely weakened. It is common practice for girls to leave home at an early age. It is, therefore, a great *mitzvah* to teach girls *Chumash, Tanakh,* and the ethical sayings of the Sages, such as Tractate *Avoth* and the book *Menorath HaMaor*, so that they will internalize our holy faith. Without this education, they might depart completely from the path of God and transgress, God forbid, the basic principles of our religion."

   In a letter dated 23 Shevat, 5693, the last year of his life, the *Chafetz Chayim* writes: "When I heard that a number of God-fearing men donated their time and services to establish a *Beith Yaacov* school in order to teach Torah, *mitzvoth* and fear of God to Jewish girls, I praised their excellent work. May God grant them strength that their work be successful. Theirs is a great undertaking of vital importance in our day, for the need to counteract the heretical ideas that are spreading is of the utmost importance...It is a great *mitzvah* to teach women...We should expend every effort to increase the number of such schools in order to salvage our tradition of learning."

   HaGaon Rav Zalman Sorotzkin, of Sainted Memory, adds a pertinent thought in *Moznayim LeMishpat*, Vol. 1, No. 42: "Since many [female] students — even those who attend religious day

Sheb'al Peh.[13] Women are, however, discouraged from delving into the complexities of Talmudic logic.[14]

8. A woman who wishes to study *Torah Sheb'al Peh* in order to more fully understand the truths of the Torah is permitted to do so. The spiritual reward for her endeavor is equal to that of performing a *mitzvah* from which one is halakhically exempt.[15] Jewish history abounds with women

---

schools from an early age — do not come from homes that are based on a conscientious dedication to scrupulous Torah observance, it is the obligation of these schools to educate their students in all aspects of Jewish Law, so that these students can observe the *mitzvoth* in a thorough manner." See also *Sho'el U'Meishiv, Mahadurah Daleth*, Vol. 3, No. 41, and *Tzitz Eliezer*, Vol. 9, No. 3.

13. *Moznayim LeMishpat* and *Tzitz Eliezer, Ibid. Iggeroth Moshe, Yoreh De'ah*, Vol. 3, No. 87, discusses the permissibility of women studying *Mishnah*: "Since *Mishnah* is included in *Torah Sheb'al Peh*, it is one of the things which, according to the Sages, should not be taught to women. Only *Pirkey Avoth* and its commentaries, which contain ethical teachings and guidelines for proper behavior, may be taught to women, since these serve the purpose of awakening a love of Torah and cultivating refinement of character. Other Mishnaic tractates are not appropriate."

Nevertheless, relevant *Mishnayoth* may be taught to women as background material to a particular topic. They should not be presented in a course by themselves unless a competent halakhic authority is first consulted.

14. *Taz, Yoreh De'ah* 246:4; *Maharatz Chayeth*, glosses to Tractate *Chagigah* 3a and *Sotah* 21b. See also the Responsa of *Maharatz Chayeth*, No. 32.

15. *Prishah, Yoreh De'ah* 246:15. Since she has decided on her own initiative to dedicate herself to Torah study, she will assuredly gain more than a "tasteless", perhaps dangerous, smattering of knowledge that the Sages wished to avoid by keeping the Oral Law out of the curriculum for girls.

In light of this ruling, a female teacher of *Tanakh* is permitted to study the Talmudic passages necessary for the understanding of

who excelled in both the breadth and depth of Torah scholarship.[16]

related commentaries and to make this information available to her students.

The *Torah Temimah, Devarim* 11:48, cites a remarkable passage from an ancient work called *Ma'ayan Ganim*, written by Rav Shmuel Ben Elchanan Yaacov Harkvalti to one such enterprising woman: "The words of the Sages [discouraging Torah instruction for women] were limited to a father teaching a girl when she is young. At early ages, there is certainly fear that she may lack the proper dedication...but women who uplift their hearts of their own free will and choose to draw close to the works of God...will surely rise to the summit of God's Mountain and dwell in His Holy Place — for they are truly wonderful women. The leaders of their generation should encourage them and strengthen their hands...Go forward and be successful and Heaven should send you all necessary assistance."

16. See the *Tosephta, Kelim, Bava Kama* 14:9, and Tractate *Pesachim* 62b. These sources relate how Beruriah, the wife of Rabbi Meir, taught her students 300 passages of Jewish Law in a single day. Tractate *Chullin* 109b quotes a halakhic query posed by Yalta, Rav Nachman's wife. The *Chiddah*, writing in *Shem Gedolim*, cites the *Rashbatz*, Vol. 3, No. 78, which answers a question posed by *Tosafoth* in the name of a learned woman.

It is reported in the Responsa of the *Maharshal*, No. 3, that Rebbetzin Miriam, the *Maharshal*'s grandmother, led a yeshiva for many years. She lectured to advanced students from behind a curtain.

See also the introduction to the *Drishah*'s commentary on the *Tur, Yoreh De'ah*, written by the *Drishah*'s son. New halakhic insights concerning the laws of candle-lighting on *Yom Tov* are cited in the name of the *Drishah*'s mother, Rebbetzin Baylah. He recalls: "After prayers, she wasted no time, but went directly to her studies, the Weekly Portion with *Rashi* and the classical commentaries...She was as accomplished as any man in Torah discussions...Her lips would occasionally utter new insights into the Midrashic interpretations of the Sages...She was especially well-versed in laws pertaining to women, particularly the laws of *niddah*. Her erudition approached that of the recognized halakhic authorities of the day."

9. Some authorities maintain that a daughter's educational expenses may not be deducted from *Ma'aser Kesafim* (the 10 percent of a person's income separated for charitable purposes), just as a son's tuition may not.[17]

10. A woman is permitted to study Torah when she is a *niddah*.[18]

Encouraging Others to Study

11. A woman who sacrifices material desires and uncomplainingly runs the home herself so that her husband and children can devote themselves fully to Torah study is

---

17. All authorities agree that it is forbidden to use *Ma'aser Kesafim* for a son's education since the ten percent of a person's income that is separated for charitable purposes may not be used to discharge financial obligations. Since a father is obligated to teach his son Torah, *Ma'aser Kesafim* may not be used when paying for his educational needs. But a father has no specific obligation to teach his daughter Torah, so it should be permissible to use *Ma'aser Kesafim* for her Torah education. *Iggeroth Moshe, Yoreh De'ah*, Vol. 2, No. 113, argues, however, that since a father is bound today by secular law to send his daughter to school — and he must choose a school with God-fearing teachers — her Torah education is considered a financial obligation, and so *Ma'aser Kesafim* funds may not be utilized to pay the cost.

It is clear that this stipulation applies only to basic tuition. For special lessons, fees may be taken from *Ma'aser Kesafim*, and this exception applies equally to girls and boys.

The above ruling of *Iggeroth Moshe* is contrary to *Beith Avi*, No. 99, which concludes that since a father is not halakhically bound to teach his daughter Torah, her education is not considered one of his financial obligations and may be funded from *Ma'aser Kesafim*.

It is stated in the *Shulchan Arukh, Yoreh De'ah* 251 and 157, that a woman is not responsible for her children's educational expenses. See Chapter 10, paragraph 1.

18. *Tzitz Eliezer*, Vol. 6, No. 8.

considered an equal partner in their *mitzvah* of *Talmud Torah*. Her spiritual reward is equivalent to that which accrues to her husband and children for their studies.[19]

12. Although a woman is not obligated to teach her son Torah,[20] *Chazal* guarantee that if she makes his study possible by transporting him to his place of learning, she merits a place in the World to Come.[21]

Honoring Torah Scholars

13. A woman is obligated to rise when a Torah scholar or elderly person passes or enters the room she is in.[22]

---

19. *Remah, Yoreh De'ah* 246:6; *Shulchan Arukh HaRav, Hilkhoth Talmud Torah* 14.

The *Chaye Adam* 10:4 states: "A pious woman has the opportunity to save her own soul as well as her husband's. When he returns home exhausted from a hard day's work, he does not always think about devoting time to Torah study. If she encourages him to do so, she will save him from failing to perform the positive commandment of Torah study on that day. The transgression of omitting Torah study is more serious than the omission of any other *mitzvah*."

In the introduction to his book *Chanukah V'Megillah*, HaGaon Rav Chaim Aharon Turtzin relates how the *Chazon Ish* once reprimanded a young Torah scholar: "Your spouse has entered into a partnership with you similar to that of Zevulun and Yissakhar. If you waste time from your studies, you are in breach of contract!" (Zevulun and Yissakhar, two of the twelve tribes of Israel, made a "contract" with each other that Zevulun would devote itself to business and finance full-time Torah study for the people of Yissakhar. The spiritual reward for Yissakhar's Torah study was divided equally between them.)

20. *Remah, Yoreh De'ah* 246:1. According to the *Shulchan Arukh, Orach Chayim* 343, and the *Mishnah Berurah*, transportation is actually the father's obligation.

21. Tractate *Berakhoth* 17a. See also the *Sefer HaChinukh* 419.

22. *Sefer Chassidim* 578: " 'Before an elderly person you shall rise up,

A woman's Torah students are obligated to show her the same respect they would a male teacher. They rise when she enters the room and are forbidden to address her by her first name.[23]

14. People are obligated to rise for a woman who is learned in Torah and for a woman who has reached the age of seventy.[24] Men and women are equally obligated in this.[25]

Some authorities require people to rise before the wife

---

and you shall give honor to a wise man' (*VaYikra* 19:32) — a woman shall also rise." See also the *Rambam, Sefer HaMitzvoth* 209, and the *Sefer HaChinukh* 257.

23. In *Y'chaveh Da'ath*, Vol. 3, No. 72, it is explained that the law requiring students to show a female teacher respect is based on a *Gemara* in *Bava Metziah* 33a, in which *Chazal* explain that a student must show respect for his teacher, "for he brings him to the World to Come." This principle is equally applicable to a female Torah teacher.

Divrey Malki'eil, Vol. 4, No. 80, points out that the obligation to show respect is not conditional on whether the teacher receives a salary.

The prohibition against referring to one's teacher by his first name is found in Tractate *Sanhedrin* 100a. It is also cited in the *Shulchan Arukh, Yoreh De'ah* 242:15.

When a teacher boards a bus, her students should rise — and if there is no place for the teacher to sit, a student must offer her a seat.

24. *Sefer Chassidim* 578: " Before an elderly person you shall rise up and you shall give honor to a wise man' (*VaYikra* 19:32) — also before an elderly woman you shall rise."

Halakhoth Ketanoth, Vol. 1, No. 154, however, discusses whether a man must rise for his elderly grandmother and concludes that there is no obligation to rise for an elderly woman unless she is the wife of a Torah scholar. The author notes the contrary position taken by the *Sefer Chassidim*.

25. *Sefer HaChinukh* 257. This is also indicated from the language of the *Rambam* in *Sefer HaMitzvoth* 209.

of a Torah scholar, even if she herself is not well-versed in Torah.[26]

15. Since the obligation to support Torah institutions is related to the *mitzvah* of honoring Torah scholars, some authorities rule this obligation applies to women as well as men.[27] It is reasonable, however, to assume that a married woman fulfills her obligation through her husband's donations.[28]

Deciding Halakhic Questions

16. A woman cannot serve as a judge,[29] but if she is an acknowledged expert in a particular area of Jewish Law,

---

26. From the *Gemara* in *Shevuoth* 30b, it appears that one should rise for the wife of a Torah scholar even after her husband's death. See also *Halakhoth Ketanoth*, Vol. 1, No. 154 (cited in note 24), *Urim V'Thumim* 17:11, and *Shevet HaLevi*, Vol. 5, No. 130.

27. This question is discussed at length by Rav Elyakim Dvorkis in *Aspaklarith HaTzedakah*. He writes that although it may be argued that women, who are not themselves obligated in *Talmud Torah*, should be exempt from the *mitzvah* of supporting Torah study, they are nevertheless obligated to give support as part of the *mitzvah* of honoring Torah scholars.

   An additional source for the obligation of women to support Torah institutions is found in Tractate *Kethuboth* 11b, where *Chazal* discuss the *mitzvah* of clinging to God: "How is it possible for one to cling to the Divine Presence, for is it not written, 'The Lord your God is a consuming fire'? Yet, by clinging to Torah scholars and their students, it is considered as if one were clinging to Him." The *mitzvah* of clinging to the Divine Presence, as explained in *Sefer HaChinukh* 434, is incumbent on both men and women.

28. A single woman who is supported by her father definitely fulfills this obligation through her father's donations.

29. *Shulchan Arukh, Choshen Mishpat* 7:4, based on the *Rambam, Hilkhoth Melakhim* 1:5, which states that only men may assume

she may, if necessary, render halakhic decisions pertaining to her area of expertise.[30]

17. With certain stipulations, a woman who is an expert in the laws of *kashruth* may serve as a *kashruth* supervisor.[31]

---

public office. *Tosafoth*, in Tractate *Yevamoth* 45b, asks how Devorah served as a judge for the people of Israel. He offers two explanations: either Devorah instructed the judges how to judge; or this was a special situation based on an explicit instruction from God to a prophet. In Tractate *Bava Kama* 15a, *Tosafoth* offers a third explanation: if the people accept a woman as a judge, as was the case with Devorah, she is permitted to fulfill that function.

Concerning the disqualification of women from giving testimony in a Jewish court, see the *Shulchan Arukh, Choshen Mishpat* 35:14. For an in-depth analysis of this subject, see HaRav Moshe Meiselman's work, *Jewish Woman in Jewish Law*, p. 73-83.

30. For example, in matters of *kashruth* or family purity. See *Sefer HaChinukh* 152; *Birkey Yosef, Choshen Mishpat* 7:12; *Pithchey Teshuvah, Choshen Mishpat* 7:5.

31. *Iggeroth Moshe, Yoreh De'ah*, No. 44-45, discusses the case of a woman who wishes to continue in her deceased husband's position as a *kashruth* supervisor. *Iggeroth Moshe* permits it, provided that the company signs the contract with a Rabbi who receives her salary and passes it on to her. In this way, the Rabbi remains ultimately responsible for the *kashruth* of the product.

CHAPTER 10
Training Children

" 'So you shall say to the House of Yaacov' — this refers to the women. 'And speak to the Children of Israel' — this refers to the men. Why are the women spoken to first? Because they are more diligent in the performance of *mitzvoth*. Another explanation — they train their children to fulfill the Torah" (*Midrash Rabbah, Shemoth, Parsha* 8:2).

A Mother's Mitzvah to Train Her Children

1. Some authorities maintain that a mother and father are equally obligated to train children in the performance of *mitzvoth*.[1] Others say that it is solely the father's responsibility.[2] According to all opinions, a wife is not

---

1. *Magen Avraham* 343:1; *Orukh HaShulchan* 343:1, based on *Rashi*, Tractate *Chagigah* 2a; *Me'iri*, Tractate *Nazir* 28b. The *Kaf HaChayim* 225:14 states that a woman is obligated to train and reprimand her son. If she fails to do so, she is liable for his sins.
2. *Magen Avraham, Ibid.*, and 616:2; *Mishnah Berurah* 616:5. See also the *Orukh LeNeir*, Tractate *Sukkah* 2b.

required to spend her own money on children's education. Financially-independent women are required to contribute their *Ma'aser Kesafim* funds towards the cost of their children's education. This is considered to be the most appropriate way to disburse such funds.[3]

2. Some of the authorities who rule that *mitzvah* education is solely the father's responsibility agree that if the father dies or forfeits his responsibilities, the obligation of *mitzvah* education becomes the mother's.[4]

Although a mother is halakhically exempt from teaching her son Torah, she nevertheless plays an active and essential role in his schooling, particularly when he is young.[5]

3. A mother must be prepared to reprimand her children strongly to guide them along the proper path so that they will refrain from wrongdoing. Occasionally, it may be necessary to use physical punishment. It is considered cruel to act leniently at such times.[6]

---

3. *Shulchan Arukh, Yoreh De'ah* 251:3, and 251:4; *Shulchan Arukh HaRav, Hilkhoth Talmud Torah* 1:14. Although exempt from the obligation to pay for her child's education, a woman is obligated to give charity.

4. *Kaf HaChayim* 343:9, and *Sha'arey Teshuvah, Orach Chayim* 640:2.

5. The two opinions cited in paragraph 1 refer exclusively to the obligation to train a child in the performance of *mitzvoth*. All authorities agree that a mother is not responsible for her son's Torah education. See Chapter 9, paragraph 12.

   As the *Sefer HaChinukh* 418 states: "It is fitting for every woman to expend great effort in the Torah education of her children so that they will not grow up ignorant of their religion. Although she is not halakhically required to do so, she will receive great reward for her efforts."

6. It is fitting to quote the words of the *Sh'lah, Sha'ar HaOthioth, Oth Derekh Eretz*: "Mothers, even more than fathers, are obligated to

4. The Torah does not obligate a woman to teach her son a trade.[7]

A Father's Mitzvah to Train His Daughter

5. A father's obligation to train his children in the practical performance of *mitzvoth* applies equally to sons and daughters.[8]

---

reprimand their children, for they spend more time with them. If the father is a Torah scholar, he is intensely involved in his studies and unable to supervise his children's actions. If a professional, he is often away from home. We are taught in Tractate *Berakhoth* 17b, 'God has given greater promise of reward to women than to men... What is the great merit of women?...They bring their children to the synagogue.' Since women are usually gentle by nature, it is especially difficult for them to stand in for their husbands and reprimand their children in a strong manner. They must be prepared to punish their children physically when doing so is essential to their proper upbringing.

"The source for the use of physical punishment is indicated in the verse, 'Merciful women cooked their children' (*Eichah* 4:10). This refers to women who are overly 'merciful' toward their children and fail to reprimand them when necessary. Such women are guilty of 'cooking' them (destroying their character)."

7. *Ran*, commenting on Tractate *Kiddushin* 29a. The *Me'iri* sheds further light on this exemption, commenting that if a mother were required to supervise her son's apprenticeship, she would have to visit the craftsmen frequently in order to follow her son's progress. This could lead to a violation of the principles of modest behavior.

8. *Magen Avraham* 343:2; *Tosafoth Yeshanim, Yoma* 82a. The *Meshekh Chokhmah, Bereshith* 18:19, cites the biblical source for this obligation: "For I know him [says God of Abraham], that he will command his sons and his household after him so that they will guard the way of God to perform righteousness and justice." A person's "household", explains the *Meshekh Chokhmah*, includes his wife and daughters.

6. Some authorities maintain that a father is obligated to teach his daughter all parts of the Torah that she is required to learn.[9]

7. Although a father is not actually obligated to teach his daughter a trade,[10] it is proper for him to guide her toward an occupation suitable for a Jewish woman.[11]

8. A father who supports his grown sons and daughters, enabling them to study Torah and attend proper schools, fulfills the *mitzvah* of *Tzedakah* (Charity) in one of its highest forms.[12]

Some Specifics of Mitzvah Training

9. Some parents have the custom to wash the hands of very small children when they awaken in the morning. This

---

9. *Sefer Chassidim* 313. This includes all negative commandments, non-time-bound positive commandments, and any other areas of Jewish Law that pertain specifically to women.

10. *Maharsha*, cited in *Sefer HaMakneh, Kiddushin* 30b.

11. *Maharam Shick, Orach Chayim*, No. 163; *Sefer HaMakneh, Ibid.*
    While the Torah requires a man to support his wife, it is beneficial for her to have an occupation of her own as well. She will thus be assured of livelihood in the event of widowhood or divorce, God forbid, and will have something to keep her creatively occupied, preventing the boredom that leads a person to sin. If she merits to marry a Torah scholar, she will be able to assist him in supporting the household, enabling him to devote himself to his studies.
    "An occupation suitable to a Jewish woman" refers to one in which neither the training nor practice are contrary to Jewish Law, especially the standards of modesty detailed in Chapters 4 through 8.

12. *Rambam, Hilkhoth Matanoth Ani'yim* 10:16; *Shulchan Arukh, Yoreh De'ah* 251:3.

is praiseworthy, since it instills a spirit of sanctity in children at an early age.[13]

10. It is proper to train children not to touch their shoes or those parts of the body that are normally covered. If they have done so, they should be taught to wash their hands before praying or reciting blessings.[14]

11. By the age of three, a boy should be accustomed to wearing a head-covering.[15]

If a young boy whose head is not covered wishes to say a blessing, his mother should place her hand on his head while he recites it.[16]

12. Once a girl has reached the age of six, her parents must train her to dress in accordance with all the requirements of *Dath Yehudith* discussed in Chapter 4.[17]

---

13. See Chapter 1, note 18, for a detailed discussion.
14. *Chanokh LeNa'ar* 5, citing *Eshel Avraham, Mahadura Tinyana*, No. 5. But *Salmath Yosef*, No. 25:3 and 26:1, rules that one need not pressure a child who has touched his shoes or scratched his head to wash his hands before reciting a blessing.
15. It is evident from Tractate *Shabbath* 156b that training a child to keep his head continually covered instills the fear of Heaven in him. This is in addition to the obligation to train a child not to recite blessings with his head uncovered. See *Shulchan Arukh, Orach Chayim* 91:3.
16. This ruling is based on the *Shulchan Arukh, Orach Chayim* 91:4. A child cannot simply place his own hand on his head for, as explained in the *Mishnah Berurah*, "The head and hand are part of the same body, and one part of the body cannot serve as a covering for another part." The *Mishnah Berurah* continues, "If he pulls his sleeve over his hand and covers his head with it, it is an acceptable covering."
17. This ruling regards a *parent*'s obligation to educate a child in these matters. In Chapter 4, paragraph 15, however, it is explained that some authorities forbid men to say *devarim shebikdushah* in the

13. It is proper to bring young children to places where they will hear the sound of Torah study and other holy words.[18] When they are brought to the synagogue, they should be taught to stand with awe and respect.[19]

14. When children are very young and likely to cause a disturbance, it is best not to bring them to the synagogue. Not only will they acquire the bad habit of acting boisterously there, but they will disturb the congregation.[20]

---

presence of an immodestly dressed girl over the age of three. See also Chapter 4, paragraphs 12 through 14.

18. The *Mishnah, Avoth* 2:8, relates that the teacher of Rabbi Yehoshua ben Chananya enumerated his pupil's merits, and one of these was *ashrey yoladto* — happy is she who bore him. The *Tiffereth Yisrael*, in his commentary to the *Mishnah*, cites the Talmud *Yerushalmi*, which explains, "When Rabbi Yehoshua was still an infant, his mother would bring him to the study hall so that the words of Torah would fill his ears."

Another source for this custom is found in the passage in the Torah concerning the *mitzvah* of *Hakhel*. We are commanded by the Torah, once in seven years, to "Gather together the nation — the men, the women, and the children...And the children who do not understand shall hear and learn to fear the Lord your God" (*Devarim* 31:12-14). Tractate *Sofrim* 10:6 infers from this that even children who are too young to understand will benefit from being present to absorb words of Torah.

The *Remah, Orach Chayim* 149: "It is proper to bring young children to kiss the *Sefer Torah*. This trains them to be diligent in the performance of *mitzvoth*." See also the *Shulchan Arukh, Orach Chayim* 699, which discusses the practice of calling children for an *aliyah* on *Simchath Torah*. This custom was also instituted to inculcate in children love and respect for Torah and *mitzvoth*.

19. *Mishnah Berurah* 124:28. In 489:18, the *Mishnah Berurah* cautions that educating children in the synagogue is only effective when the father sits with them and supervises their behavior.

20. The *Mishnah Berurah* 98:3 cites the *Sh'lah*: "When children play and misbehave in the synagogue, they profane the sanctity of the place and disturb the concentration of the worshippers. This

15. It is forbidden to kiss one's children in the synagogue. This is to teach them that love of God transcends the love of parent for child.[21]

16. When teaching a child to recite blessings, one may say the entire text, with *shem* and *malkhuth*. The blessing is recited for educational purposes and does not constitute a blessing said in vain.[22]

17. Children should be taught to answer *amein* to blessings — for it is said that once a child learns to respond with *amein*, he is assured a place in the World to Come.[23]

18. An adult should not answer *amein* to the blessing of

---

negative behavior will become second nature, and it will be difficult to correct when the children grow older. Children should be trained to sit with awe and reverence and answer *amein* to *Kaddish* and *Kedushah*."

21. *Shulchan Arukh, Orach Chayim* 98:1. The *Mishnah Berurah* 96:4 adds that for the same reason a child should not be allowed to stand directly in front of his father during prayers.

22. *Shulchan Arukh, Orach Chayim* 215:3. The *Mishnah Berurah* comments: "This only applies when educating a child. An adult who is studying the laws of blessings in their Talmudic sources may not recite them with *shem* and *malkhuth*. On the other hand, when reciting an entire Scriptural verse, one may say the name of God that is found there." For an explanation of *shem* and *malkhuth*, see Chapter 2, paragraph 15.

23. The *Remah, Orach Chayim* 124, cites this Talmudic saying from Tractate *Sanhedrin* 110b: "From what age does a child merit the World to Come? We have been taught in the name of Rabbi Meir that it is at the age when he begins to answer *amein*. It is written, 'Open the gates and the righteous, the guardians of the faith (*shomrey emunim*), shall enter' (*Yeshayahu* 26:2). Do not read 'guardians of the faith', but read 'those who answer *amein* (*she'omeir amein*)'."

a child who is too young to comprehend the meaning of his words.[24]

19. Even very small children should not be exposed to music or performances that are inconsistent with modest behavior, as these experiences will accustom them to evil and engender negative habits.[25]

20. When a parent overhears a child engaging in forbidden speech — idle gossip, lying or cursing — the

---

24. The *Mishnah Berurah* 215:16 infers this from the language of the *Shulchan Arukh* 215:3: "But when they recite blessings on their own, after they have reached the age of *chinukh* (education), we may answer *amein*."

   Yabiah Omer, Vol. 2, *Orach Chayim*, No. 13:12, elaborates: "One should not answer *amein* to the blessing of a child younger than six...but one may answer a child over six who knows to Whom we bless...If we are unsure whether the child understands what he is saying, *amein* should not be said until the age of nine, when we can be sure that he comprehends the idea behind the blessing. There is no difference in this regard between a boy and a girl."

   Since today's children attend religious schools from the age of three or four, comprehension can be assumed by the time they are six years old.

   HaGaon Rav Ben Zion Abba Shaul suggests a way to answer *amein* even to the blessing of a younger child. While the child recites the blessing the parent can recite the verse *Barukh HaShem l'olam, amein v'amein* (Blessed is God forever, *amein* and *amein*.), saying the verse silently and the final word out loud.

25. Parents should be very careful to oversee what a child hears or reads. The *Sha'ar HaTziyun* 560:25 even says, "One should not sing immodest lullabies to a baby as this will encourage a bad nature in him...Be conscientious about this...and instruct all family members in this regard."

   Shevet HaLevi, Vol. 5, No. 129:1, discourages bringing children to magic shows because they show manipulative deception. See the *Shulchan Arukh, Yoreh De'ah* 179:15.

parent should admonish the child to refrain from such speech in the future. If a parent is lax, the child may, God forbid, become habituated to this behavior.[26]

21. In order to establish a foundation of trust and consistency in the home, parents should not promise a child something such as a gift and then fail to keep their word. This teaches the child dishonesty.[27]

22. One should not frighten a child, especially with the threat of harm from a non-kosher animal. For example, one should not tease or discipline a child with the threat that a dog or a lion will kidnap him. There are numerous sources to the effect that this has a negative effect on the purity of the child's soul.[28]

23. It is permissible to take a child to visit a zoo.[29]

---

26. *Mishnah Berurah* 343:3. The *Mishnah Berurah* bemoans the negligence of his contemporaries in this area: "It has become second nature for children to lie and engage in forbidden speech. When these children mature and realize the seriousness of their behavior, they are unable to change habits which have become ingrained through the years."

The Vilna Gaon writes in a letter to his wife: "I strongly request that you teach the children not to curse or take oaths. Neither should they speak falsely or in ways that will cause strife. Everything should be said in a spirit of peace and love..."

27. See Tractate *Sukkah* 46b and *Yevamoth* 63a.

28. *Kitzur Shulchan Arukh* 33:14; *Shulchan Arukh HaRav, Hilkoth Shemirath HaGuf*. The original source for this ruling is found in the *Sh'lah, Sha'ar HaOthioth, Oth Derekh Eretz*.

29. The *Chiddah* describes his visit to the London Zoo in *Midbar K'deimoth, Ma'arekheth* 2:22.

Although *Arugoth HaBosem, Orach Chayim*, No. 39, forbids attending a circus or visiting a place where animals are caged, this ruling only refers to situations where the animals are mocked and ridiculed. In the case of a zoo, we may apply the statement of *Chazal* in Tractate *Eruvin* 100b that much can be learned by

24. Children should not be allowed to eat foods forbidden by the laws of *kashruth*. Even if a child is too young to be held accountable for his sins, those foods intrinsically deaden the finer qualities of the soul and can cause long-lasting spiritual damage.[30]

---

observing animals: modesty can be learned from the cat, honesty from the ant, marital fidelity from the dove, and strength of character from the rooster. This is expressed explicitly in *Iyov* 35:11: "I have learned from the animals of the earth. From the birds of the sky, I have gained wisdom."

There are many sources in the Talmud which indicate that the Sages were knowledgeable about the nature of various animals. See also the *Nodah BeYehudah, Kama, Yoreh De'ah*. No. 10, cited in the *Pithchey Teshuvah, Yoreh De'ah* 28.

30. The *Remah, Yoreh De'ah* 81:7, and the *Chatham Sofer, Orach Chayim*, No. 83, both state that a mother who must eat forbidden foods for medical reasons should not nurse her child during this time unless absolutely necessary.

When a child is not yet old enough to understand the significance of his actions — before the age of two or three — it is not necessary to confront him each time he eats non-kosher food or transgresses some other prohibition of the Torah. Once he is old enough to understand that he is doing something wrong, a parent is obligated to stop him from transgressing even a Rabbinic prohibition. When the child reaches the age of six or seven, it is incumbent on any observer to prevent him from transgressing a Torah prohibition, but not laws that are prohibited by Rabbinic Law. See the *Mishnah Berurah* 343:7.

The *Orukh HaShulchan, Yoreh De'ah* 89:7, *Chelkath Yaacov*, Vol. 2, No. 88-89, and *Yabiah Omer*, Vol. 1, *Yoreh De'ah*, No. 4, and Vol. 3, *Yoreh De'ah*, No. 3, all conclude that a child may drink milk an hour after he eats meat. He should recite the blessing *Borey nefashoth* after the meat meal, which establishes a separation between the meat and the milk. HaGaon Rav Shmuel Wossner arrives at a similar conclusion in *Shevet HaLevi*, Vol. 4, No. 84. He rules that very young children have no obligation to wait between meat and dairy.

According to the *Chokhmath Adam* 40:13, an adult who is indisposed is also permitted to eat dairy foods one hour after eating meat, provided that she cleans her teeth and rinses her mouth

25. Parents should pray to God tirelessly that their children grow in the ways of Torah and become God-fearing adults of refined character.[31]

26. Some parents have the custom to bless children at the beginning of *Shabbath* and *Yom Tov*, reciting the verse, "May God bless you and keep you..." For a son, they begin, "May God make you like Ephrayim and Menasheh." For a daughter, "May God make you like Rachel and Leah."[32]

27. We conclude this chapter with a quotation from Rabbenu Yona in *Iggereth HaTeshuvah, HaDrash HaSh'lishi*:

" 'So you shall say to the House of Yaacov.' Why was Moshe commanded to speak to the women first? Because they send the children to school and look after them when they return home. They influence their children with pleasant words and develop in them a desire to study Torah. They protect them so that they will not waste time from their studies, and they teach them fear of Heaven when they are young. It is written that one must 'educate a child according to his way, for then, even when he grows old, he will not turn away from it.' From here we see that the Jewish woman, the primary contributor to the child's early education, establishes the foundation of Torah study and fear of God."

---

between the two dishes. Pregnant and nursing women who are in need of the nutrients contained in milk products may also exercise this option when necessary.
31. *Mishnah Berurah* 47:10, based on Tractate *Shabbath* 156b.
32. *Siddur Otzar HaTefilloth*, commentary of the *Besamim Rosh* on the *Shabbath* Eve service. The *Besamim Rosh* cites the custom of placing two hands on the child's head during the blessing.

CHAPTER 11
Bath Mitzvah

The Bath Mitzvah Celebration

1. A girl who has reached the age of twelve is considered an adult, and she is obligated to fulfill all the *mitzvoth* of the Torah.[1]

---

1. Tractate *Niddah* 45b; *Rambam, Hilkhoth Shevithath Asor* 2:11, and *Hilkhoth Ishuth* 2:1; *Shulchan Arukh, Evven HaEzer* 155:12, and *Orach Chayim* 616:2.

   The age of maturity, twelve for a girl and thirteen for a boy, is a *Halakhah LeMoshe MiSinai* (an oral tradition transmitted to Moshe on Mt. Sinai). See *Teshuvoth HaRosh*, No. 16, and *Maharil*, No. 51.

   Various interpretations are offered to explain why women attain adulthood a year earlier than men. In Tractate *Niddah* 45b, *Chazal* comment, "God has given greater understanding to women." Some attribute the more rapid emotional and intellectual maturation of girls to this fact, and this would also explain why the Torah obligates them in *mitzvoth* at an earlier age than boys. See also the *Torah Temimah*'s commentary on *BaMidbar* 30:4.

   Actually, the Torah recognizes a girl's passage into adulthood only if she has also reached a certain level of physical maturity. The basic criteria is that she have at least two pubic hairs. Details of this requirement are discussed in the *Shulchan Arukh, Evven HaEzer* 155:12. For a young woman to perform Torah obligations on

2. A *bath mitzvah* celebration is not a *mitzvah*, and it should not be held in a synagogue.[2] There is no prohibition against celebrating a *bath mitzvah* as long as the celebration conforms to standards of modest behavior.[3]

---

behalf of others, for instance, to exempt another person in the *mitzvah* of *Kiddush*, it must be definitely established that she has attained physical maturity. For her to perform Rabbinic requirements on behalf of others, we may assume that she has attained physical maturity at the age of twelve. See the *Remah*, *Orach Chayim* 55:5, and the *Mishnah Berurah* 55:31 and 55:41. This assumption is known as *chazakah d'Rava* (Rava's assumption) and is discussed in Tractate *Niddah* 46a.

2. *Iggeroth Moshe, Orach Chayim*, Vol. 1, No. 104, Vol. 2, No. 97, and Vol. 4, No. 36. This event is no different from other birthday parties, which may not be held in the synagogue since they are not *mitzvoth*. See also *S'ridey Aish*, Vol. 3, No. 93, which arrives at the same conclusion.

3. *Zaken Aharon*, Vol. 1, No. 6, forbids the celebration of a *bath mitzvah* on the grounds that it mimics pagan practices, which commemorate a girl's passage into puberty. Imitation of this heathen custom, according to *Zaken Aharon*, constitutes a violation of the injunction, "You shall not walk in their statues" (*VaYikra* 18:3).

Iggeroth Moshe, Orach Chayim, Vol. 4, No. 36, and *S'ridey Aish*, Vol. 3, No. 93, disagree. In their view, the celebrants do not intend to copy the gentiles, and the practice does not relate to any form of idol worship. *S'ridey Aish* concludes, "Especially in our generation, the celebration should be encouraged as a means to further motivate young girls to lead a life dedicated to Torah values."

Iggeroth Moshe, Ibid., rules that in the United States, where parents customarily make a *kiddush* in the synagogue on significant family occasions, a *kiddush* may be made to celebrate a *bath mitzvah*. The girl may speak in honor of the occasion, as long as she does so from the *kiddush* table and not from the *bimah*.

Kol M'vaseir, Vol. 2, No. 44, objects to large *bath mitzvah* parties due to their unnecessary extravagance. In the author's opinion, it is sufficient to mark the day with a modest gathering of family and close friends. *Iggeroth Moshe* cautions that where there is a possibility that the celebration will bring about laxity in the laws of *tzniuth*, it should be cancelled.

On this occasion, it is fitting to discuss the significance of reaching the age of *mitzvoth* and to encourage the young woman to follow the path of Torah and fear of Heaven.[4]

3. It is not customary for a father to recite the blessing *Barukh shep'tarani mei'onsho shel zeh*[5] on the occasion of his daughter's *bath mitzvah*,[6] even though some authorities

---

4. *Yechaveh Da'ath*, Vol. 2, No. 69, encourages celebrating the *bath mitzvah* with a festive meal at which words of thanks and praise to God are spoken.
5. "Who has relieved me from this one's punishment." The father recites this blessing on the occasion of his son's *bar mitzvah*. Its source is not found in the Talmud but in the *Midrash Rabbah, Parshath Toledoth*. For this reason, the *Remah, Orach Chayim* 225:2, advises that *shem* and *malkhuth* be omitted. The *Kaf HaChayim* 225:16 reports that omission is also the Sephardic practice. The *Mishnah Berurah* 225:8, however, points out that both the Vilna Gaon and the *Maharil* include *shem* and *malkhuth*. The *Chaye Adam* concludes that a father who recites the blessing with *shem* and *malkhuth* has done nothing wrong.
6. This issue is first discussed by the *Pri Megadim* in *Eshel Avraham* 225:80. He explains that a father recites this blessing when his son reaches *bar mitzvah* to mark the fact that he no longer bears the heavy responsibility for educating his son. The *Pri Megadim* postulates that the dispute over a father's responsibility for his daughter's education is the reason it has become customary to omit the blessing at her *bath mitzvah*.

   The *Kaf HaChayim* discusses the *Levush*'s explanation of the reason for this blessing. The *Levush* cites *Chazal*'s statement that a young child may be subject to punishment for his father's sins. From the day of his *bar mitzvah*, however, the child may only be punished for his own sins. The father recites the blessing to God for freeing him from such a heavy responsibility. A girl's destiny, explains the *Kaf HaChayim*, is primarily shaped by the spiritual level of her future husband, who has been selected by Divine Providence, not by her father's actions. She is less likely to experience the consequences of her father's actions, and the blessing does not apply to her.

permit it.[7]

A mother does not recite the blessing for a daughter or for a son.[8]

4. Some authorities recommend that young women wear a new garment or eat a new fruit on their *bath mitzvah* day so that they may recite the blessing *She'he'che'yanu* with the intention that it also cover the occasion of becoming obligated in *mitzvoth*.[9]

---

7. *Noam*, Vol. 7, p. 4, and Vol. 8, p. 272; *Yabiah Omer*, Vol. 6, *Orach Chayim*, No. 29. *Yabiah Omer* points out that the Sephardic practice is never to recite this blessing with *shem* and *malkhuth* anyway, so there is nothing wrong with a father reciting it. It appears that even those who follow the view of the Vilna Gaon, and normally recite the blessing with *shem* and *malkhuth*, should omit *shem* and *malkhuth* for a daughter.

8. *Pri Megadim, Ibid.* Since a mother may not be halakhically obligated in the *mitzvah* of *chinukh* (See Chapter 10, paragraph 1.), she does not recite the blessing, which, in the *Pri Megadim*'s view, marks the end of this obligation. It would also seem that a child is not punished on account of his mother's sins (It is written that God "visits the sins of the *fathers* on the children".), so even according to the *Levush*, a mother would not recite the blessing at her son's *bar mitzvah*.

9. *Kaf HaChayim* 225:12; *Ben Ish Chai, Shanah Rishonah, Parshath Re'eh* 17. The *Kaf HaChayim* adds that a child should increase the amount of time spent in Torah study on the *bar* or *bath mitzvah* day. The *Biur Halakhah* 25 also recommends increased commitment to Torah study on the day that a boy begins to wear *tefillin*.

CHAPTER 12
Mourning

The Funeral

1. A woman's funeral takes precedence over a man's,[1] unless he is a Torah scholar.[2]

2. A woman may be eulogized.[3] If she was married to a Torah scholar, the eulogy may be given in a synagogue or

---

1. *Shulchan Arukh, Yoreh De'ah* 354. This applies even if the man passed away before the woman. The reason, as explained in Tractate *Semachoth* 11, is that a woman's body decomposes more rapidly than a man's. The *Tashbatz*, Vol. 2, No. 11, adds that no distinctions are made among women in this regard — old or young, pregnant or nursing, etc. See also the glosses of Rabbi Akiva Eiger on the *Shulchan Arukh, Yoreh De'ah, Ibid.*
2. *Chatham Sofer*, Vol. 6, No. 59.
3. *Shulchan Arukh, Yoreh De'ah* 344:2. The first eulogy mentioned in the Torah honored a woman — "And Avraham came to eulogize Sarah" (*Bereshith* 23:2). *Gesher HaChayim* 13:8 adds that this is among the obligations a husband has to his wife.

study hall,[4] but the coffin should not be brought into these places.[5]

3. A woman should not deliver a eulogy.[6]

4. A woman whose father is a *cohen* may enter a cemetery or be in the room with the deceased.[7]

5. Men and women should sit separately during the eulogy and walk separately in the funeral procession.[8] It is customary for women to walk behind the coffin[9] and not to view the grave until it is closed.[10]

6. It is not customary for women to pass through the consolation line formed after the burial, even if they are accompanied by male mourners.[11]

7. A woman does not customarily visit a cemetery while she is a *niddah.*[12]

---

4. *Shulchan Arukh, Yoreh De'ah* 344:19. This applies even when she is a widow. The *Taz, Yoreh De'ah* 242:14, cites *Maharam Mintz,* who rules that there is an obligation to honor the wife of a Torah scholar even after her husband's death.

5. *Har Tzvi, Yoreh De'ah,* No. 266.

6. *Kol Bo Al Aveiluth* 7:9, citing *Otzar HaChayim.*

7. *Shulchan Arukh, Yoreh De'ah* 373:2, based on Tractate *Sotah* 23b.

8. See Tractate *Berakhoth* 51a, and the *Shulchan Arukh HaRav,* Vol. 5, *Hilkhoth Shemirath HaGuf V'Nefesh,* paragraph 10, citing the *Zohar.* See also *Minchath Yitzchak,* Vol. 2, No. 20.

9. *Shulchan Arukh, Yoreh De'ah* 359:1.

10. *Shulchan Arukh, Yoreh De'ah* 359:2.

11. *Gesher HaChayim,* Chapter 16, 7:4. One explanation for this custom is that it is immodest for women to walk between two rows of men. Even when there is only a single line of comforters, women do not walk along it.

12. *Chaye Adam* 3:38, cited in the *Mishnah Berurah* 88:7; *Pithchey Teshuvah, Yoreh De'ah* 195:19, citing *Chamudey Daniel.* According

Tearing the Garments

8. A woman must tear her garments on the death of a relative.[13] At the loss of a parent, the accepted practice is to tear all upper garments except the undergarments. A woman should fold back the tear so that her undergarments are not visible.[14] The torn garment is worn

---

to the *Chaye Adam*, a woman should not visit a cemetery until her menstrual period has ended and she has immersed in a *mikvah*. *Kol Bo Al Aveiluth*, p. 167, however, rules that widows or virgins, who do not normally attend the *mikvah*, may visit a cemetery as long as they are not actually in their menstrual period, even though they still have the halakhic status of *niddah*. It appears from other authorities that even a married woman who has not yet immersed in a *mikvah* may visit a cemetery. See also the *Pithchey Teshuvah, Ibid.*, and the *Beith Barukh*, commentary on the *Chaye Adam*, citing *Leket HaKemach HaChadash*.

Nachamu Ami cites a halakhic ruling of HaGaon Rav Shlomo Zalman Auerbach that a woman may enter a cemetery during her menstrual period if the visit is on the day of an unveiling or a *yahrzeit*. This ruling is also cited by *Shulchan Melakhim*, Laws of *Niddah* and *Yoledeth*, No. 5. These sources also permit a menstruating woman to visit a cemetery during the days of *Selichoth* prior to *Rosh HaShanah*, since it is customary at this time for people to pray at the graves of their ancestors. The *Mishnah Berurah* and the *Chaye Adam*, however, do not note these exceptions.

See the introduction of the *Maharam Shick* to *Orach Chayim*, where he discusses the esoteric reasons behind this custom. He also notes that a woman should not be present at the time of a person's death, especially if she is a *niddah*.

13. This refers to those relatives for whom one is required to observe the laws of mourning, i.e., parents, siblings, children, and spouse.

14. According to the basic law, as stated in the *Shulchan Arukh, Yoreh De'ah* 340:11, one is required to tear all one's garments over the loss of a parent. The *Remah* qualifies this, pointing out that it is no longer customary to rent the undergarments. The *Shakh* adds that a woman should fold back the tear so that her undergarments are not visible.

throughout *shiva*. It may be mended with a temporary patch immediately after the funeral.[15]

The Seudath Havra'ah

9. A woman should not receive the *seudath havra'ah*[16] from a man unless her husband, son or brother is eating with her.[17] She should not receive this meal from her husband. Similarly, a man should not receive the *seudath havra'ah* from his wife.[18]

On the death of other relatives enumerated in note 13, the mourner is only required to tear the outermost garment.

Only clothing that is worn throughout the day is torn. Thus, a winter coat does not have to be torn, even for the loss of a parent.

Nachamu Ami 10:7 advises that another woman should help the mourner tear her garments.

15. If the clothing is repaired at this time, it should not be sewn with a straight stitch.

HaGaon Rav Moshe Feinstein rules that women should wear the torn garment throughout *shiva*, even when mourning other relatives. It is explained in the *Shulchan Arukh, Yoreh De'ah* 340:14, that if a person changes clothes while sitting *shiva* for a parent, the new garment must also be torn.

16. This is the first meal eaten by the mourner after the funeral. It is not prepared by the mourner, but sent by neighbors.

According to the *Orukh HaShulchan* and the *Chaye Adam*, only the mourner's *first* meal after the funeral must be donated by neighbors. Rabbi Akiva Eiger and the Vilna Gaon rule that all meals eaten during the first day of mourning should be donated. The generally accepted custom is that of the *Orukh HaShulchan*.

17. *Shulchan Arukh, Yoreh De'ah* 378:2.

18. *Orukh HaShulchan, Yoreh De'ah* 378:3. This is because a meal received from a spouse is not considered to have been donated. A son or daughter who is not supported by parents may send the *seudath havra'ah* to them.

The *Ba'er Heytev, Yoreh De'ah* 378:1, cites the *Taz*, who remarks that if no one sends a *seudath havra'ah* to the mourner, or if she has no acquaintances in the city, she is certainly permitted to prepare her own meal.

10. A woman may deliver a *seudath havra'ah* to a man who is not related to her.[19] She need not request permission from her husband before performing this *mitzvah.*[20]

Comforting Mourners

11. A man does not customarily pay a condolence call to a house where only women are mourning. If prayers are held in the house, the man may attend these prayers and fulfill the *mitzvah* of comforting the mourners after the service.[21]

A woman may pay a condolence call on a man, providing that they are careful to avoid *yichud.*[22]

Restrictions During Shiva

12. Since mourners are forbidden to engage in laughter and other enjoyments during *shiva*, a woman should not play with children during this time.[23]

---

19. *Gesher HaChayim*, Chapter 20, 2:7, deduces this from the fact that authorities only describe a prohibition against a man bringing the mourner's meal to a woman. When she brings the meal to a man, however, she must be careful to avoid *yichud.*

    Shulchan Melakhim, No. 378, on the other hand, does indicate that a woman should not deliver a *seudath havra'ah* to a man. It appears that this more stringent view applies only in the Sephardic community. There it is customary for the one who delivers the meal to eat alone with the mourner. Those who do not follow this custom would permit a woman to deliver the meal.

20. *Orukh HaShulchan, Yoreh De'ah* 378:3. A woman may not donate a large sum of her husband's money to a charitable cause without his permission, but a *seudath havra'ah* is considered a small donation. If her husband specifically objects, she may not send the meal.

21. *Gesher HaChayim*, Chapter 20, 5:2.

22. See Chapter 7, paragraph 27.

23. *Shulchan Arukh, Yoreh De'ah* 391:1. It is forbidden to *play* with a child, but holding a child is permitted.

13. When necessary, she may wash dishes, sweep, mop the floors, make the beds, cook and bake during *shiva*.[24]

Haircuts and Make-up

14. The restriction against haircuts during mourning applies equally to men and women.[25]

15. During *shiva*, combing the hair is permitted.[26]

16. Widows or single women in mourning may not use make-up for thirty days after the funeral. Married women may use make-up immediately after *shiva*.[27] So may a woman seeking a husband.[28]

17. A woman who has been married for less than thirty days may apply make-up during *shiva*.[29]

Bathing and Cutting Fingernails

18. The prohibition against bathing during *shiva* applies equally to men and women.

---

24. *Shulchan Arukh, Yoreh De'ah* 380:24.
25. *Remah, Yoreh De'ah* 390:5. The Ashkenazic custom prohibits haircuts for at least thirty days after the funeral. When mourning a parent, haircuts are forbidden unless the hair grows so long that it elicits negative reactions from neighbors. The Sephardic practice is to permit haircuts immediately after *shiva*. The *Shakh* adds that even according to the Ashkenazic custom, if a woman's hair is exceedingly long, she may cut it after *shiva*.
26. *Shulchan Arukh, Yoreh De'ah* 390:6.
27. *Shulchan Arukh, Yoreh De'ah* 381:6, based on Tractate *Kethuboth* 4b. The leniency for a married woman is based on the principle that a woman should not appear unattractive to her husband.
28. *Shulchan Arukh, Ibid.*
29. *Shulchan Arukh, Ibid.*

19. A woman whose night to attend the *mikvah* occurs during *shiva* should postpone her immersion until after *shiva*.[30]

20. A woman is permitted to wash herself internally during *shiva* for the purpose of making a *hefsek taharah*.[31]

21. After *shiva*, she may wash and shampoo her hair as usual to prepare for immersion in the *mikvah*. She should, however, make a slight change in her normal manner of bathing.[32]

22. Some authorities rule that, when necessary, a married woman may bathe in warm water immediately after *shiva*.[33]

23. Cutting fingernails is forbidden during the thirty days following the funeral.[34] A woman who needs to immerse in the *mikvah* should ask a neighbor to cut her

---

30. *Shulchan Arukh, Yoreh De'ah* 381:5.
31. *Shakh, Yoreh De'ah* 381:3, based on *Mas'ath Binyamin* and contrary to the *Remah, Yoreh De'ah* 381:5. The *hefsek taharah* is the internal examination that a woman makes to begin the seven clean days after her menstrual flow has stopped. Its purpose is to establish that bleeding and staining have completely ceased.

   The *Shakh* emphasizes that during *shiva* a woman must be careful only to wash the areas between her legs where staining might appear. She may use warm water.
32. *Or Zarua*, cited in the *Remah, Yoreh De'ah* 381:5. According to the basic law, men and women are permitted to bathe immediately after *shiva*. The general custom is to refrain from bathing the whole body at one time until thirty days have passed. Instead, the body is washed part by part. See the *Remah, Yoreh De'ah* 386:1.
33. *Chokhmath Adam* 168.
34. *Shulchan Arukh, Yoreh De'ah* 390:5.

nails for her. If this is not feasible, she may cut them herself.[35]

Some authorities maintain a woman may cut her own fingernails after *shiva* in any case.[36]

A Woman Who Has Recently Given Birth

24. A woman who sits *shiva* within thirty days after giving birth may wear leather shoes if she feels they are necessary.[37] If necessary, she may also bathe in warm water.[38]

Kaddish

25. It is not customary for a daughter to recite *Kaddish* for a parent in the synagogue or at home, even if the parent requested that she do so.[39]

26. Some authorities note that if a woman attends synagogue services and answers *amein* to the men's

---

35. *Chokhmath Adam* 165:30. The *Taz* notes that women are generally lenient and cut their own fingernails.
36. *Nodah BeYehudah, Kama, Yoreh De'ah*, No. 99.
37. *Shulchan Arukh, Yoreh De'ah* 382:2. This leniency applies when non-leather shoes do not offer sufficient comfort.
    During the first thirty days after giving birth, a woman is classified as a "sick person whose life is not in danger." When it is important for their well-being, Rabbinic prohibitions are waived for such people.
38. Since she is not bathing for pleasure, the *Shulchan Arukh, Yoreh De'ah* 381:3, permits this. The *Shakh* adds that if she feels uncomfortable, she may even bathe on the first day of mourning.
39. *Sha'arey Teshuvah, Orach Chayim* 132:5; *Ba'er Heytev, Yoreh De'ah* 376:3; *Teshuvah MeAhavah*, Vol. 2, No. 229:10; *Shevuth Yaacov*, Vol. 2, No. 93; *Sdeh Chemed*, Vol. 6, *Ma'arekheth Aveiluth*, No. 160; *Gesher HaChayim*, Chapter 30, 8:5.

Kaddish, she will bring merit to her departed parents: "The reward of one who responds is greater than the one who recites."[40]

Remarriage

27. Although a woman only observes a thirty-day mourning period after the death of her husband, she must wait a minimum of ninety days before remarrying.[41]

After the death of his wife, a man must wait until three major festivals have passed before he may remarry.[42]

28. A remarried widow may visit her first husband's grave to pray for the elevation of his soul as long as her second husband does not object.[43]

---

40. *Mateh Ephrayim, Diney Kaddish Yathom* 4:8.
41. *Shakh, Yoreh De'ah* 392:2, based on the *Shulchan Arukh, Evven HaEzer* 13. If she remarried immediately after her husband's death, we would be in doubt as to whether a child born seven months after remarriage is a premature baby of the second husband or a full-term baby of the first husband.
42. *Ibid*. This ruling is based on the *Mordekhai*, who believes it is easier for a woman than for a man to start a new life after the loss of a spouse. If not for the possible question of paternity, a thirty-day waiting period would be sufficient for her. A man, however, needs to experience the joy of the three major festivals — *Pessach, Shavuoth* and *Sukkoth* — before he can begin a new life with another woman.
43. This question is discussed at length in *Gesher HaChayim*, Chapter 29:8, and *Nachamu Ami*, p. 95. They conclude that a woman should not light a memorial candle to honor the anniversary of her first husband's death in the presence of her second husband. She may light a candle in the synagogue without asking his permission. A man, on the other hand, may light a *yahrzeit* candle for his deceased wife, even in the presence of his second wife.

In the notes to *Nachamu Ami*, the author recounts a remarkable story from *Zikhron LeMoshe*, a biography of the *Chatham Sofer*:

Yizkor

29. On days when *Yizkor* is recited in the synagogue, a woman may recite it at home.[44]

"Once the *Chatham Sofer* noticed that his third wife, the widow of the author of *Tiv. Gittin*, had lit a memorial candle on 25 *Tishrey*, the *yahrzeit* of her first husband's death. Being a sensitive person, the *Chatham Sofer* was taken aback, but in his righteousness he said nothing, so as not to cause his wife additional sorrow. Inexplicably, he became extremely despondent over this incident. To our great misfortune, the *Chatham Sofer* himself died on that same date a number of years later."

The *Chatham Sofer, Yoreh De'ah*, No. 355, implies that a remarried woman should not visit her previous husband's grave. He explains that once she has remarried, she is no longer considered a relation of her first husband. Citing *Evven Yaacov*, No. 28, the *Gesher HaChayim, Ibid.*, brings contradictory evidence. He even cites authorities who rule that a woman who has had two husbands should be buried near the first one.

Even according to the *Chatham Sofer*, a man is permitted to visit his first wife's grave after he remarries. *Nachamu Ami* cites the *Tashbatz*, No. 443, who calculates the numerical value of the verse (*Tehilim* 31:13), *Nishkachti k'meith mi'lev* — "I have been forgotten as a departed soul [is forgotten] from the heart" — to be equal to the phrase *chutz min eisheth ne'urim v'hi chavivah* — "Except for the wife of my youth for she is dear to me." He uses this *gematria* to support his ruling that a man's second wife will not object if he observes the anniversary of her death, since it would be unnatural for a man to forget his first wife.

44. *Gesher HaChayim*, Chapter 31:2.

CHAPTER 13
Challah

The Mitzvah

1. The *mitzvah* of separating *Challah*[1] from dough is directed primarily to women.[2] Therefore, although her husband is the legal owner of the dough,[3] a woman may separate *Challah* without his permission.[4]

---

1. "From the first of your dough you shall set apart *Challah*" (*BaMidbar* 15:20). Originally, the separated portion of the dough was given to a *cohen*, but today it is burned. (See note 18.)
2. *Mishnah, Shabbath* 2:6. In the Talmud *Yerushalmi*, Adam is called the "*Challah* of the world" (the portion of the world separated for Divine Service). R. Yose says that God formed man from dust of the earth just as a person separates *Challah* from dough. Because Eve caused Adam to transgress by giving him fruit from the tree of knowledge, she was given the *mitzvah* of separating *Challah*, as a means of rectifying her sin.
3. The *Shulchan Arukh, Yoreh De'ah* 328:3, points out that one who separates *Challah* without the owner's permission does not sanctify it.
4. *Kaf HaChayim, Orach Chayim* 242:24; *M'lo HaOmer* 328:1; *Chalath Lechem*, No. 7:7. The *Kaf HaChayim* explains that since this *mitzvah* is the wife's responsibility, a husband must ask *her*

2. A husband may separate *Challah* without his wife's permission, if she is not at home. By the same token, if there is fear of spoilage, a third party may separate *Challah* without formal permission.[5]

3. A minor may not separate *Challah.*[6]

4. A woman who is a *niddah* may separate *Challah*[7] and recite the appropriate blessing.[8]

---

permission if he wishes to perform it.

Mahari Assad, Vol. 1, No. 121, allows a woman to appoint her own agent to separate *Challah*, because with respect to this *mitzvah*, she is considered the "owner" of the dough and not merely the husband's surrogate.

5. *Kitzur Shulchan Arukh* 35:8. The *Misgereth HaShulchan*, commenting on the *Kitzur Shulchan Arukh*, cites the *Shakh* and the *Bach*, who only apply this leniency when the dough will certainly spoil before the woman returns. In such a case, we assume that the woman would prefer that the *Challah* be separated. If there is only a slight possibility that the dough will spoil, it is forbidden to separate *Challah* without the owner's permission.

According to the *Misgereth HaShulchan*, this restriction does not apply to a Jewish maid: "If the woman regularly allows her Jewish maid to separate *Challah*, the maid may do so without prior permission, even where only a slight possibility that the dough will spoil exists."

6. According to the *Shulchan Arukh, Yoreh De'ah* 331:3, if a boy of twelve or a girl of eleven takes *Challah*, the separation is valid. The Vilna Gaon, however, maintains that a child's separation is ineffective unless he or she has actually passed *bar* or *bath mitzvah* age.

7. *Rambam, Hilkhoth Bikurim* 5:12; *Magen Avraham* 263:6; *Remah, Orach Chayim* 88. In ancient times, it was required that the *Challah* be ritually pure (*tahor*). Therefore, a *niddah*, who is classified among those who are ritually impure (*tom'ey*), did not perform the *mitzvah* herself. Today, all people are presumed to be *tom'ey* (See Chapter 3, note 10.), so this restriction no longer applies.

8. See paragraph 5 for the minimum amount of dough which necessitates a blessing.

The Dough

5. One must separate *Challah* from a dough made from the "five types of grain",[9] if more than 1200 grams (2.64 pounds) of flour was used.[10]

6. A blessing is recited over separating *Challah* only if the dough was made from a minimum of 2250 grams (4.95 pounds) of flour.[11]

---

9. *Shulchan Arukh, Yoreh De'ah* 324. The five types of grain are wheat, barley, spelt, oats, and rye.

10. The Talmud calls for the taking of *Challah* when the flour content of the dough is equal to the volume of 43.2 eggs. Halakhic authorities not only disagree, but have their own doubts as to the proper method of converting the Talmudic measure into grams or ounces. Each authority establishes a minimum amount of flour, which might necessitate separation, and a larger amount, which definitely necessitates separation. With the lesser amount, the *mitzvah* is performed without a blessing, in accord with the general halakhic principle that no blessing is recited when a *mitzvah* is performed in a situation of doubt.

The *Chazon Ish* maintains that *Challah* should be separated without the blessing when 1200 grams (2.64 pounds) of flour were used in preparing the dough. HaRav Chaim Naeh requires *Challah* separation without the blessing for a minimum of 1250 grams (2.75 pounds), adding that this was the accepted practice in Jerusalem. According to HaGaon Rav Y.M. Tikotzinski, 1050 grams (2.3 pounds) of flour necessitates separation without a blessing.

11. According to the *Chazon Ish*, the dough must contain a minimum of 2250 grams (4.95 pounds) of flour to warrant a blessing. HaRav Chaim Naeh, however, permits the blessing when the dough contains 1666 grams (3.66 pounds) of flour and HaGaon Rav Tikotzinski rules that it may be said over 1570 grams (3.45 pounds). The *Chazon Ish*'s opinion is cited in the text because it includes *all* opinions and therefore avoids the possibility of reciting an unnecessary blessing.

Sephardic authorities introduce still different amounts. The *Ben*

7. *Challah* is separated only if the dough was kneaded with the intention to bake it in the oven. A dough that was kneaded with the intention to boil or fry it, for noodles or blintzes for example, is exempt.[12]

8. *Challah* must be separated from a dough even if the dough is to be divided into small pieces. If the intention is to bake the small pieces at separate times,[13] there is no obligation to separate *Challah*.[14]

Ish Chai, Shanah Rishonah, Parshath Sh'mini, maintains that a blessing should only be said if the dough contains a minimum of 2487 grams (5.47 pounds) of flour. The *Kaf HaChayim* reports that in Syria and Yemen the practice was to recite a blessing if there were 1750 grams (3.85 pounds) of flour.

12. According to the *Shulchan Arukh, Yoreh De'ah* 329:3, the obligation to take *Challah* depends on the woman's intention at the time of kneading the dough. If she intended to bake the dough, *Challah* must be separated, even from a thin or loose batter. If her intention was to fry or boil it, *Challah* is not separated, even from a thick batter.

The *Shakh* and *Pithchey Teshuvah* cite the opposing view of Rabbenu Tam, who rules that *Challah* must always be separated from a thick batter, even if it is to be fried or boiled, and never separated from a thin batter, even if it is to be baked. The *Pithchey Teshuvah*, citing the *Panim Me'iroth*, concludes that a careful person should be stringent and separate *Challah*, without the blessing, from dough made from a thick batter which she intends to boil or fry, i.e., when making *kreplach*.

Leket HaOmer, p. 16, cites the view of the *Shulchan Arukh*, who rules that if the intention at the time of kneading a thick dough is to bake it, *Challah* must be separated even if the dough is subsequently boiled. On the other hand, if the intention at the time of kneading dough from a thin batter was to bake it, *Challah* is only separated if it was actually baked. If instead, the dough is boiled, it is exempt from *Challah* according to all opinions.

13. *Pithchey Teshuvah, Yoreh De'ah* 326:2.
14. *Remah, Yoreh De'ah* 326:4.

9. A dough which does not have the required amount of flour is exempt from *Challah* even if it later expands in volume.[15]

10. If a dough is kneaded with a liquid[16] other than water, *Challah* should be separated without reciting the blessing.[17]

11. One should add a small amount of wine, honey, olive oil, milk or water to any dough which has fruit juice for its liquid ingredient.[18]

---

15. *Shulchan Arukh, Yoreh De'ah* 324:13. This rule applies regardless of whether the dough expands before or during the baking process.
16. Such as fruit juice, eggs, butter, or margarine, without water added.
17. *Shulchan Arukh, Yoreh De'ah* 329:9. The *Shakh* cites a dispute among the *Rishonim* as to whether there is an obligation to separate *Challah* from such a dough. Therefore, the separation should be made without reciting the blessing. The *Pithchey Teshuvah* 329:2 cites authorities who rule that if the dough was kneaded with wine, honey, olive oil or milk, a blessing should be recited over the separation.
18. In ancient times, *Challah* was presented to a *cohen* to be eaten by him and his family. Both the *cohen* and the *Challah* had to be ritually pure (*tahor*). Today, all people, including *cohanim*, are classified as a ritually impure (*tom'ey*). They are assumed to have had direct or indirect contact with a dead person. Consequently, *Challah* is no longer given to the *cohen*. Instead, it is burned after being separated. Although the Torah forbids burning *Challah* that is *tahor*, since whoever prepares the dough today is *tom'ey*, *tum'ah* is transmitted to the *Challah*, and it may be burned.

In *VaYikra* 11:38, we are taught that food cannot receive any form of *tum'ah* unless it has come into contact with a *mashkeh* ("liquid"). *Chazal* list only seven liquids that are called *mashkeh*: blood, water, olive oil, dew, milk, wine, and honey.

If a dough is kneaded without adding one of these liquids, it cannot receive *tum'ah* and remains in a *tahor* state. The *Challah* separated from this dough is also *tahor*, and it cannot be burned. Even a small amount of added *mashkeh* allows *tum'ah* to be

12. If two small doughs cling to one another, so that one stretches when the other is moved, they are considered as one in determining whether *Challah* must be separated.[19]

13. Two small loaves baked from separate doughs and placed in the same basket may together make up an amount which necessitates the separation of *Challah*.[20] (See paragraph 15.)

If two loaves are wrapped in separate bags and placed in the same freezer, they do not combine.[21]

Order of Separation

14. One first recites the blessing for the *mitzvah* of separating *Challah* — *asher k'dishanu...v'tzivanu l'hafrish*

---

transmitted to the dough. But if only a small amount of *mashkeh* was added, no blessing is recited over the separation, as explained in paragraph 10.

19. *Shulchan Arukh, Yoreh De'ah* 325:1. The *Mishnah Berurah* 457:7 emphasizes that for purposes of *Challah* it is not sufficient for the doughs to be loosely touching; they must be attached to one another.

20. *Shulchan Arukh, Ibid.* According to the Vilna Gaon, cited in the *Mishnah Berurah* 457:7, the two loaves must touch in the basket in order for the cumulative principle to take effect. The *Pri Chadash* and the *Taz* maintain that loaves in the same basket combine whether or not they are actually touching.

Machazeh Eliyahu, No. 110-117, and *Moadim Uz'manim*, Vol. 2, No. 187, rule that breads placed in the same refrigerator or car do not combine.

This principle has specific application on Purim, when families often receive many different gifts of cake. The givers may have only kneaded small doughs and not separated *Challah* at home. When the receiver places all the cakes in one container, they combine to make an amount which necessitates the separation of *Challah*. When many cakes are placed in a container, *Challah* should be separated without a blessing.

21. This ruling is based on a decision of HaGaon Rav Shlomo Zalman Auerbach. See *Machazeh Eliyahu, Ibid.*

Challah. (Who has sanctified us...and commanded us to separate *Challah*)²² — then separates a portion of the dough and burns it. It is customary to separate a *k'zayith.*²³

15. If *Challah* was not separated from the dough, it should be separated from the bread after it is baked. If a blessing was required, it should be said at this time.²⁴

16. If separated *Challah* is taken by a child or an animal before burning, a new separation need not be made.²⁵

Separation on Shabbath and Yom Tov

17. It is praiseworthy to bake loaves of bread on *Erev Shabbath* to fulfill the *mitzvah* of separating *Challah* with a blessing.²⁶

---

22. *Remah, Yoreh De'ah* 328:2; *Kitzur Shulchan Arukh* 35; *Orukh HaShulchan* 328:2.
23. *Shulchan Arukh, Yoreh De'ah* 322:5. Since the *Challah* has become *tom'ey* (See note 18.), it must be burned rather than given to a *cohen.* It is customary to burn the *Challah* in the oven before baking the dough. It should be wrapped in aluminum foil so the oven won't absorb the flavor of the burning *Challah.*

HaGaon Rav Y. Steiff, writing in *Sh'eiloth U'Teshuvoth HaMaor,* rules that the *Challah* should be burned until it turns to ash. It may then be thrown into the waste basket. If it has not been burned completely, it should be wrapped in two layers of paper and thrown away.

Moadim Uz'manim, Vol. 3, No. 268, maintains that in *Eretz Yisrael* one is *required* to separate no less than a *k'zayith.* Nevertheless, if less was removed, the *mitzvah* has still been fulfilled. A *k'zayith* is a dry volume measurement equal to approximately 1 ounce, 28 cubic centimeters.
24. *Shulchan Arukh, Yoreh De'ah* 327:5.
25. *Birkey Yosef, Yoreh De'ah* 322:3.
26. *Mishnah Berurah* 242:6. As noted in paragraph 1, the *mitzvah* of

18. It is forbidden to separate *Challah* on *Shabbath*.

19. *Challah* may be separated on *Yom Tov* from a dough that was kneaded on *Yom Tov*.[27] *Challah* may not be separated on *Yom Tov* from a dough that was kneaded before *Yom Tov*.[28] If the *Challah* was separated in error, the bread or cake may be eaten.[29]

20. Outside *Eretz Yisrael*, *Challah* must be separated before sunset on Friday evening. In *Eretz Yisrael*, the separation may still be made during twilight.[30]

---

separating *Challah* is directed primarily to women as a rectification of Eve's sin, which took place on *Erev Shabbath*.

The *Ben Ish Chai, Shanah Rishonah, Parshath Lekh L'kha*, cites the custom of placing coins in a *tzedakah* box before fulfilling the *mitzvoth* of separating *Challah*, lighting *Shabbath* candles, and immersing in the *mikvah*.

27. *Shulchan Arukh, Orach Chayim* 506:3. The *Mishnah Berurah* 457:10 adds that if a small dough was kneaded before *Yom Tov* and placed in a basket with another small dough on *Yom Tov*, *Challah* may then be separated since the obligation took effect on *Yom Tov* itself.

28. *Shulchan Arukh, Orach Chayim* 339:4, 524:1 and 506:3.

29. *Mishnah Berurah* 339:25 and 506:8. If the *Challah* was removed in willful disregard of these prohibitions, the bread or cake may not be eaten until after the conclusion of *Shabbath* or *Yom Tov*.

30. See paragraph 22. If a person living outside *Eretz Yisrael* forgot to separate *Challah* before *Shabbath*, the bread may be eaten as long as a small amount is put aside so that *Challah* can be taken from it after *Shabbath*. In this situation, because the bread may be eaten prior to taking *Challah*, the separation is not deemed urgent, and taking *Challah* is not permitted during twilight. In *Eretz Yisrael*, the separation of *Challah* is a Torah Law. Therefore, if *Challah* is not separated before *Shabbath*, the bread may not be eaten. Here, the separation of *Challah* is urgent, and *Chazal* permit it during the twilight period of *Shabbath*, which lasts for approximately one half-hour after sunset. Separating *Challah* during twilight should only be done if there is no other bread to eat. (See the *Magen Avraham*

21. A woman who has lit candles and accepted *Shabbath* on herself may ask someone who has not accepted *Shabbath* to separate *Challah* for her, but there is a doubt as to whether the blessing may be said.[31]

22. If *Challah* was not separated on *Erev Shabbath* or *Erev Yom Tov*:

In *Eretz Yisrael*, where separation is Torah Law, it is forbidden to eat the bread.[32] On *Yom Tov*, however, one may knead an additional dough and make a separation from it that covers both doughs.[33]

Outside *Eretz Yisrael*, where separation is Rabbinic Law, a small piece from which *Challah* will be separated after *Shabbath* or *Yom Tov* should be set aside, and the rest of the bread may be eaten.[34]

---

and *Machatzith HaShekel* 261:2.) The *K'tzoth HaShulchan* adds that when there is only sliced bread in the house, *Challah* may be separated during twilight in order to have whole loaves for the *mitzvah* of *Lechem Mishneh*.

31. *Shevuth Yaacov*, Vol. 3, No. 19. This issue is discussed at length in Rav Tzvi Cohen's work, *Erev Pessach She'chal B'Shabbath*.
32. *Shulchan Arukh, Yoreh De'ah* 323.
33. *Shulchan Arukh, Orach Chayim* 506:2, and *Mishnah Berurah*.
34. *Shulchan Arukh, Yoreh De'ah* 323. If the loaves were made from separate doughs, a piece of each loaf must be set aside.

Appendix

The following are synopses of halakhic opinions of HaGaon Rav Moshe Feinstein that appear in *Iggeroth Moshe, Evven HaEzer,* Vol. 4, and *Choshen Mishpat,* Vol. 2. They were prepared by Rav Fuchs for the English edition of *Halichos Bas Yisrael.* This latest volume of the Responsa of HaGaon Rav Feinstein appeared in print after the manuscript of *Halichos Bas Yisrael* had been prepared for publication. It refers to many issues dealt with in the book, and we would have been remiss if we had not included synopses of these responsa in this volume.

Chapter and paragraph references within parentheses at the end of a synopsis are to *Halichos Bas Yisrael.*

The obligation of a divorcee to cover her hair

A young divorcee may uncover her hair if she is afraid that covering it, as required by Jewish Law, will cause her difficulty in finding a husband. She must realize, however, that whenever this fear is unfounded, she is obligated to cover her hair in accordance with the Law. (*Evven HaEzer* No. 62:4. See Chapter 5, paragraph 6.)

A married woman who does not cover her hair

Today, married women who do not fulfill the obligation to cover their hair do not forfeit their *kethubah*. Moreover, a

Appendix

husband may no longer divorce his wife against her will for transgressing this law. This is especially true in the United States where many women, even those who are otherwise observant, are negligent in this area. (*Evven HaEzer* 62:6. See Chapter 4, paragraph 1, and Chapter 5, paragraph 14.)

Bathing where there is a male lifeguard

It is praiseworthy for God-fearing women, especially wives of Torah scholars, to refrain from bathing at a separate beach where there is a male lifeguard. If they can do so in a peaceful manner, their husbands should prevail on them not to bathe in these places. (*Evven HaEzer* 62:1. See Chapter 7, paragraph 25.)

Flesh-colored stockings

One must abide by the modest practice of a particular community and wear, at a minimum, flesh-colored stockings if the custom of women in that community is to wear them. These stockings constitute covering for the legs since they give only the *appearance* of flesh. Since the exposed part of a woman's body below the knee does not induce erotic thoughts in a man, there is no prohibition against wearing these stockings. (*Evven HaEzer* 100:6. See Chapter 4, paragraph 4, note 12.)

Training children not to wear clothing of the opposite sex

From the age at which parents are particular to dress them in clothes of their own sex and the age at which they feel shame when they are dressed in clothes of the opposite sex, children should be trained in the prohibition against wearing clothing of the opposite sex. (*Evven HaEzer* 62:4. See Chapter 7, paragraph 2.)

Dieting and plastic surgery for cosmetic reasons

It is permitted, indeed an obligation, to refrain from food and drink for reasons of health. One should not object to a woman dieting purely for the sake of beauty and attractiveness, even if she refrains from nutritional food, not only from sweets and the like.

A woman who wishes to undergo surgery for cosmetic reasons may be permitted to do so. (*Choshen Mishpat* 65 and 66. See Chapter 7, paragraph 30.)

184

Miscellaneous Laws of Yichud

1. It is reasonable to assume that there is no prohibition of *yichud* between a father and daughter who have both converted to Judaism. (*Evven HaEzer* 64:1. See Chapter 8, note 9.)

2. A man who rears an orphan girl in his home must refrain from *yichud* with her if his wife dies. The same applies to a woman who rears an orphan boy. As long as both spouses are alive and living together, there is generally no problem of *yichud*. (*Evven HaEzer* 64:2. See Chapter 8, note 12.)

3. The law permitting *yichud* between siblings on "a temporary basis" is defined as follows: As long as it is clear that the sibling is "visiting", and the duration of the visit is not longer than normal, it may be considered "temporary", even if it lasts longer than thirty days. This would depend on where the sibling is coming from; it is obvious that an out-of-town visitor usually stays longer than a visitor who resides in the same city. When a sibling "moves-in" on a permanent basis, *yichud* is forbidden, even for one day. One should be stringent in questionable situations. When one of the siblings is old and sick they may live together on a permanent basis. (*Evven HaEzer* 64:3. See Chapter 8, note 9.)

4. Parents with two children at home, a boy and a girl, should not leave for extended vacations unless *yichud* is avoided. They could, for example, ask a friend or relative to stay with the children. (*Ibid.*)

5. *Yichud* is permitted when a woman's mother, daughter, or granddaughter is present. But *yichud* is forbidden between a man and two sisters. (*Ibid.*)

Additional comments on the Laws of Yichud, from Evven HaEzer 65

1. A woman should not make an appointment with a doctor outside his regular visiting hours, when no nurse or secretary will be in his office. If she must make an appointment at such times, she should be accompanied by her husband or one of her children. (See Chapter 7, note 23, and Chapter 8, paragraphs 19-21.)

Appendix

2. The exclusion of a "door open to the street" does not apply to an open window facing the street if people on the street cannot see through it into the house. If the window is low enough to allow people to see into the front room, it is permitted. (See Chapter 8, note 16.)

3. It is preferable to avoid *yichud* in a car, even on a highway where other cars pass by. When necessary, however, for instance, when a neighborhood woman needs a ride to the same place to which a man is driving, or when it would appear mean and selfish to turn down a request for a ride, one should be lenient. This applies even if the woman who requests the ride is not Jewish. (See Chapter 8, paragraph 22.)

4. As long as people might enter and sometimes do, the exclusion of a "front door open to the street" applies even when the door is closed for protection. At those times when people are not entering the building, *yichud* is only permitted if the door is actually open. (See Chapter 8, note 16.)

5. The presence of a man's wife only removes the prohibition of *yichud* if she is actually in the house. It is not sufficient for her to be in the same city. This is evident from the words of the *Shulchan Arukh, Evven HaEzer* 22:8. (See Chapter 8, paragraph 15, note 29.)

6. If a woman's husband is imprisoned in the same city, and it is certain that he will not be freed for a considerable time, the prohibition of *yichud* applies to her. (See Chapter 8, paragraph 14, note 26.)

7. In a large city like New York, even if her husband is in the same city, if the wife knows that he has traveled to the other end of the city and could not return for a few hours, *yichud* is forbidden to her. This also applies when the husband is at work and unable to return home for a number of hours. Only when the husband has the freedom to come home at any time and could indeed arrive at any time, is the prohibition of *yichud* lifted for his wife. (See Chapter 8, paragraph 14, note 26.)

8. The prohibition of *yichud* applies to an old and weak person, unless he is sick in bed and could therefore not engage in sexual relations.

9. It is customary to be lenient and allow a man to instruct young girls even when his wife is out-of-town or in the hospital after giving birth.

10. In practice, one should adopt the ruling of the *Rambam* and the *Shulchan Arukh* forbidding *yichud* between one man and many women. But if a man's wife is present, it is permitted, even if he comes in contact with women in the course of his occupation. (See Chapter 8, paragraphs 15 and 18.)

11. The ruling of the *Shulchan Arukh, Evven HaEzer* 22:6, permitting *yichud* between many men and many women applies when there is a minimum of three men and three women. (*Choshen Mishpat* 65:9. See Chapter 8, paragraph 17-18.)

12. When there is only a possibility of intimate contact, short of actual sexual relations, for example, in an elevator, there is no prohibition of *yichud*. (See Chapter 8, paragraph 27.)

13. A woman whose husband is in the city may give lessons to boys in her home. One may certainly be lenient in the United States where most people drive cars, and it is possible that the husband will return home at any time. (See Chapter 8, paragraph 14.)

Glossary

Akhilath pras — A dry volume measurement equivalent to three or four times the volume of an egg

Aruthah — A betrothed woman

Arvuth — A principle of mutual responsibility which allows one person to recite a *birkath ha'mitzvah* on behalf of another

Birkath HaMazon — Grace after meals

Birkath ha'mitzvah — A blessing upon performing a *mitzvah*

Birkath hoda'ah — A blessing of thanksgiving

Birkhoth ha'shachar — Morning blessings

Birkath HaTorah — Blessing recited before Torah study

Challah — The *mitzvah* of separating a portion of the dough

Chatzitzah — A separation between a part of the body and the water

Chinukh — Religious training

Dath Moshe — Requirements of modesty mandated by the Torah

Dath Yehudith — Standards of modesty adopted by Jewish communities

Devarim shebikdushah — Literally, "words pertaining to holiness", which include prayers, words of Torah, and blessings

Ervah — An erotic stimulus

Hakhel — The commandment that all Jews gather in the *Beith HaMikdash* once every seven years to hear the King read the Book of *Devarim*

Hefsek taharah — The internal examination made by a woman after her menstrual flow has stopped

Kaddish — A prayer which includes the highest form of praise of God

Kiddush levanah — Blessing for the new moon

K'betzah — A dry volume measurement equivalent to the volume of an egg

Kethubah — The Jewish marriage contract

K'zayith — A dry volume measurement equivalent to the volume of an olive

Ma'aser kesafim — The ten percent of a person's income separated for charitable purposes

Ma'ariv — The evening *Shemoneh Esrey*

Mar'ith ayin — Acting in a suspicious manner

Mayim acharonim — Washing the hands before *Birkath HaMazon*

Middath chassiduth — An expression of piety not an obligation

Mikvah — Ritualarium

Minchah — The afternoon *Shemoneh Esrey*

Minyan — A group of ten adult Jewish men

Mitzvah — A commandment of the Torah

Mechitzah — A partition between men and women

Motzie — The act of fulfilling a religious obligation on behalf of others

Mussaf — The additional *Shemoneh Esrey* added on *Shabbath* and holidays

Niddah — Halakhic status of a woman from the onset of her menstrual period until she purifies herself through immersion in a *mikvah.*

Negelvasser — Literally, "waters for the nails", popular Yiddish term for the washing of hands in the morning

Netilath yadayim — Washing the hands

Nussach — The prescribed order and liturgical tradition of the prayers

Panim chadashoth — A person attending the *sheva berakhoth* who was not at the wedding
Parutz — A person lax in any sexually-related matter

Revi'ith — A volume equal to 86 or 150 cubic centimeters (3 or 5.3 fluid ounces)
Ruach ra — Impure spirit that rests upon a person during sleep

Seudath havra'ah — First meal eaten by a mourner after the funeral
Sifrey kodesh — Holy books
Shacharith — The morning *Shemoneh Esrey*
Shem and *malkhuth* — Elements of a blessing referring to God's name and the declaration of His kingship
Sheva Berakhoth — Nuptial blessings recited after *Birkath HaMazon* for one week following the wedding
Shiur sevi'ah — An amount of bread that satisfies
Shiva — The seven day mourning period that begins immediately after the funeral
Shoke — Literally, thigh
Sotah — A woman whose husband suspects her of infidelity

Tefach — Measure equal to a handbreadth (approximately four inches)
Tom'ey — Ritually impure
Torah shebikhthav — The Written Law
Torah sheb'al peh — The Oral Law
Tum'ah — Ritual impurity
Tzniuth — Modesty

Yahrtzeit — The anniversary of a death
Yichud — A situation in which a man and woman are alone, unaccompanied
Yizkor — Memorial prayer
Yetzer hara — The evil inclination
Y'tziath Mitzrayim — The Exodus from Egypt

Zimun — The introductory sentences to *Birkath HaMazon* where one person "invites" the others to recite with him

Index

Numbers before a colon refer to chapters; numbers after a colon, to paragraphs; "n" after a number refers to note. Thus, "10:13, 14n; 11:5" means: Chapter 10, paragraph 13 and note 14; Chapter 11, paragraph 5.

Index